DARING HONOR

DIANA MUÑOZ STEWART

Daring Honor, copyright 2023, Diana Muñoz Stewart
Published by Diana Muñoz Stewart
Cover by Elizabeth Mackey (www.elizabethmackey.com)
Edited by Mackenzie Walton (http://www.mackenziewalton.com)
Interior Design by Judi Fennell at www.formatting4U.com

All rights reserved. Thank you for respecting the hard work of this author. No part of this book may be reproduced in any form or by any electronic or mechanical means, including information storage and retrieval systems—except in the case of brief quotations embodied in critical articles or reviews—without permission in writing from the author. This book is a work of fiction. The characters, events, and places portrayed in this book are products of the author's imagination and are either fictitious or are used fictitiously. Any similarity to real persons, living or dead, is purely coincidental and not intended by the author.

Books by Diana Muñoz Stewart

HIDDEN JUSTICE (Spy Makers Guild Book 1)
RECKLESS GRACE (Spy Makers Guild Book 2)
DARING HONOR (Spy Makers Guild Book 3)
FIGHTING FATE (Spy Makers Guild Prequel Novella)
BROKEN PROMISES (Bad Legacy Series)
AMOR ACTUALLY (Holiday Anthology)

Prologue
Tony

You'd think the jumpy, aggressive, snot-nosed guard was half-naked, unarmed, and being marched through the barb-wired gates of a Mexican compound in order to "perform" for a sadistic sex-slaver. Hell, if that were the worst of my problems, I'd be less terrified.

So young his acne glistens under the dull yellow floodlights, the kid shoves me, then Victor, toward the golf cart waiting to take us inside to his soon-to-be-dead boss.

Victor glares at Young-and-Pimply, but I let the push roll off my back. No sense in getting bent out of shape because of one aggressive guard, not when we're surrounded by a half-dozen more.

I got bigger things to worry about. Namely, keeping my sisters, Gracie and Justice, alive during this operation. *And* killing the man who's brought more misery to those I love than anyone on the planet.

Walid is a dead man.

Then again, so am I.

Once I administer the poison that takes Walid out, I'm going to bite down on the small pod hidden in my molar, ingesting the drug that will make me look dead.

Leaving everyone I love behind is the price I'll pay for betraying my family. Though, to my mind, sneaking behind my family's back to prevent Justice from making a mistake that could have gotten her killed wasn't betrayal; it was an act of love.

My naked ass cheeks hit the weathered golf cart seat, and I begin to pray everything goes smoothly from here on out.

The compound alarm goes off.

I lower my head and curse under my breath.

That blaring pulse kicks Young-and-Pimply into freak-out mode. He begins to look around frantically. His gaze settles on me and Victor.

Shit.

Wearing a USA baseball cap and the attitude only a 6' 5" jacked dude can manage, Dusty, my inside man and also head of security here, orders me and Victor out and onto our knees.

Victor flashes me a look of alarm, but he follows my lead when I get out and drop my knees onto the rough, dry soil.

"Stay put," Dusty says as he directs his men to secure the gate.

I know why Dusty's keeping us down here; he needs to reassure those under his command that he has control of us, but he's also making us look guilty as hell.

Alarm… Dusty's reprimand… Jittery guards… Not a good combination.

Young-and-Pimply wastes no time bending down to get in my face.

My turn to freak out. I know it—know it like I know my sister's temper. If Young-and-Pimply wants to avoid the wrath of Justice, whose scope is on him and who takes a threat seriously, he needs to stop acting like a macho idiot. Because, as agitated as he is, it's nothing compared to Justice, who wants into the compound to destroy the human trafficker who kidnapped her boyfriend and killed her biological sister.

Reasons number one and two she should've been banned from this operation. I've said it from the get-go. She's too close to the mission. I've said it after every mistake she made. Said it as I came up with an alternate plan. Said it as she nearly got herself—and others—killed again and again. Hell, I even wrote it down in a letter to our momma.

But when no one in my family of spies listened, I'd stopped

talking and did something about it. I'd organized a plan that should've forced my family to do it my way. The safer way. The keep-Justice-alive way.

I'd sent word to Walid, letting him know where to go to escape Justice's assassination. I'd believed once Walid had been alerted, The Guild would reevaluate everything. I'd believed they'd see that the better way to run this op was to take out Walid and his brother separately, not have Justice do them both together. And yet... it hadn't worked.

Momma had sent Justice after Walid and his brother Aamir anyway. Justice had gotten one of the two brothers, but, in the process, had drawn Walid's ire. So much so, our quarry became the hunter.

He'd found Sandesh and kidnapped him. Which is how I ended up in Mexico stuck between Jittery-Guard and furious Justice.

"Knock it off," I whisper to the kid over the ball of panic rising into my throat.

He curses at me and spittle flies from his mouth.

I see it in his eyes; talking to him had been a mistake; he takes my words as a threat, not a warning.

He lifts me to my feet.

I raise my hands to show him I'm no danger.

This, too, he sees as a threat.

He reaches for his gun.

Pop.

Justice shoots him center forehead.

His blood strikes me in the face and spatters across my lips. My stomach drops.

Another guard goes down and the rest scramble. Justice lays down cover fire, and I sprint toward the closest building.

The pops of gunfire recede behind me. I duck behind the building, pressing up against wood shingles as I catch my breath.

Victor pulls up beside me. "Coño," he whispers. "What do we do now?"

We?

I have no idea. Unless…

The plan forms quickly—station Victor as backup while I make my way to Walid. I'll tell Walid the truth, that I was the one who'd sent the initial warning on how to avoid assassination. Hell, I can prove it. If he listens—he *will* listen—I'll tell him I'm on his side. Tell him I'm here to offer him the one thing he can't resist—his brother's real killer. The woman who, for forty years, has been adopting children from all over the world and training them as her own secret society of spies and assassins.

Momma.

Sounds like a dick move turning on the woman who'd rescued me from the streets, but I know Momma would approve. If it keeps the others alive, Momma will understand.

I turn to Victor. "I have a plan."

Chapter 1
Tony

I crack open bleary eyes then slam them shut against a red-hot stab of sunlight. Okay, so it feels like a jackhammer mated with a battering ram to create whatever's assaulting the inside of my skull right now.

Licking dry lips with my sandpaper tongue, I taste copper and salt--*blood*?

I open my eyes again. Blinking away tears, I turn my head and find I'm sprawled on the ground near a bullet-torn leather couch and blood-soaked yellow drapes. The smell of death's bowels and the lingering scent of gunpowder curls my nose hair.

What the hell happened here?

Like an old Ford on a below-zero January morning, my drug-addled brain misfires, turns over, then restarts.

Oh fuck, right. That op in Mexico. Kill sex slavers, fake my own death, and escape my family before they can take revenge on me for doing what I thought was right.

That explains the empty pit in my stomach, the sour stench, and the stone silence—a roomful of dead sex traffickers isn't generally loud.

It'd worked. My plan fucking worked.

Shit had gotten a little out of hand, so says the condition of this room, but the basic plan had still worked. I'd poisoned Walid, bit down on the zombie drug, then pretended the poison that'd killed Walid was also killing me.

Of course, I'd thought the zombie drug would've worked faster. Thought I wouldn't have had to see… Justice… Her tears…

Fuck. I hate that I hurt her. Hate that Gracie is likely torturing herself with regrets after this mission. I fling an arm over my eyes. I'm going to miss those crazy bunch of people.

I shift and my nerve endings fire brutal rebukes at me.

Yeah. Yeah. Shake it off. I roll my head against the floor, teasing out an ache, and a flood of relief sweeps my body. They'd left me. I'd worried my sisters would take my body back or bury me.

As far as those two options went, the first had been more terrifying. The second meant I'd go to sleep permanently. The first meant they'd realize I wasn't dead, take me home, and use The Guild's advanced technologies to rob me of my memories, replacing them with who they thought I should be.

No fucking thanks.

Oh, damn. I can't feel my leg.

I look down to make sure it's still there. It is. I must've fallen on it while the drug took effect. It's bent under me and so numb I can't move it.

Sitting up, I grab a fistful of the green cargo pants I'd *borrowed* from one of Walid's guards, lean to the side, and straighten my leg. Blood flows back into the limb with dagger-sharp pins and needles lancing my thigh and calf.

Biting off a curse, I rub my leg to help return the blood flow.

A figure crosses into the room, and I cringe as Dusty, carrying a tarp, walks behind the couch and finally sees me.

"What the fu—" He drops the tarp, takes out his gun, then points it at me. "You're not dead?"

So not what I want to deal with when my stomach is giving me the middle finger, pins and needles teeter me between laughter and tears, and my heart is pretty much broken.

I put a hand to my temple and rub my throbbing head. "They teach you those kinds of expert evaluations in the bur… bureau?"

Throat is so dry I sound like Momma's righthand man, Leland. Guess it makes sense since it turns out we're related.

I look up at Dusty. "Stop pointing your gun at me."

He does, but he keeps it out. Can't blame him. Probably his first encounter with someone coming back from the dead.

"What's going on, Tony?"

I'm stalling, trying to figure out my next move. Probably shouldn't go with that. Our partnership was an exercise in both of us using the other—Dusty pretending he'd left the FBI to join my family, me pretending I believed him. But Dusty isn't stupid. So, him knowing I'm still alive isn't an option. "The poison I gave Walid must not have transferred enough to work on me."

Dusty frowns and looks back toward the doorway. "Your sisters are already gone, but we can call them once we're clear."

This is a problem. Dude is big. Like, *gladiator* big, and I'm in in no shape to take him on. I've got a couple of advantages—Dusty has no idea what's really going on, and it isn't like I hadn't considered I might wake up in Mexico with someone nearby.

Bending over to cover the movement, I work my fingers under the waist of my pants to my live entertainer G-string—most humiliating cover ever. I one-handed release the tiny, modified syringe hidden inside a sex tool. "Just help me up."

Dusty puts his gun away and comes over to me. "You're one lucky son of a bitch."

Don't feel lucky. Feel like a douche that's about to do to this guy what I wouldn't want done to me. But this is temporary. If my family got ahold of me… The mindfuck would be permanent.

I say, "Must've been scary to walk in here and find me alive."

According to Zuri, my mad-scientist sister, the first step in temporarily erasing a memory is getting the person to recall the memory. After that, I'll administer the drug that'll disrupt Dusty's mind from storing the memory again, allowing me to replace it with my own.

Dusty comes over and takes my hand. "Granted, it's not a regular occurrence. You scared the life out of me."

He pulls me to standing and I bring my hand to his shoulder as if to steady myself. Actually, it does help. I stab Dusty with the tiny needle, press down and simultaneously pretend to fall. "Sorry, didn't mean to scratch you."

He automatically tightens his hold, helping to support me. "Dagger claw you got there."

Getting my feet under me, I slip Dusty's gun from its holster He rears back, rubs at his neck, and falls onto this ass. "You…" He trails off and sits there blinking. It takes only a few more seconds before he's completely malleable.

Bending over him, I edit the story of what just happened, and whenever Dusty looks confused or uncertain of this version, I follow Zuri's instructions—not that she knew I'd use them for this—and give him a mantra, "Leave it be, man. Leave it be."

I do this over and over, then ask Dusty what happened here. He repeats what I told him. When I ask him if he's certain that's what happened, he whispers, "Leave it be, man. Leave it be."

Holy shit. It worked. Dusty's memory is disrupted.

Apologizing to him, I put him into a choke hold and he goes to sleep.

I lay him onto the ground and pat his shoulder. "I really am sorry, man."

Poor guy. Well, he won't remember any of this, not for a while anyway, and, by that time, I'll be long gone, having set sail for warm beaches.

Chapter 2
Honor

Rain pounds the beach in El Tuque, Puerto Rico. The lack of sun combined with the wind from the retreating tropical storm lashes me with a deep, nagging chill.

Tightening the straps on my jacket, drawing the slick red hood into an outline around my rain-drenched face, I push through the last brutal gusts.

Stacked lounge chairs clack in the distance and striped cabanas snap in the tempest. No sane person should be out here today, but I needed to be alone. Anyway, it's an appropriately cold and miserable day.

It's like the sky and heaven wail with me, tears of sadness and fury. Has it really been two years today? Two years since I lost Mom and ran to my grandfather, my abuelito's home, looking for guidance from the man who'd lost, first, my grandmother, then my mother. I thought Abuelito could teach me to live a life without the ache of missing mom.

He couldn't.

Oh, Mom, I miss you. I wish you were here to share your wisdom. What should I do about the confounding offer on Loco for Cocoa?

To accept the ridiculous money an anonymous buyer offered for our family business is to give up not just on me, on my vision of selling chocolate from Puerto Rico worldwide, but on my grandmother's vision, of years rebuilding the inn and the cocoa farm, and on everyone who works for us.

It's also to give up on our family, Abuelito, on the life I've grown to love, and of course, the cocoa. But to *not* take it means to keep scraping by, desperate for money with only our tours and the cruise ship patrons keeping us afloat.

Ducking my head as if from the weight of this decision, I avoid puddles in the sand as the indents from my sneakers create smaller puddles.

"Follow your heart, mija," Mom's voice whispers in my head, as if it could ever be that easy for me. I ran from my heart when she died. Ran from the wound straight through my center that never heals and is easily torn open—as proved by this anniversary of her death. The media reaching out through phone, email, and texts for quotes about the unfortunate death of my famous mother was too much.

It was their painful harassment more than the offer on my business that caused me to come out here, hoping the ocean would provide some certainty.

Instead, it's provided a distraction.

A kiteboarder, rash and daring with a bright-yellow sail, glides across the rough ocean water. His dark hair flies back as his agile body, covered in a wetsuit, maneuvers his board with and against wind and waves.

He's so skilled and confident that he creates an ache, a desire, inside me. What I wouldn't give to be that strong, that free, and that daring.

A gust, and the kiteboarder leaps into the air, flies up and up.

I gasp as my heart rises with him. He's too high. He has too far to fall.

He slams back down to the surf, angling his athletic body this way and that as he skims along the waves.

He did it! Mom would've loved watching him—another confident, courageous soul, just like her and nothing like me.

Mom stomped through puddles; I've always hung back, worried about consequences. Mom went boldly after love, spoke her desires aloud, and gave her heart away again and again. I secret away my heart and my true desires because I remember her tears, the drink, and the therapy she needed to get right after every failed relationship.

With every exciting new relationship, Mom had seemed to forget that. I never forget.

Still, when the winds of time had swept Mom's fierce soul back into the *nunca-nunca*, as she had always called death, it hadn't been her wild and crazy lifestyle that had caught up with her. No. She'd been hit by a car as she'd walked the streets of her quiet neighborhood.

One less brave and daring light in the world. Today, I feel the dark cold of that extinguished warmth in my skin, my bones, and my heart.

Maybe, that's why I can't stop watching the kiteboarder. Anyone that wild and free and exciting, anyone like Mom, calls to me like a siren song to my soul.

He continues to work with the energy of the waves, weaving himself among them even as he wrestles his second opponent, the wind.

My breath fans out in sheets of white as he, explosive and strong, leaps with sail and board into the wind. A thrill of terror grips me as he flies through the air.

A moment later, he hits the waves and the sail jerks his arms straight, then he leans his body almost flat against the roaring ocean.

I clap and jump up and down.

Then the wind turns, snaps his kite, and yanks him backward.

I watch in stunned disbelief as the man is tossed up then beat down against an outcrop of rocks. His strong body, suddenly flimsy and fragile, slips from the rocks into the waves.

Racing toward the ocean, I fling off my shoes and rain slicker. Knee-deep in cold water, I stop to get my bearing. Where is he? The sail bobs against the waves, but where is he?

There.

He's floating face-down. A wave rises up and crashes over him, and he disappears beneath the water.

I take a deep breath and dive under the surface. Using muscles conditioned by years of swimming, I fight forward. Saltwater stings my nose and throat, and the ocean pushes against me with an insistent, *Turn around.*

Surfacing, I tread water and look around to make sure this is where he went under. It is; I know it.

Diving again, I look around. Green and gray, a surreal, muted picture stretches out before me, then I spot him, a blob darker than the rest of the ocean.

I swim deeper and deeper to get to him.

This day is already an anniversary of one tragic death; I won't let it take another life.

Ears muffled with pressure, I grab the collar of his wetsuit, capturing a fistful of his hair in the process.

I kick up and pull. His limp body comes even with mine. I grasp him under his armpits and swim.

My head angled as high as I can get it, I race for the surface and much needed air. The weight of him slows me. He's too heavy. If I'm to survive, I need to let him go.

I can't.

I absolutely cannot.

The edges of my vision began to dim. I'm too far from the surface. The drag of him is too much. We're not going to make it.

Heart and lungs desperate for air, I kick harder, propelling us toward that glassy ceiling.

We break the surface. I gasp for breath with the kiteboarder silent against me. His head bobs in the water.

Legs as insubstantial as seaweed, I roll onto my back. Keeping his head up, I kick weakly toward the shore.

It seems forever before my butt hits the beach and an exhausted cry escapes me. Sweeping my feet under me, I crouch-pull the kiteboarder onto the sand. Waves roll into us, nearly toppling me.

"Déjame ayudar," someone says, and I turn to find an older, dark-skinned man offering me help. I can't even nod my acceptance, but he doesn't need me to. Together, we drag the kiteboarder out of the waves and drop him onto the rain-soaked beach.

The bystander pants beside me so deeply I worry for him.

"Enfisema," he says, pointing at himself. He coughs roughly, before advising me that he called emergency services.

With a nod of understanding and praying the EMTs hurry, I start CPR. My knees grind into the sand as I pinch the kiteboarder's nose, put my mouth over his, and force air from my aching lungs into his lifeless body. I begin compressions on his chest.

Drops of water slide across his handsome, too-pale face, but not one muscle twitches in response.

Please live, please, please.

Desperate tears sting my eyes as the rain whips my hair. I repeat the process again and again until he convulses once, hard enough to look like I'd hit him with electric paddles.

He coughs dramatically and spits out water.

I quickly roll him onto his side.

He spits out more water, and I pat his back repeatedly. When he's done, the kiteboarder groans and flops onto his back, eyes closed, breathing heavy.

Breathing.

"They're here," the old bystander says, standing and walking up the beach to wave at the EMTs.

I did it. I'd saved a man's life. If I can do that, I can do anything—even save my failing business.

That's it, then. I'm not taking that offer.

Feeling a surge of happiness and a connection with this human, I brush the sand from his jawline, cheekbones, and lips. The most perfect shape of lips. The most perfect feel.

He's beyond handsome with a muscular build that fills out his wetsuit like a superhero. Mom would've declared him good enough to eat.

His eyes pop open, blink, and catch me with a finger still on his lips. I pull my hand back.

Deep hazel eyes ringed with the longest lashes I've ever seen stare at me. His eyes turn to slits as if trying to puzzle something out, then he sighs, "Yeah, they are. Silver eyes."

He closes his eyes and, smiling to himself, whispers, "So fucking beautiful."

Chapter 3
Tony

It's been a long time since I've had this nightmare. Ten years of therapy taught me how to unwind it usually. But I make a rookie mistake; I listen.

And just like that, I'm six years old again.

Thunk and thuck and umphs fill the small kitchen, making my stomach turn. Hidden by the dingy blue tablecloth, my small heart pounds loud enough that I imagine it pointing fingers and waving arms in my direction.

No one can hear me over Daddy hurting Mommy. And, this time, I feel like he won't stop. I have to do something.

Curling my fingers into fists, I charge out with a, "Stop!"

My bony shoulder slams into Daddy's kneecap and a sharp zing of pain slingshots up to my neck.

Daddy and I fall then slide across the linoleum.

Quick as a squirrel running from a vicious dog, I spin up and away.

Not fast enough.

His hand latches onto me, drags me back, and hoists me up.

I see Mom for an instant, curled up on her side. She's not moving.

"Teach you to stay in bed," Daddy slurs, *carrying me toward the laundry room door. A hole punched long ago into its center allows me to clearly hear the low growls on the other side.*

I fight and twist like a fish on a line. "Not in there. Not in there!"

No use. Daddy is just bigger and stronger. He tosses me into the laundry room and slams the door shut.

Thor, the pit bull Daddy bought from an abusive drug dealer, latches onto my leg, all teeth and fury. Pain slices into my calf, and I scream.

A God's honest yell escapes me as I jolt up in the hospital bed and it takes me one paralyzed second to realize where I am. Who I am. That I'm no longer a scared kid unable to defend himself.

No, I ran away from that murderous bastard. And after he died, I ended up being adopted by one of the wealthiest women in the world, AKA Momma, AKA Mukta Parish. A woman whose covert society, The Spy Makers Guild, trained me to be able to defend not only myself, but people who needed me.

And I loved it. Until I fucked up.

I scrub my face with two hands. Christ. Guess, trauma only needs a near-death experience to bring it back to the surface.

Shaking off the dream, I lie back and tune into the pounding in my head. Seems like I've been here before: headache, waking up without a clue, trying to piece together what happened to get me here.

This time, the hospital lights shout down at me, hitting me like a fistful of *wake up, dumbass* and the memory comes quickly.

Tropical storm.

Kiteboarding.

Idiot.

With a groan, I roll my head, forgetting why that simple action is a mistake. I swallow the warm moisture in my mouth, listening to the beep of the heart monitor as the rocking feeling settles.

No one to blame but myself. Shouldn't have gone out, but I'd been anxious and frustrated by my inability to get off the island because of the storm. Not just the storm, but also by my decision to visit home one last time to see everyone. That's how I'd ended up so close to the States when the storm hit. Furious at myself, I'd gone looking for something so deep, so wild and filled with adrenaline, I couldn't think anymore.

Basically, I'd wanted to kill my thoughts. It'd worked. For a little while, anyway. I have the headache to prove it.

"Knock, knock."

My gaze snaps to the door and I do what I've been trained to do: assess. I take in tanned legs, wrinkled white shorts, a rain slicker tied around a slim waist, and a drying brown T-shirt tight against large… A smile springs to my lips. Heat shoots through my body.

Not for nothing, she is gorgeous. And those eyes—silver? I thought I'd dreamed those eyes. Here is the fierce angel who'd saved my life then brought me back from the dead.

Beginning to become a bad habit of mine.

"Come in, come in," I say, waving her inside. I try to sit up, but the room tilts, and I'm forced to use the remote to inch the bed up. There's a *click* and *whir* as I bring myself to seated. "I want to thank you for saving my life."

Is that my voice? Sounds as rough as sand. As rough as my uncle Leland's. *Uncle?* Still doesn't sound right to call him that. After all, I spent the better part of twenty years not knowing we were related.

My angel, her loose brown curls caressing a delicate, almost regal neck, walks across the room and, oh man, I feel something. Something big. Something wild and filled with adrenaline and a zing of lust that has my heart monitor galloping.

I don't believe in love at first sight. It's absolute bullshit. This, what I'm feeling, is what happens when your gratitude is life-saving big. That's all. It's Nightingale syndrome or something.

Silver eyes flick to the monitor. No way to deny that frantic beat, but other than a flush of pink in her cheeks, she doesn't bring it up.

She swallows and holds out her hand, "Hello. I'm Honora Silva. Honor for short."

"My hero has a name worthy of her."

I extend my own hand, noticing she has a tattoo, a date that starts at the base of her thumb and runs up her wrist. It's today's date, but two years ago.

Staring at it, I take her hand almost absently. The hot silk of her skin ignites flames in my palm that spread through my body like a wildfire.

Attention gotten. Seriously, I could hold her hand all day. I actually want to.

With a twinge of regret, I let go and give her my alias. "Lazarus Graves. Laz for short."

She leans comfortably against the bed rail. "Lazarus?" She laughs. "How wonderfully appropriate. I have a cousin named Jesús. You two simply must meet."

I can't help but laugh. She's a smart-ass. *Me like.*

I say, "You got the States in your voice. Let me guess... You're on vacation and determined to get every day you can from Puerto Rico even during a tropical storm?"

"I grew up in California," she says smoothly and points at her tattoo. "But I moved back to my grandfather's posada—*inn*—after my mother's death, and, to be honest, that's why I was on the beach today. I needed to clear my head."

Some unnamed emotion breaks in my chest, pulling me toward her, seeing this day through her eyes. This has been a bad day for me, but it's been an incredibly shitty day for her. This grieving woman threw herself into the ocean to save my life. Can't help it, I put a hand to my chest. "I'm so sorry for your loss."

That *I'm sorry* hits in a way that has her shoulders slumping and tears swimming into her eyes. She quickly casts her gaze away and brushes aside the tears.

Her body's visible ache stings deep. That, right there, that pain, is what I've done to my family. By faking my death, I hurt them like that. I whisper through a tight throat, "I shouldn't have been out there today. I didn't mean to make your day worse."

"You definitely shouldn't have been out there," she says,

raising her eyes and smiling, "but you actually did me a favor. Because of you, I found an answer to a question I had, and you also transformed the meaning of this day. Now, it's not only about Mom's death, but also about the life I saved."

She's blowing me away right now. "It's also about you," I say. "Your mother's fearless daughter."

A startled, snort-laugh breaks from her like a crack of thunder. "Dios. I am not fearless." She covers her mouth and laughs softly. "In fact, Mom used to call me la León Cobarde, the Cowardly Lion."

I can feel the furrow between my eyes. The nickname makes no sense; she's anything but cowardly. "You jumped into the ocean to save an idiot stranger during a tropical storm. I call that fearless." I find myself racing to defend her, even it's from… her. "And the Cowardly Lion was tough, too. He just needed to find the right situation to bring it out. Trust me, you're daring, Honor."

At this, she laughs, so surprised and maybe delighted that her head tilts back as her chin lifts to the ceiling. When she brings her head down, her silver eyes are alight, like twin moons, and I am absolutely captured.

She says, "Well, this Daring Honor makes chocolate for a living."

I smile back at her. There's no way not to. "Ah, so you're sweet *and* brave. I must be the luckiest survivor in the world. Who you makin' chocolate for?"

She tips her head to the side. "We ship pretty much anywhere. We, my abuelito and I, own a cocoa farm, inn, and agro-touring business in the mountains."

Wanting to know more, wanting her to keep talking, wanting her to stay around a bit longer, I roll my hand in a tell-me-more gesture. "What kind of tours?"

She shrugs. "Tours of our cocoa farm along with outdoor adventures, canyoneering, rappelling, hiking and climbing in Bosque Estatal Toro Negro."

"You just described my dream job. Rappelling, spelunking,

anything to do with the great outdoors and adventure, I'm your guy. Gotta say, I'm a little jealous."

Self-consciously, she fingers the bit of blanket poking through the metal guardrail. "And you? Are you on vacation?"

I have my cover. Of course I do. And yet, she's been so honest with me, saved my life, in fact, and she's asking so sweetly that I can't bring myself to lie to her. I lower my voice as if confiding in her, which, honestly, I am. "Don't tell anyone, but I ran away from home, changed my name, and set sail. I was forced to port with the storm."

"Mr. Graves—I knew that name couldn't be real." Her eyes brighten. "But that sounds like an adventure story. I love adventures stories."

She opens her mouth to ask a follow-up, a question I'm sure I don't want to answer because, really, why isn't she running out of the room right now?

Brave as hell.

I cut her off with my own question. "Your eye color—is that real?"

Her eyebrows go up to kiss the curls hanging across her forehead. "Of course they are."

Sensitive. "That offends you? Me asking?"

"The idea that I am a person who puts in contacts to impress others offends me."

Oh, man, I like the way she talks—clipped and absolute and kind of formal. Reminds me of the girls at the Mantua Academy, the private school my family runs which serves as a cover for The Guild's clandestine operations.

"Never said it was to impress anyone. Maybe people who wear colored contacts just like the way they look. Like I like my tattoos."

She swishes her chin around as if sampling my words, almost like a sommelier tasting wine.

Okay, that is freakin' adorable.

She must find the comparison to her liking because she nods and says, "My eyes aren't that unusual."

"You can't actually believe that. They're silver."
"Some would call them a light gray."
"Some would be wrong."
"I think my skin tone might lend them to seeming lighter."

Darker than even mine, her skin is a tawny island tan so pristine her body seems draped in silk. Can't help the longing to run a knuckle across the swell of her high cheekbones, collarbone, and cleavage.

"You have great skin," I say like an idiot.

She raises a dark eyebrow over one silver eye. The gesture gives her a dangerous, seductive quality that's hard to resist.

Not sure I want to.

Not sure I have a choice.

A squawk from the hall announces visiting hours are over. I expect her to make her excuses, but her gaze dips to my bicep and the tattoo beneath the hospital gown.

"Your tattoo, 'One for all,' like the Three Musketeers. Does it have meaning beyond that?"

"It means my life for others. Used to be my motto."

She frowns. "But not anymore?"

I wish she hadn't asked, but she did and the way I'm feeling right now—grateful and turned on and fuzzy enough in the head that this whole conversation seems surreal—I say, "I told you, I ran away from home. So, I guess I'm looking after myself, making myself number one for a while."

I wait for her to accuse me of being a selfish prick, but, instead, she looks me in the eyes, almost sadly.

"You say that like you're admitting a crime. You don't seem the type to run away from a wife or children."

"I'm not." I shake my head a little too quickly and my stomach sloshes. "Never been married. There's just me." And my big, crazy spying family.

She does frown now. "You feel badly about living *your* life for *you*?"

Shit, yeah, I do. Every day I wake up with this stomach-turning guilt. Guilt at the wrongness of it, of not doing what I'm good at, what I can to help. "I was raised to care. I do care. It doesn't feel right to have even one day that's focused solely on me."

Her gaze seems puzzled, as if she's trying to figure me out. "I don't understand that guilt, but if you feel that way, why leave?"

"It wasn't really my choice. It was run or lose my mind." *Literally.* "Now I'm sailing around the world. Maybe sailing forever, and every day is a fight to let go of those things I grew up believing."

She takes a deep breath like she's preparing to dive, then exhales long and low. "Do you know the Loco for Cocoa shop near where the cruise ships dock?"

"I docked at a small marina. Haven't really been here long enough to learn the layout. Why?"

"Oh." She blinks at me and, after a moment, continues. "I have a cocoa shop near where the cruise ships dock. I'm there Mondays, Wednesdays, and Saturday mornings. If you stop by, I'll take you on a personal tour, an adventure through the rain forest, show you my business, and even share some of my personal chocolate with you."

Personal chocolate? Let's hope that's a euphemism for what I really want to taste. "Hold on. You asking me out?"

Her cheeks pinken.

I grin wide. "You *are* asking me out." Aw, man, the absolute worst time for it, too. If they haven't already, my family will soon figure out I'm alive. Once they do, they'll be gunning for me, so staying in one place, especially this close to the States, is too dangerous. "Totally makes my injuries worth it, but..." This is killing me. "I'm not sure I'll survive another adventure."

She swallows and her eyes widen. "I won't let anything happen to you."

My heart trips in my chest. I honestly can't remember the last time someone thought to protect me. That's *my* job. "You saving my life once is enough, Honor."

She flushes, starts to protest, but I cut her off. "And, honestly, I wish I could, but I have to set sail, ASAP."

She frowns, bites her lip, then, in a move so sudden I nearly jerk away, she leans over and presses a kiss to my cheek.

It happens in one hot, blinding instant. Something I haven't allowed myself to feel for a long, long time uncoils from where it's been tightly wound inside me—selfish desire.

I want her. I want to feel those soft, full lips working against my body, want to take her in all the best ways, slow and fast, as she gasps and moans beneath me.

Leaning back, she smiles and her eyes travel down my body. "I saved your life. I think you owe me."

Wait. What does that mean? Is it my male ego or did she just proposition me?

Our eyes lock and I see the blatant, unrestrained desire for me clearly reflected in her eyes. It almost propels me out of the bed. My greatest weakness is a woman who knows what she wants and puts it out there. My heart feels like it's filled with helium.

Love at first sight doesn't exist.

This is lust.

And I'm okay with that. "Yeah. I'll pay that debt," I growl. "With interest."

She glances down at my lips, then leans toward me again, slow this time, giving me the opportunity to say no.

My body is saying hell yes, and so am I.

Like my heart—and, of course, the monitor picks up its beat.

"Se acabaron los horarios de visita." A no-nonsense nurse enters and announces our time is up. Wheeling a blood-pressure machine into the room, she looks at Honor with a shake of her head. "Todos fuera."

Honor startles like she got pinched in the butt, then takes a step away.

Is that regret in her eyes? That makes two of us.

Before I can think of a thing to say or a reason to say it, Honor heads for the door.

I watch her walk away.

When she reaches the door, she looks back. Catching my gaze on her ass, she grins. "I hope to see you at the shop. Until then, try to stay out of the grave, Lazarus."

Her flirty intention has the opposite effect. It snaps me back to the reality of running from my family and The Guild. It reminds me that I'm in danger, a danger that extends to anyone around me. Which is why I'm on a sailboat, to keep away from any civilians who might get hurt when/if my family finds me.

That'll be a lot easier if I leave the island. Which means, as hot as this smart-ass chocolatier is—hot enough to make me regret every life choice I've ever made—this is the last I'll see of her.

Chapter 4
Tony

One of the things I love most about my new life is that I don't have a clock. I've thrown away the schedules. So, to be woken by my cell at butt-crack a.m.—two hours after I snuck out of the hospital—first annoys then terrifies me.

Only one person has this number, the one person who knows I'm still alive. That person wouldn't call without an absolutely valid reason.

A pit bull of dread tears a hole the size of a lost lifetime through my chest. Guilt, regret, and fear roil inside as I roll over in my bunk.

Grabbing my earpiece from the side table, I slip it on over my right ear, sit up, swing my legs out, and accept the call, cutting off *Aladdin*'s "Friend Like Me."

Beneath me, the sailboat sways and pitches. Kind of matches my stomach right now. "What's the bad news, Rome?"

There's a beat of silence, a steeling of resolve or a moment of dread or a lag in connection before my younger brother's voice filters through my headset. "You're no longer dead."

"The family knows I'm alive?"

"Yep."

"Justice?"

"Everyone. I don't think I've ever seen Justice so angry, and she spends ninety percent of her life pissed off."

Dread and relief slam into me. Relief because I'd rather the family be pissed off at me than sad and mourning. Dread because now they'll be looking for me, and I've been stuck on this island for days. Now I have to *run*, not just hide because if they find me, they'll strap me in the chair and erase my memory.

"What gave me away?"

There's a long pause. "Short or long version?"

I should ask for the long one, but I don't have the heart for it this morning. Pain pounds my skull like a Moroccan drum. "Short and sweet."

"Sweet? You haven't been gone that long."

With a grunt, I climb out of my bunk and promptly hit my already throbbing head on the doorjamb as the boat pitches. Holding my head, I stumble to the bathroom.

Rome speaks into my ear. "Gracie fell in love with an FBI agent, the one who helped you in Mexico."

"Wait. Gracie fell in love with Dusty? No. Nope. She needs to be careful with him. He's—"

"He's chipped, and he's been down to the dungeon, where they restored his memory and got a beat on you. By the way, he's definitely not a fan of yours."

Grabbing a Motrin bottle from the cabinet, I glance at the lump under my skin where my disabled chip, a GPS system that allowed The Guild to always know where I was, sits as a distorted reminder of how hard it is to run from them. I pour three pills into my hand as the disbelief settles in my chest. "Dusty, the FBI agent, has been chipped, basically allowed into The Guild, into our illegal global operations to rescue women around the world?"

"Yeah. It looks like we found your replacement."

Even though I know he's saying that as a joke, it hurts. I pop the pills and dry swallow. "How much time do I have?"

"Dude, you were adopted into a wealthy family of spies, with enough technology and contacts to run secret operations around the world. You have zero time. That's why I'm calling—to tell you to run and keep running."

Easier said than done.

Crossing the living area and galley, I climb onto the deck.

The marina is abuzz with early morning activity. I blink at the sun and steam heat. The connection goes fuzzy.

"Tony?"

I press my earpiece deeper into my ear. "Has Momma talked about erasing my memory?"

There's a long moment of silence before he whispers, "They did Bridget."

Cold washes down my body along with a deep sense of guilt. They took my sister Bridget's memory? Obviously, because she helped me carry out my plan to save Justice.

"She agreed to it. She said to show her remorse, she had no problem complying with The Guild's rules. That's messed up, right?"

Bridge. Of *course* she let them do that to her. She's all about loving people, even when they don't show the same back.

When I don't say anything, Rome continues. "She doesn't seem different or anything. She's still herself, but she doesn't remember her part in the betrayal stuff. They'd probably do the same for you. It might not be that bad."

I close my eyes against the sharp stab of grief in my chest. He's a teenager, a kid, and I'm the only brother he knows. I swallow the lump in my throat. "I miss you, too, Rome. I do. But I can't let them take me anything from me, not even a little bit. You feel me?"

"Yeah." He curses. "You better go deep, brother. As deep as you can, like Amazon-deep, or Greenland."

"I will." Which means getting out of this marina and getting out of Ponce. "Keep me in the loop but stay safe. Ditch this number. You got the other phone numbers I gave you?"

"Yeah. I'll move onto the second number if I need to contact you."

Good thing the kid is such a brainiac. "Okay, but don't risk yourself. You've done enough."

Another pause before Rome clears his throat and says, "It's better now since you left. I mean, even The Troublemakers

Guild—the badass unit to end all badass units—has stopped looking at me like I'm the enemy. Like I'm someone who needs to be trained and kept in line. They're treating me like I'm a real person."

My heart responds without my say. The thing about The Guild is it's made up of girls and women who've all had some shit experiences with men, so, sometimes, they put up walls around the only two men adopted into the family—me and Rome. And those walls sometimes feel like a punch in the face. That I'd shaken up the family enough to make a space for Rome and reevaluate the way things work... it means something.

Bending down, I open the cooler strapped to the deck rail and take out a bottle of water. "I'm glad it's better." I sip. "But remember what I told you. They don't mean it. The suspicion, the anger... They're looking at you through damaged glass. To them, you'll always reflect the pain they experienced at the hands of other men."

"That's dark, man."

No shit. "Just be careful. I love you."

"Love you, too," Rome says without a moment of awkward teen hesitation. "Dead or alive."

I try to swallow over the lump that sticks in my throat but can't. Unable to say a word—there are none to express how much I appreciate the kid's support, how much I regret having to leave, how much I miss them all—I hang up.

Chapter 5
Honor

I'm late to open our small shop by the pier, so I press the gas on my red Hyundai Accent, which sputters before swinging around a bend. The road is mostly cleared of damaged trees, torn electrical lines, and shattered glass. It's still a hot mess out here, but clean-up crews have done enough to get us all back to routine. So says the two docked cruise ships.

I'm glad they're here. We sell more chocolate on arrival days, and the main purpose of opening the satellite store near the dock is to introduce our chocolate to a wider audience.

With a turn of my wheel, I pull into the asphalt parking lot of the standalone Loco for Cocoa chocolate store. Football-shaped like a cocoa bean, the lower half painted in colorful yellow and purple with a white upper half and roof, as if the raw cocoa inside the shell has been revealed, the store is undamaged. If only I could say the same about myself.

I made the mistake of calling Angelica Torres, the real estate agent who presented me with the offer on Loco for Cocoa, this morning. That was a nightmare. She would not take no for an answer, and I found myself arguing with her. It was unbelievable. Plus, she made me late because I couldn't head down the mountain without losing cell service.

Annoyed with the memory, I turn off my car, try not to dwell on the conversation, but fail.

Sure, Angelica lost a big commission on my decision, but she was so rude, acting as if turning down the offer was the dumbest thing she'd ever heard. I would've told her exactly where she could shove her opinion, but she also happens to facilitate tours for the cruise ships. Right now, I need that business.

Pocketing my keys, I swing the car door open, and the metal hinges on the rusty old car squeak loud enough to almost drown out the ring of my cell. It's going to be one of those days. I look at the screen and answer with a frown. "Junior, shouldn't you be headed up into the mountains with our guests?"

"Sí, pero there's a problem."

Yep. One of those days. "¿Qué pasa?"

"I'm the only one here. No one else showed up."

"None of the guests? Is the cruise ship docked?"

"Oh, no, the guests are all here, but I'm the only tour guide who showed up for work. I'm good, cousin. You know I'm good, but I can't run the whole tour by myself."

My keys dangle from my hand as I freeze in place. "Are you telling me all three of our tour guides haven't shown up for work today? Even Tito?"

"Yep. And Tito was the only one who didn't text and tell me he was sick."

"Okay. All right." I turn on my heels to head back to the car. The store will have to stay closed. "I have outdoor gear in my car. I'll change and be there in a minute."

"The two of us? Is that safe?"

He's right. It's not, but we can't lose these gigs. The cruise ships don't take kindly to disappointing their customers, and if Loco for Cocoa is kicked off the approved tours list, we'll have to go through the grueling application process all over again, costing us time and money we can't afford. "I'll find us a third person. You get the guests to sign the forms, give them the preliminary instructions, and load them into the truck. If you need to keep them happy, dip into the midpoint chocolate stash."

"Got it."

I hang up and let out a breath as I scroll my contact list. Dios.

It's really not easy to find someone in Ponce who's free early morning on a weekday and who actually knows how to rappel and…

Wait a minute. There *is* someone who's available and knows how to do the things I need him to do, and, bonus, he's not far from here. He told me his boat was docked at the marina. That's five minutes away.

Jumping back into my car, I tear out of the lot, hoping Laz is the answer to my prayers.

Chapter 6
Tony

One arm laden with my purchased provisions, which include a big box of mouthwatering Slim Jims, I cross the parking lot toward the dock. Despite wearing shorts and a sleeveless T-shirt, I have sweat dripping down my back. Humid as hell out here.

Mentally running through the list of things I need to do, it takes me longer than it should to sense someone coming up behind me.

But when that someone clears their throat, my heart starts to pound. They've found me already. I've got one shot. Throw the bag at whoever is behind me and reach for my concealed carry. And then what? If it's one of my sisters, all I can do is threaten, because there's no way I'll shoot. I'd rather die, and they know this.

"Lazarus?"

Not my sisters.

Every muscle in my body packs up its briefcase and quits for the day and I almost fall down.

Adrenaline still coursing through my body, I turn.

Honor wears a brown Loco for Cocoa T-shirt, tan cargo shorts, and brown hiking boots. Her silver eyes beam at me from under her Loco for Cocoa baseball cap.

My heart flips in my chest. "Hey." I go for casual. "Whatcha doin' out here?"

Car keys in hand, she waves them at me. "I'm really sorry to bother you, and please don't feel like you have to say yes, but I need a favor."

My heartbeat picks up to a yes-please-right-now-boat's-over-there pace.

Down, boy. She probably wants to borrow a cup of sugar or something. "Anything. I owe you my life, after all."

She shakes her head. "You owe me nothing, and I don't want you to say yes if... it's inconvenient or if you're still too injured."

Her cheeks flush. Freakin' adorable.

Inconvenient? She saved my life, and, despite what she says, I *do* owe her. Man, I really wish I could stay and get to know her better. Nope. No. Shove that shit down and bury it. I can't afford that kind of thinking. This could just as easily have been Justice, Gracie, or any number of my sisters. "I feel right as rain. What's up?"

"My tour guides haven't shown up, and I have a tour from the cruise ship scheduled for this morning. I can't afford to cancel it, but I also can't run the tour with only me and my cousin. It wouldn't be safe."

Oh, shit. This isn't an hour or two. This is an all-day thing. A job, basically. This is a delay I can't afford.

"It's too much. You're obviously preparing to go. I don't—"

"I'm in," I say because I know she wouldn't be asking if she weren't desperate. And, honestly, even if she hadn't saved my life... Well, I might not be part of The Guild anymore, but that doesn't mean I can't help someone when they need me. "I'm all in."

"Are you sure? Are you recovered enough? I don't want to ask anything too extreme of you."

Too extreme? That's basically my home address. "I want extreme, Honor. That's exactly what I want you to ask of me. All day, every day."

Smiling, she cocks her head to the side with a flounce of the ponytail sticking from her cap. "Don't tempt me, Lazarus. I have a feeling we could end up in serious trouble."

I'm sure she didn't mean that to sound dirty, but that's where my mind went, right to dirty trouble.

Swallowing, I hitch a thumb toward my boat. "Can you give me a sec to put my supplies away?"

"Of course. I can't thank you enough. Really."

"No problem."

Well, slight problem. This is a mistake. Logic is shouting at me to leave, but logic is a selfish prick. Honor saved my life on a day when she was grieving. She jumped into the ocean during a storm. She risked her own life to save min,. so, logic can kiss my ass on this one.

Oh, hell, I'm becoming as undisciplined as Justice.

Chapter 7
Honor

Our Loco for Cocoa tour truck is an old, slat-sided, open-air, green military vehicle with seats running along the inside. Parked outside the pier gates, it's crammed with guests when I arrive with the handsome Lazarus Graves.

So handsome that it hurts my heart to look at him. So handsome that he makes me afraid. So handsome that my desire shushes that fear. Not even my anxiety can stand up to the insistent need that keeps wanting to get closer to him.

Walking around the truck, I wave to Junior, who's standing in the center of the bed, collecting forms. Slim as a reed in his Loco for Cocoa uniform—brown baseball hat, tan cargo shorts, brown tee, and hiking boots—he waves back before securing the papers to a clipboard and jumping down.

"Hola, prima." He hands me the clipboard and the keys to the vehicle. There's no question about who's driving. Tipping up his hat, dark skin slick with sweat, he casts a wary look at Laz. "¿Quién es Robin Hood?"

I'm not sure why he has to compare strangers to people he's seen on television or in the movies, but it's pretty consistent theme with him. Though, now that I think about it, Laz *does* kind of look like a muscular version of Robin Hood, with his wavy dark hair, amazing smile, and confident swagger.

"Mira, he's a volunteer who is saving our culos, so show some respect."

Laz snorts. "Always thought of myself as a dark hero." He

holds out his hand. "Lazarus Graves. Your newest tour guide and a quick study."

Cracking his own smile, Junior shakes his hand. "Let's see how quick a study. Climb on the back and make sure everyone is strapped in. There's a mic back there, so unless you're shy, try to charm them."

Despite Junior being rude, bossy, and giving Laz the speaking guide job that takes way more training, Laz doesn't hesitate. "Not for nothin'," he says, grabbing onto the side of the slat-sided truck. "Charm, I got."

So says my melting heart as Laz lifts himself onto the truck with a flexing of arm muscles that causes my hormones to swoon like a teenaged girl at a boy band concert.

"You sure about this?" Junior asks me while rolling his eyes toward Laz.

"Sí." I nod and head toward the cab of the truck.

He follows, obviously not convinced.

"I already grilled him, Jesús." I use his given name so he knows I'm serious. "He knows how to rappel, climb, and has experience with mountaineering that's better than my own."

I open the door to the cab of the truck, put the papers on the front seat, then turn back to him. "It's okay. Really."

Junior's gaze travels toward the big tread of the truck's tires. "Bien. If you're sure..."

As sure as I can be. I climb into the cab. He's still standing there. Dios. "Mira, if he can't hack it," I say, "we'll call the tour early and take everyone back to the posada. They'll love the inn, and Abuelito will fill them with chocolate and charm until they can't see straight."

Junior grunts. "I've been there."

"Haven't we all."

As spry as a cat, he climbs into the back of the truck then, bangs onto the roof of the cab, giving me the all-clear.

I slam the door shut and turn the truck over. It roars to life with a rumble that travels up through my body. As much as I'd rather be making and selling chocolate, I do love driving tours. With the big, black plastic wheel comfortable in my grasp, I shift forward with a bounce as we take off.

After about five minutes of Junior using the microphone to welcome and inform the guests, I hear Laz's voice come through the speaker.

He begins narrating the tour, talking up the island as if he's been giving tours to diverse personalities his whole life. He's a natural.

Before too long, I hit the winding road that leads up the mountain. It's an older road that's more scenic for tourists and a little scary for them, too. I know this road like the back of my hand. I even know how people will react to the scenery before we get there. On my mental cue, the guests, including chatty Laz, grow silent.

I smile because the only way to enjoy this particular section, a downward view so lush with green, so startling in fertile beauty that it captures your heart, is silently.

I love the stillness of this moment... When people from all over the world are touched by what can't be denied—the hand of God Himself crafted every divine leaf, every sun-streaked bit of verdant green, every hill and rock in Puerto Rico.

The moment of awe passes, and I hit the horn twice, signaling Junior to start the chant.

He calls out, "I'm loco for..."

And the group calls back, "Cocoa!"

My heart is light as I swing the truck expertly around a huge stone outcrop that squeezes far into the road, causing us to practically hug the drop. We look closer than we actually are to the edge. It's the first of many sight-unseen turns up the mountain. The first of many times I'll hit the horn and Junior will start the call and response.

We've explained to the group that this is to alert any trucks coming down the other side that we're coming up. The chant is also to keep people calm. The steep drop is terrifying to most people, and it's not like they'd believe me if I told them I could probably drive this road with my eyes closed.

I likely could. Some people have a photographic memory when it comes to words or ideas, but I have that same kind of didactic memory with trails and roads and scenery. If I walk a terrain even once—paved or dirt or stone—I will remember its every dip, rise, curve, and swell.

I pull into the trail parking lot, and, after adjusting my hat, I climb down from the cab. Before I know what's what, Laz rushes over to me, picks me up, and twirls me around.

I'm breathless as he sets me back on my feet and stares at me in wonder. He blurts, "Honor, the way you drive catches my breath. It's like you're one with the earth. The way you pause in the road right before a dip... It's absolutely..."

Maybe realizing what he's done, what he's said, he stops and shakes his head. "I'm sorry. I shouldn't—p"

I stop his words by putting a hand on his chest. "No one has ever noticed that before," I tell him. "You're the first."

He winks at me. "I like being your first."

Laughing, I reach up and tug down the Loco for Cocoa baseball cap he's now wearing. He tips it back up, and we exchange a look that sends a deep longing through me. I want to be closer to him. I want to hear his heartbeat racing with desire. I want to hear his blood pulsing want through every cell of his body. I want to hear his laughter as I rest my head against his chest.

Our stare goes on much too long, but it's not until Junior clears his throat that we break away.

Laz slides me one last grin before he goes around the truck, releases the liftgate, props up the stairs, and begins to help people down.

When the guests have all lined up, Junior hitches up his camo backpack and, in a musical voice, singsongs, "I'm loco for..."

The twenty guests shout, "Cocoa!"

With their laughter and chatter filling the air, we start down the trail to the repelling station.

Chapter 8
Tony

The cliff where Honor and Loco for Cocoa set up their rappelling station is kind of genius. It's high enough to give a thrill and a great view, but not so high as to put the fear of God into their clients.

Stationed at the bottom of a rocky cliff dotted with green moss, I work the belayer, securing the rappelling ropes for each guest and encouraging the hesitant ones. I'm kind of loving this. The thing about sailing to escape your family's wrath is you don't always get to stop and enjoy the view.

A day spent outside, hiking, diving into warm pools of water, repelling, laughing, and hanging out with the enchanting and scorching-hot Honor Silva isn't going to be easy to top. Or forget. Sucks that tomorrow I'll be all by my lonesome, sailing away from Puerto Rico and her.

A pit lodges in my throat at the thought. It's weird, but even though everyone calls me Laz, being here makes me feel like me again. Like Tony. It might be because the activities remind me of the underground training facility back home. Especially this, the climbing. Like I told Honor, climbing is one of my skills. It's also another reason the kids I trained in the gym called me Monkey Man.

Damn. Must not think of home. It brings down my mood, and I'll have plenty of time to brood when I'm sailing alone tomorrow.

Craning my neck, I wait as Junior signals that the last

guest—a big guy named Roger but nicknamed Bud—is ready. I feed the line and keep my feet wide enough to balance as Bud begins to rappel.

Behind me at the edge of the forest, Honor has set up a folding table with chocolate and booze. The other guests, helmets and harnesses off, talk, eat, drink, and mingle loudly, barely paying attention to the last of their group.

Bud doesn't need their encouragement anyway. He's got a decade on me, but has prior military training and has even worked on movie sets, so he knows what he's doing. I like the guy. He's been giving me a hard time all day. Still is.

He calls down, "Make sure you get right under me to catch me if I fall."

"No worries," I call back up, working the rope. "These rocks are super soft. Like cushions."

Bud laughs and continues to lower, walking himself back. He's slow at first, but once he gets the feel of it, he drops quickly, lands feet against stone, then pushes off again.

Halfway down, something in his demeanor shifts. He tucks his feet into a rock, pulls his fingers off the line, and grips stone. It's as if he suddenly decided to free climb.

Sweat rolls from under my helmet, and I blink it from my eyes. "You okay up there, Bud?"

Junior encourages the big man from above with, "Got some beer down there."

His body weight supported on a thin outcrop, Bud calls, "My carabiner."

His carabiner? The piece of metal securing him and his harness to the rope?

"What's going on?" Honor says.

I startle, realizing she's somehow next to me. "Bud has an issue with his carabiner."

We exchange a look. I know what she's going to say before she says it, so I cut her off. "Attach to the belay device. I can climb up to him."

Shaking her head, she looks nervously up at Bud. "No. I'll go."

That's what I knew she was going to say.

Already grabbing her carabiner, I lock her in, hand off the safety line, and unhook myself. "Trust me, I got this."

Well accustomed to supporting my own weight, even by my fingertips, I grasp hold of an edge of rock and pull myself up. It's slippery as all get-out, but I make good on my Monkey Man nickname and ascend rapidly. I find handholds and footholds, almost without thought. In no time, I'm parallel with Bud.

Shit. His legs are trembling, and it's not adrenaline. If you aren't moving, aren't used to climbing, and can't find subtle ways to shift weight, you're going to find your weaknesses quickly.

I wedge my own feet. "What's up?"

Without turning his head, fingers digging into stone so hard they've turned white, he says, "Need another carabiner."

I instantly see what he means. The thing he's wearing is junk. I doubt there's even enough strength in it for me to take time to tie a safety knot. Palms slick with sweat, I keep my voice calm. "No worries, man. I've got one right here."

Honor automatically gives me the feed as I tug the rope from below. Bud doesn't need to be told what to do—he simply eases back, giving me the space to secure the new equipment.

My fingers expertly spin the clasp on the new carabiner and loop it around the line. The moment it's set, Bud relaxes and the new equipment takes his weight. I reach for the old one, and, *bam*! it gives way. I barely manage to catch the bigger pieces.

Damn. That was close.

Bud looks down below. "I'm good to go?"

Can't blame him for wanting out of here. Double-checking his equipment, I signal Honor. She gives me a thumbs up. "You're good," I say, and he continues down.

I stare at the broken carabiner in my palm. It's stressed and old. If Bud hadn't been paying attention, it's likely he would've fallen.

Pocketing the pieces, I free-climb back down. At the bottom, I find Honor hugging Bud. "I'm so sorry. This equipment…"

She stops whatever excuse she'd been about to issue. Honestly, what can she say? The guy could've died.

Bud shakes his head. "You need to check your equipment more often. I won't start any trouble, but that could've been bad."

Chastised and confused, she nods. "Thank you, Bud. This will never happen again. I promise. And if you ever need a place to stay on Puerto Rico, you have a free room at Loco for Cocoa."

Bud nods once, then turns and scoops me into a bear hug that nearly cracks my ribs. "Thanks," he says with obvious emotion in his voice.

"No problem, man. Sorry this spoiled the adventure for you."

He puts me down and scratches his salt-and-red-pepper beard. "I need a drink." Legs looking a little wobbly, he joins the others at the table, picks up a bottle of whiskey, and pours himself a cup.

Taking the pieces of carabiner out of my pocket, I hand them to Honor.

Her silver eyes run over the distressed pieces in confusion. "This isn't one of our carabiners. Ours are brand new because we've only been doing tours for about a year."

"Coming down," Junior calls, and Honor readies the lines. Once he's down, she holds out the broken equipment to show him. "Didn't you check?"

Junior disengages, steps from the lines, and looks at her hand. He shakes his head. "We checked them last night."

Honor holds up the old stressed piece. There's no mistaking the condition of the equipment, and Junior has had his hands all over it. She whispers harshly, "You didn't notice this wasn't one of ours?"

"No. Coño." Junior removes his safety helmet and wipes sweat from his forehead. "The guy kept chatting with me, and I was trying to do two jobs at once. We are a few people short, you know."

Honor twists the metal in the waning light of day. "What

about when you opened the equipment locker under the seats in the truck? Did it look like anything had been tampered with?"

"No. The harnesses were there, stacked and ready. I just assumed..." He shakes his head. "Lo siento. It's my fault. I should've been paying more attention."

"Okay. But we need to make sure there's no way for anyone to steal our equipment again and replace it with their own used stuff." She pockets the pieces with her face a cross between angry, confused, and frightened. "Let's get everyone to the hotel so they can get some food and visit the chocolate shop before we take them back to the ship."

After packing everything up, we begin to hike back through the jungle. I'm not surprised to find most of the guest have no idea what happened. They'd been talking and drinking, and danger hadn't seemed close at hand. That's the way it works with most people, but I'm not most people, and I can't dismiss what happened.

I drop back to talk with Honor. "You leave your equipment in the truck?"

She lets out a breath heavy with tension. Or regret. "Yeah. It's locked, but obviously not well enough. It never occurred to me that someone would need money badly enough to steal our equipment and pawn their old stuff off on us."

Okay, so maybe I grew up in a suspicious environment, but I'm not ready to jump to that innocent a conclusion. "Honor, you don't have anyone who would want to sabotage your business, right? I mean, first your guides don't show up and now the equipment fails. Seems kind of suspicious."

She gapes at me, and it's obvious this is the first moment she's considered these things as connected. She says, "Where do you come from?"

Right there, I see it. Now that I introduced the concept, she has her own suspicions. Still, she doesn't know me well enough, or maybe doesn't want to get into it right now to answer my question.

I play along. "No place near as fun as being with you."

Chapter 9
Honor

A spin of my steering wheel and I direct the tour truck up the long road that cuts between acres of cocoa trees. I proceed slowly, so people can watch the men with poles tending the trees. I slow more as we pass the covered porch with vats used for fermenting cocoa beans lined up under the red steel roof. The architect in charge of this process—Tío's self-description—works among the vats.

Expecting nothing, I wave at Tío José. Of course, he turns his back on me. He's been annoyed with me ever since I moved here and took a hand in running Loco for Cocoa. Oh well, can't win everyone over.

I pull up to the yellow-walled and white-trimmed, thirty-six-room posada with its charming farmer's porch. Seated at one of the outdoor tables, Abuelito stands and moves down the front stairs to greet the truckload of people.

He looks like a man twenty years younger, with a straight spine and thick, mostly gray hair swept into a ponytail. As usual on tour days, he wears his trademark white hat, white shirt, and white pants,

After parking, Laz and Junior get the stairs in position to help the guests out, and I run around the truck to Abuelito. This has been the kind of day where I need a hug.

He draws me in and holds me tight. "¿Esta bien, mija?" he says, kissing me on the top of my head, rubbing my back.

I take in his reassuring cocoa butter scent before answering, "Bien, Abuelito."

And I *am* fine. Well, now at least. It doesn't erase what happened or the suspicion Laz put in my head, but there's nothing like the feeling of my grandfather's hug to put things in perspective.

We move around to the back of the truck and Abuelito turns on his charm, greeting the guests with a big smile as Laz and Junior help them down the stairs. His excited words roll over me.

"¡Bienvenido! Welcome to Loco for Cocoa. This posada was begun by my wife, Flor Marie, who purchased the abandoned structure nearly forty years ago. My granddaughter"—he motions to me, and a few people make noises of surprise that he's my grandfather—"expanded the business two years ago. One year ago"—he holds up one finger—"we opened Cocoa Casa, our chocolate store, located behind the posada. Shortly after, we started our agro-tours." He opens his arms wide. "I hope you all enjoyed your tour today."

There's a cheer among the group, and even Bud is smiling. Thank God. It's a relief to hand the group over to my grandfather's expert care. If there's one thing he knows how to do, it's how to make a guest feel welcome.

Abuelito leads them away, pointing out architectural details as he smoothly takes them to the white covered porch and the tables set up under ceiling fans, so they can comfortably eat and drink. Our staff quickly circulates among the guests, offering hand towels to clean themselves and handing out chocolate lemonade.

It's a joy to watch people try my perfect lemonade recipe. They sip and smile and sip again. I invented that recipe as a tween. That's what hooked me on creating treats for people. I mean, you can enjoy a good meal, but it can't put a smile on your face like chocolate.

"This place is great," Laz says, coming up beside me. "I love the combination of the surrounding dense forest and the posada's fairy-tale charm."

"Ay." I put a hand over my mouth, because I'd forgotten. "You've never been here before. Me olvidé."

He laughs. "You forgot?"

"You fit so perfectly into the tour"—not only the tour but my life and my world—"that it seems like you've been here before." *Forever.*

The tour truck starts up with a rev of its engine, saving me from myself as Junior pulls it away from the front of the inn.

"Feels familiar to me, too," Laz says softly, then nods toward Abuelito. "Your grandfather is a snazzy dresser."

I throw my head back and laugh. "He calls it his costume. When he first came up with the idea of doing tours for extra income—he ran tours in San Juan where he grew up—he also came up with his farmer persona. As silly as it sounded to me, he was right. Guests love it."

"Hard not to," Laz says, "He's so damn charming. I almost joined the group."

Smiling, I say, "Would you like your own personal tour?"

"I would."

Bouncing happily on my toes, I lead him up the front porch and inside. We nod to our guests, who are now looking at menus. They're going to love the food. Abuelito's a fine chef who trained the other cook who works here. And I can't help but notice many of the guests have already finished their drinks. Looks like we rescued this tour.

"Wow," Laz says when we enter. He's staring at the handcrafted wooden front desk that seems to grow into the matching banister and railing. Made out of wood from the surrounding jungle, the desk extends out in rough branches that are bound together, climbing up along the steps. It's as if the railing is a tree that sprang to life, curving and reaching out as it grew.

I can't help but beam. "That's all original. Wela wanted it to seem like an extension of the woods."

"Wela?"

I take in a pained breath as heat rises into my face. "That's what I called my grandmother. It was my way of saying abuela as a child because my Spanish was nearly nonexistent." He doesn't ask and I don't explain. My bilingual mom only spoke Spanish to express extreme emotions, joy or anger, or when we came to visit here, about once a year.

"You're an Olympic archer?"

I follow his gaze to the trophy case behind the desk filled with various-sized trophies, a picture of my Olympic team, and my compound bow. "I was only an alternate."

He grunts a laugh. "Slacker."

Joy bubbles up inside me as it's obvious he's joking, and I can see the wonder in his eyes. It feels good, this sharing of my world and myself with him.

Eager to lead him through the posada, I grab his hand. Heat washes down my body, tugs at my center, and an "Mmm" escapes my lips.

His eyebrows shoot up.

At this point, why hide it? "Good enough to eat," I whisper under my breath, and pull him down the hall. We walk through the dining room, the quaint library/conversation area, and go onto the back patio. Wedged between large-leafed trees and ferns is an enormous tree with an enormous tree house built atop it. Beyond that is my store, the Cocoa Casa.

"I love this place."

Happy with his response, I lean into him, and I don't even think about it. It feels so natural.

He runs his nose along my cheek. "Your grandfather mentioned that you'd done some renovations."

My heart, like my steps, grows lighter as I lead him to the tree house. "After Mom died, I needed a project and Loco for Cocoa needed a lifeline. I invested my inheritance and my desire to build something beautiful from all that pain."

He squeezes my hand. "You succeeded."

My throat fills with emotion as we walk hand-in-hand down the stone walkway. Now that I think about it, it's not only that Laz fits into this place, my world, it's like this place, my world, has been waiting for him all along. Everything somehow feels better, more complete, with him here.

That's a crazy thought. A rash and dangerous thought because, as he's already explained to me many times, he can't stick around. He's sailing around the world maybe forever. My heart trembles with regret and an unnamed fear.

What is happening to me? I'm not my mother. I do *not* rush into a relationship knowing it will end badly. I do not go boldly after what I want despite the prospect of pain. I cannot afford to have my heart, still repairing from the loss of Mom, shattered again.

And yet, I want him more than any of my fears and prospects of future pain. Maybe, and this is an odd thought, it's never been that I wasn't like Mom. Maybe I've never before met anyone I wanted enough to do what she did—toss caution to the wind.

What was it Laz said? *The Cowardly Lion was tough, too. He just needed the right situation to bring it out.*

Consider me brought out. I'd rather *one* night with him than *no* nights with him. No matter what the cost.

Chapter 10
Tony

Loco for Cocoa is like a homey bed-and-breakfast, but also has some unexpected areas that are whimsical and unique, like the yoga room, built up high and supported by the trees. We climbed a winding staircase to get into this room that's open on all sides, with wood floor, beams, and pitched roof.

"It's a tree house," I say.

"An expensive one," she says. "Half of the cost of our renovation went into this casa del árbol. I wanted guests to have a place to really connect with the jungle. To really feel the trees and the aliveness of everything. And Abuelito is a practitioner of yoga."

Dude does yoga? "I love that letting people connect with this place, the realness of it, is important to you."

She points at the bamboo slats rolled up along the glassless window. "Well, we only allow so much realness. There are some seasons that are buggier than others and rain is frequent." She walks over to flick on the fans along the ceiling.

Bridget, a yogi herself, would freakin' love this tree house, uh, casa del árbol.

Must not think of Bridget. Or the fact that her mind has been altered and she's been robbed of the most sacred part of herself—her memories—because she'd been trying to save her hot-headed sister.

"Who teaches the yoga classes—you?"

She laughs. "No. During classes, I'm usually in the Cocoa

Casa kitchen making chocolate. Abuelito hired a yoga teacher, Lanie. She's forty years younger, but I'm pretty sure she has a crush on him."

"That's it. I've got to start eating whatever it is this guy is eating."

She laughs. "I think it's chocolate." She dips her head toward the windows in a *this-way* gesture then, silent as a cat across plush carpet, walks to the edge of the room and looks out into the distance.

I watch her go—because I like to watch her. I like the way she glides those sleek curves and long limbs.

When she sees I haven't moved, Honor points at the view. "You can almost see forever from here."

It's obvious she wants me there, so I stroll across the room and look out over the trees and at the distant speck of ocean. "That's incredible."

Unexpectedly she turns toward me, closes the two inches between us, and lifts her chin as if inviting me to kiss her.

Licking my lips, I look down at her. I know what she wants, what *I* desperately want, but I need her to make that move. It's not only because I like it when she's bold, but because I need her to take what she wants. Because, when I leave Puerto Rico tomorrow, I don't want to feel like an absolute shit.

Her breathing picks up.

Mine, too. I stand my ground as color rises into her cheeks. This might be the hardest thing I've ever done—holding still when all I want to do is crash into her, drag her body against mine, claim her mouth, and run my hands all over her.

I silently sent her a do-it-please-fucking-do-it signal.

She steps away.

Shiiit.

She says, "Would you like to see the chocolate store?"

"Your lead," I tell her, because it really, really is.

Chapter 11
Honor

Coño. I curse myself as Laz and I descend the last step from the yoga casa del árbol and walk the stone pathways between chalets.

Why didn't I kiss him? I could see he wanted me to—there's no way *not* to feel the scorching heat between us—but when he looked down at me, too handsome to be real, I froze with uncertainty. Cowardly Lion indeed.

Keeping close enough to him that our arms rub together, I direct him toward my chocolate store. I tangle our hands and manage to hold his. He looks down at our joined fingers and grins. Okay, so maybe I am trying to make up for the failed kiss. What of it?

"I've saved the best for last," I tell him.

His eyebrows go up and his smile widens.

I shove him playfully as we walk. "Honestly," I say, "the jungle is steamy enough without the looks you keep sending me."

"That's the only look I've got when it comes to you, Daring Honor."

Ha! Daring, my culo. But it's nice to know my mind isn't the only one so consumed with thoughts of sex that everything sounds dirty.

I stop at the door to the Cocoa Casa because I want him to know something before he goes inside. "This place, this store, has always been my dream. Redoing the lodge and even the tours came about because of this dream. Every recipe inside is mine."

He nods his understanding, then chucks me under the chin. "I can't wait to get my lips around your recipes."

There's a growl in his voice that sends heat shooting down my body and warmth tingling between my legs. I lean into him and whisper, "You're going to enjoy every minute of it."

He makes a choked sound, and I can't help the wave of triumph. I finally get why Mom was so spontaneous with her romantic relationships. Just this flirting feels amazing. I'm so keyed up, I'm not sure how my skin is containing me.

Opening the door, I pull him inside.

My assistant and the posada's part-time staff and yoga teacher, Lanie, greets us with a wave as she continues to stack colorful boxes on the counter.

I wave back to the slim blonde, then close my eyes and inhale deeply. The cool air smells of sugar and chocolate and spices. And well it should, with cases of chocolate, shelves of wrapped chocolate, fudge and elaborate displays of truffles, and red-and-black boxed chocolates lining the walls.

I open my eyes and find him staring at me with his mouth open. Everything around me seems to still as the air between us buzzes with electricity. I should've kissed him. I wish I had. Maybe now? I step closer.

Laz reaches for me—

And the chimes over the entry door ring.

I jump away from Laz as an old family friend, Ford Fairchild, enters the store. A trim man, with a razor-straight nose peeling from a bad sunburn, Ford is one of my favorite people.

He meets my eyes and jokingly says, "Store's packed." He winks or tries to wink, but it turns into a blink. Ford has some quirky social awkwardness, but it's part of his charm. That and his loyalty.

When I put the word out to my mother's wealthy friends in the States that I could use a few bodies to fill rooms, he was one of the first to respond. He's been here for almost three weeks now, renting his room, buying drinks for other guests, and doing everything he can to pour money into my business.

Leaving Laz, I greet Ford with a kiss to his cheek. "Is it true you're leaving next week?"

"Afraid so." He smiles and a deep dimple appears on the left side of his mouth. "My Uncle Winthrop is insisting I come home for an important meeting. Apparently, he needs to see my face to believe that I still work for him." He laughs.

I don't. I met his Uncle Winthrop, a movie financier, when I was younger, and I've never forgotten the dismissive way he spoke to me. Ford is much too kind to work for such a jerk. "We'll be sad to see you go, but I'm sure your wife and daughter will be home soon."

"Yes. They're due back from Japan next week, and I'm eager to see them."

His wife is an illustrator for graphic novels. She travels a lot, going to conventions and exhibits. Ford's coming here to help me is one of the few times he's been without his wife and five-year-old daughter on tour.

Grabbing his hand, I say, "I really appreciate you coming here. It's been wonderful spending time with you."

He takes a moment, clears his throat, and says, "You, too, Honora. It's been amazing getting to know you better."

Lanie, blonde hair cut close around her fair face, walks over. "Hi, Ford, did you need help with something?" She flicks light blue eyes toward Laz, letting me know she has this covered.

I smile in gratitude because I can see Ford tomorrow, but I know Laz is only here for tonight.

Leaving her to help Ford, I catch up to Laz who's examining the contents of the cases. "You like?"

He jumps at the sound of my voice, and his eyebrows draw together. "You're, like, ninja quiet."

I laugh, something that I've done over and over again today with so little effort. I'd forgotten I could laugh so much. "Funny, I've been told I'm mouse quiet, but I like ninja much better."

"You are no mouse," he says with determination, then adds quietly, "It's a great store."

"It is," I say. "Every time I come in here, my chocolatier's heart beats faster. I'm so glad you like it, but one thing is making me nervous."

"Just one thing?" he says, hooking a finger around a strand of my hair and twirling it.

Well, many things about him make me nervous, but right now... "What's your favorite?" I point at the rows of dishes in the glass case, white china-filled with different types of chocolate and truffles.

"My favorite?" He looks around. "Would it disappoint you if I said I'm not a huge chocolate fan?"

I take a step back. "Are you trying to cause me physical pain?"

He laughs. "I love chocolate." He closes the distance, getting so close I can almost feel his front against my front. "Do you have anything with some bite?"

Biting. Yes. What? I'm losing my mind. How can I not? He is hotter than anything I have in this store. But this is my chance to make up for the missed opportunity in the yoga casa. *Bold, Honor. Be bold.*

Leaning left, I gather up a jar of chocolate sticks from a shelf and take one out. Putting the jar back, I hold it up. "I invented this."

He looks doubtfully at the straw. "I've seen them before. It's a small, chocolate straw that you dip in coffee, right?"

I shake my head and pull off the paper wrapper. "Nope. It's a kissing stick. The middle is filled with a warm surprise, but as you can see, it's a little large for one mouth to suck on."

Nodding, he says very seriously, "I think I need a demonstration."

Oh, good. That's exactly the response I wanted. I feign annoyance, though I can feel my cheeks burn, and say, "The things I do for my craft."

I put the chocolate straw into my mouth, up to the red line at the center. I tilt up my chin, and he doesn't hesitate. He dips down and captures the other end of the stick, so that his lips are flush with mine.

Heat.

Heat like I've never felt before shoots through my body. I clutch him because I have no choice. There's no way *not* to bring him closer, *us* closer. My body has taken over, and my mind has closed down.

Closer. More. Closer. Now.

The chocolate reacts instantly, melting, and he moves his slippery lips against mine, then darts his tongue in and out, licking the chocolate.

I am on fire.

The cayenne warms my tingling mouth, and I find a boldness I have never, ever known. I open my mouth, tangle my tongue with his, fist his shirt, and deepen our connection and our kiss.

He moans softly, and I move against him. He puts his arms around me, drags me tight against him.

He let me have the first move, the first kiss, but he takes control now, demonstrating his own need.

His body is hard against me, his mouth pulling at me, tasting me. He is chocolate and heat and spice, and I am so lost that the jingle of bells over the door does nothing to pull me from him.

Until he puts his hands on my upper arms and pulls back, and I remember where we are and what that bell sound means—

Likely Ford leaving after seeing me making out with a guest. Yikes.

I step back from Laz, and we stare at each other. Our breathing is heavy and much too loud. The heat in my mouth is nothing compared to the heat building between my legs. I can't utter a single word. Not one.

What is this?

What is happening to me?

I've never felt this way about a man. I thought this kind of attraction—the kind that drives away doubt and common sense—was a myth. I thought it was something my mother wanted to believe, not something real.

I've had four lovers in my twenty-six years on this Earth,

and they've all been fun and exciting, but this is *not* fun and exciting. This is fierce need and overpowering desire and an inability to think straight. All I can think about is taking him up to my room and ripping off his clothes.

But I have to be cautious. This is my first experience with these feelings, this desire, but that doesn't mean it's his. He likely does this to a lot of women.

He licks his lips and says, "Sweetest thing I've ever tasted."

I don't miss the genuine tension in his thick voice. He might do this to other women, but I definitely do something to him, and, for this night, it's more than enough. I'll hurt tomorrow. "My grandfather usually finishes the tour around five, so we have a little bit of time. Would you like me to show you the rooms?"

He hooks a finger through the loop of my cargo shorts, pulls me closer, leans down and growls. "Fantastic idea. Let's start with yours."

Waving goodbye to Lanie, I tug Laz out the door and we run hand-in-hand down the winding trail to the hotel.

I stop short and Laz does too as José appears out of nowhere. Okay, not out of nowhere; he steps out of a side door that leads to the staff offices. Clad in rubber boots, mud-green pants, and a brown shirt soaked in sweat at the armpits and around the neck, he blocks the path in front of us.

"Uncle José?"

"¿Qué pasó en la gira de hoy? Someone was hurt?"

Ay. Dios. Mío.

Chapter 12
Tony

On the walkway behind Loco for Cocoa, two steps from the door that would've led us inside Honor's room, I'm hanging back as Honor's uncle—a tall, muscular guy with white-streaked black hair and chestnut-brown eyes—shows up. His timing, considering our goal, is comical enough to require a horse-walks-into-a-bar rim shot. *Ba-dum-tish.*

Except no one is laughing. Honor glares at him before telling me, "I need to talk to my uncle in private. It'll only be a minute. Don't go anywhere."

I can't help the snort of laughter or the full-stop gesture of my upraised hands. "Even if my car was here and headed straight at me."

A smile twitches at the corner of her mouth, but her face falls to serious as she faces her uncle.

For his part, José looks equally annoyed, even a little hostile. They walk off together and head into a side door.

And though I have no intention of leaving the hotel, that doesn't mean I'll actually stand stock-still out here. Especially when I have an interest in this particular conversation.

And there *it* is. The bone-deep truth of who I am. I was raised to spy and cross every red line, including on a conversation between a woman I just met and her uncle. That *should* make me feel uncomfortable or twitchy, but it doesn't, not really. Because I don't like the resentment that guy's putting out, and what happened on the tour today has my Spidey sense tingling, so I need to know more.

Running on the balls of my feet, I catch the door they went through before it clicks shut. I swing into the hall and hang back as they turn a corner.

They don't even look around, not once. Huh. Spying on regular people is easy. Not like spying on my sisters or bad guys or law enforcement or anyone with any kind of situational awareness.

The office door they pass through closes with a *click*, and I stroll up to it. Using a special app on my burner phone, along with a small ear device, I easily listen to the conversation on the other side of the door.

As I lean against the wall, my phone shows me some game I've never played before. I pretend to play while hitting buttons mindlessly and focusing on the conversation.

"I told you, Honora. I have told you a thousand times that the tours are dangerous. Now you must see that we need to take that offer and get out while we can."

What offer?

With a deep sigh, Honor says, "Tío, you know why we had to start the tours, and why we still need them. As for the offer, I don't want to give up on Wela's dream for this place. Trust me, our business will make it past this. We're five years away from having a thriving chocolate store, and—"

"And if a storm comes? Or if the U.S. changes a law? Or if any one of a thousand things happens? We need to split the four million and go lie on a beach in San Juan."

There's a long pause, and though I don't know Honor well, not really, I picture her stunned face growing angry.

"The four million offered to buy the property and business is large, but not if you deduct the two million I've invested—"

"You've invested money." He spits the words. "My blood is here. The arthritis in my fingers. My sweat. The kink in my back. Things you can't equal. That has paid off as much as your dollars. I ferment the beans."

"Of course, Tío, I didn't mean…"

I pull out my earpiece and walk away. It's that or bust in. And that's not my place, even though he's trying to bully her into doing what he wants, manipulating her and belittling her contributions when it's obvious to me, even after only one day, that she is tireless in her efforts to make this place work. He's completely dismissing her financial contributions as well, and her reasoning. What an ass.

None of this makes me feel better about today's near miss. Could Honor be in real trouble here? I rub a frustrated hand across my face before making my way back outside.

Something isn't right; I can feel it in my bones.

Agitated, I sit on a bench by the edge of the garden path and wait for Honor to come back. Maybe I should've knocked on the office door and interrupted. I hate doing nothing and I absolutely can't stand to hear a man bully a woman like that.

Great, Tone. You were raised with a bunch of kickass women, and you revert to character the moment you leave?

Justice's voice in my head? That's new. And unwanted. Still, I mentally converse with her. "Yeah, J, I get it. Honor is capable of defending herself, not like the women we rescue— trapped by circumstance, poverty, brutality, and conditioning. But you're not here."

Truth is, if she were here, she'd probably be telling me the same thing. In this way, my sister and I are built differently. She learned to fight to defend herself, learned to be quick and skilled and a deadly shot because there was a time when her weakness made her a victim. I learned to fight to defend others, learned to use my strength to defend those who are weak because there was a time when my weakness had made someone I love into a victim: my mom.

That difference might not seem like much, but it's everything tonight. Hearing José berate and mistreat Honor reminds me of how Dad would talk to Mom, of how I could do nothing about it, of how, when I finally did try to help, it'd been too late.

To this day, it's my greatest shame—being unable to defend Mom from that abuse, then keeping quiet about her death after. It's why, when I'd realized Justice, as capable as she is, was about to go off and get herself killed, I'd risked everything to speak up and keep her safe. It'd cost me—my integrity, my relationships, and my world. But she's alive, so it was worth it.

Fifteen minutes pass before Honor comes back out, and I'm nearly pacing when she does. Her face is pinched and angry, and I'm ready to let her vent. More than ready, even though, and this is just an observation, I'm so not getting laid now.

Honor walks over. I stand and reach out to her. She reaches too, grabs me my hand, and tugs me along, throwing back, "Let's get to my room. We don't have a lot of time."

Dumbstruck with a surge of lust, I let her lead me inside. We skirt through the dining area then the kitchen, where she lets my hand go and acts like she's giving me a tour, nodding here and there to her kitchen staff. Guess it isn't easy to be the boss and have a sex life.

With a brisk and boss-like, "Follow me," she leads me up a back staircase in the corner of the kitchen.

At the top of the stairs, we enter a small, dimly lit hallway, and I realize this is where staff lives. She unlocks one of the wooden doors with a key, an actual fucking key. A two-year-old could pick that lock. I'll bring it up later. Much later.

Honor's room is more like a suite, with a large outer room that includes a sitting area, desk, fireplace, and a miniscule kitchenette. Looking through the doorway, I see another room with a big bed under a plush comforter.

She shuts the front door and steps up to me, putting her hands on my waist.

I look down at her, waiting to see what she'll do. Her face is still a little cross, but now there's something else there too. Fear.

"You're afraid," I say.

She looks down and away.

I put a finger under her chin and lift. "I get it. This day has been filled with ups and downs, so much emotion, and now this thing between us. It's a wildfire, big and fast-moving, and full of heat. And we don't have time to take it for granted because this moment is all we get. So yeah, I understand, but I think I know how to make it better."

"How?

Slowly, slow enough to set a different mood, I bend and kiss her, gentle and sure, taking my time to learn the incredible feel of her lips, her silky tongue. Taking my time to soak in her moaning response, to savor the sweetness of her mouth.

Our breathing picks up and her low moans turn to eager groans. I am so hard my shorts became uncomfortably tight. I roll my hips against her, and she grasps my sides, making soft sounds and demanding tugs.

Her need comes alive, robs her of her fear, and drives her to take control. I smile against her lips, because I am so here for it.

She slips her hands under my shirt. Wild and brash and needy, she rubs her hands along my stomach, groaning.

Her hot need, her uninhibited truth is what I want from her, so I whisper, "Take what you want."

She unzips my shorts.

Wildfire.

Chapter 13
Honor

It's a workday. Ten minutes ago, I had a fight with Tío José. I have guests from the cruise ships walking around, one of whom was nearly injured, and here I am in my bedroom, rubbing my hot hands along a man I just met.

And yet, he is all that matters. I couldn't stop if I wanted to. This man is so handsome and sexy, so sweet and attentive, so much of what I want—have always wanted, though I'm not sure I knew it—that I cannot stop demanding more of him, all of him.

Not that he's asking me to stop. He's doing the opposite. He's giving me room to explore, room to enjoy, and room to set the pace. And, for once, that's how I want it.

Furious after that exchange with Tío José, I want to be with someone who lets me take the lead and respects me enough to give me that control.

I have no idea how Laz seems to know that, but he does. And his response and encouraging patience are setting me on fire. Rubbing against his hardness, I kiss him until we're both breathing heavily and tearing each other's clothes off.

Which come off in record time.

Naked, we crash back together. He puts his hands on the sides of my face, kisses me, long and deep. I whimper at the perfect feel of him, arch against him, begging him to take me.

Laz pulls away, steps back. *What?* He reaches down and put his hand against my center, cupping me, the palm of his hand hard against my clit. Moisture pools between my legs, and I gyrate against his hand.

A challenging look settles on his face. "Ask me," he says.

Ask? No. He has to take. Asking… I know what I said about wanting to be in charge, but this…?

His finger brushes over my clit.

"I'm not sure," I say, as my eyes roll back in my head. He kisses me. A kiss for the ages. A kiss like fire. A deep and probing kiss, an expert and sucking kiss that draws need from me in a swell that breaks through all my inhibitions.

Panting, he pulls back, looks pointedly at me. "Tell me what you want."

This time, I don't hesitate. "Get on your knees," I order him, "and taste me."

He grins that beautiful smile and drops to his knees. His arms snake around and he grips a butt cheek in each palm. He brushes his tongue against my clit. I jerk with pleasure. He flicks his tongue against my clit while moaning with deep, heady vibrations.

His mouth covers me with that vibrating, sucking heat. His tongue rings my clit. Encompassed on all sides by him, appreciated, worked, worshipped by him—I lean my hands against his shoulders for support. I have to. I can no longer feel my legs.

The building pressure, the tingling need, the hot warmth has me whimpering approval. He is everywhere, his hands, his tongue, but I want more.

"Harder," I say. His hands tighten against each cheek, fingers digging into flesh as he drives his tongue harder against me. "Yes. Suck me," I say, and he sucks me so expertly, so sweetly, so perfectly, I throw my head back and have to bite my tongue to keep from screaming his name.

The pressure builds under the eager insistence of his teasing tongue, the work of his expert mouth. The orgasm breaks over me in a wave of pleasure that has me crying out, coming against his mouth as his hands hold my shaking body tightly to him. He wrings every last tremor of delight from me before gentling, releasing his hold on me, and looking up into my face.

I come back from the bliss, tingles still dancing through me, and stare down at this beautiful man. I have never seen such a naked desire in someone. It robs me of my breath. "Take me," I whisper.

He rises to me, breathing heavily. He kisses my ear. "Never been this hard in my life. Honor, do you have a—"

My two-way squawks to life. "Guests are coming back. Ready in ten."

Junior, telling me the guests are coming back from the tour and will be ready in ten minutes to head back to the ship. How has the time gotten away from me?

Laz moans a low curse against my neck. "That's my ride."

Smiling, I grasp his hard-on tight. "You're not leaving here like this."

"Honora." My name is a moan on his lips.

"Shh," I say and begin to stroke him. Judging by the hiss that escapes him, he wasn't expecting that.

I work the length of him, tightening and releasing, fast and hard. He drops his head, moans a pleasure-pained sound against my ear. Feeling a little wicked, I stop. His eyes pop open. My voice tight with desire, I say, "Put your hand over mine."

His eyes swim with approval as he places his hand over the top of mine. I'm breathing so heavily I can barely say, "With me."

We quickly find our rhythm. His beautiful, muscled body, so strong and capable, naked and willing, and his hard-on between us is the hottest thing I've ever seen.

Together, our hands move along his flesh, faster then harder. I'm so turned on that I alternate between watching our hands slide along his cock to watching the pained pleasure slide across his face, to letting my gaze slide over every beautiful muscle in his ripped body. His moans and rapid breathing tell me he is getting close.

My gaze darts back to his face. I expect to see him with his eyes closed, but they are open and staring at me. His lips are parted. His eyes dip for a moment to my full breasts bouncing with our movements.

I know exactly the moment he needs me. I pick up the pace, and he cries out, tightened his hand around mine. And together, we pump, a hard, fast, breathtaking beat that fills the room with sound and heat.

He comes with a moan so sexy it has moisture pooling between my legs. I release him. And we crash together again, spontaneously grabbing at each other and kissing. A kiss that feels like an ellipsis, the start of something that has no end. It feels like forever.

I cling fiercely to him, wanting this feeling to be true and knowing it a lie. This kiss, this embrace, is our goodbye.

Chapter 14
Tony

Knowing the tour guests and her family will be waiting for us, I dress quickly in Honor's room. She's done before me, and I catch her watching me. Grabbing her hand, I kiss it softly and begin to lead her out.

She pulls back. "We can't go down there together."

"Why not?"

Her eyes open wide, round and innocent. "People will suspect."

"Okay." I can barely stop myself from laughing. I kiss her softly on her cheek. "I'll go out first."

At the doorhandle, I stop. I shouldn't. I know I shouldn't. But I can't help myself. All of her guides not showing up, the near accident, and her uncle's anger are striking chords of warning in me. Not just chords, a gong.

I exhale, lean back against the door. "Honor, are you sure there's no one who would want to bring down your business? There's no competitor on the islands, maybe even a family member who wants you to run the business a certain way?"

Her eyes slit at me.

Yeah, fine, that wasn't subtle, but I don't have time for subtle. For a moment, I know she's going to tell me something important, then something in her eyes shifts and she says, "Don't worry about it."

Nah. I don't work that way. "If you're tryin' not to drag me into something, worried because I have to leave, don't be. I'm asking here. What crossed your mind?"

"You *do* have to leave."

"Honor."

"It really isn't anything you need to worry about."

I open my mouth to tell her to think again, but whatever she sees on my face has her shoulders dropping.

"Okay. Fine. We had an offer on the business, farm, lodge, cocoa store—the whole thing. It was a crazy offer. Way more than the business is worth right now. I declined it."

That puts what José said in a whole new context. "Could one accident, the thing with Bud, force you to sell?"

"Yes. If we'd lost the cruise ship business, I probably would've been forced to sell. I've put every dime I had into the business—not only money I saved, but my inheritance. I need the cruise business to keep the hotel up and running until I can make a name for myself with the chocolate."

She *is* in trouble. Shit. "Who would benefit most from the money from this offer?"

"Directly, very few people. The agent in charge of the offer, and me, my grandfather, and my uncle, who are all part owners of Loco for Cocoa."

Not a lot of suspects on that list. I could probably figure this thing out fairly quickly. "I'd like to help you investigate before I set sail. Interview the guides, talk to whoever made the offer—"

"I don't know who made the offer. It was anonymous. I only know the agent."

"Then we talk to the agent brokering the deal. Okay?"

"You said you have to set sail tomorrow."

"I do have to. I will. But I've got the morning free, so let's check it out. I'll feel better if I know before I set sail what's going on here. Trust me, this is what I do." I shake my head. "It's what I did."

"You protected people? And now you're trying to make sure I'm safe?"

For all the good it's done me. It seems like every time I try to do the right thing, protect people I care about, it blows up in my face. But that doesn't mean I'm going to stop trying.

"Yeah. And I still owe you a life debt, so don't mess with me."

Chapter 15
Honor

The rhythmic *whoosh* of Ponce's ocean waves slap the shoreline and spill in through my car's open windows. The drive is slow, like island life. It's also hot, but I like the weather as hot as I like my men. Well, one man.

And speaking of his hotness… There he is, almost hidden against the brown wall of the restaurant where we said we'd meet when we parted ways yesterday.

I pull into the parking lot, and Laz strolls toward me. Not stroll, that gait is *not* a stroll. He's stalking toward me with his limber, packed muscle ready for action as his eyes take in the area. I can see it now, see the protector underneath the casual kiteboarder and mountaineer I've already met. This is another side to him. Even what he's wearing is not as casual as what he had on yesterday. He's wearing military cargo pants, olive green, with a matching T-shirt, worn loosely out, and thick-soled black boots.

His outfit, along with his unruly dark hair, the stern set to his jaw, and the intensity of his walk warn me that this man is dangerous.

Should I be afraid? It was his job to protect people, so he has some kind of training and he's not Lazarus Graves.

In the hospital, that information had seemed light and fun. Or my hormone-addled brain had made it feel that way. Now… I'm worried. For him or about him, I'm not entirely sure, because I can't trust myself right now.

Sliding into the passenger seat, he leans toward me, and I lean the rest of the way to him. We meet in the middle and kiss, lightly at first, then deeper and wetter, then frantic and groping.

My body screams its desire at me. *I don't care. I'll pay whatever price there is to pay to be near him.*

A chill runs through my body, and I can't tell if it's a premonition that the price will be too high or a thrill at my growing boldness. What is the difference between boldness and recklessness?

Maybe that's something you don't know the answer to until you experience the fallout.

I pull from the kiss. "Are you sure you want to spend our last day researching when this whole thing is probably a coincidence? I can park. We can go to your boat."

He groans, moves away from me, and leans his head back. I can see him close his eyes as if in pain behind his sunglasses.

"Laz?"

"Just give me a minute to get the image of us on the boat out of my head." He adjusts himself, and I thrill to see the reaction pressing hard against his pants. He lets out a breath. "Can you put the air on?"

I do, rolling up the windows in the process. Some people only like it hot in the bedroom.

After another second, he reaches over and brushes one of my curls behind an ear. "I can't leave here knowing I did nothing when you might be in danger."

Ouch. Who knew the fallout would come this quickly? I try to swallow a big, hard ball of complicated and disappointed emotion, a feeling I won't give voice to. It's silly anyway. This connection between us is not real. "Do you have to leave?"

What the heck? Even when I tell myself not to ask, I ask.

He puts his hand over the top of mine, resting on the emergency brake. "I want to stay, Honor. I mean, if last night was the opening act, I really want to stay for the next scene. But staying isn't an option. One way or the other, it's best that I go."

Heat that feels like rejection stings my cheeks, and I pull my hand out from under his and drive out of the lot.

Laz doesn't say anything else, doesn't offer any more explanations or apologies, and that actually helps. He's being honest with me. He wishes he could stay, but he has no choice in the matter.

And even though he has to go, he's delayed his trip to go to Angelica's office with me this morning. He's taking time to help me out. That truth sinks in slowly, and since he hasn't pressed any words or explanations into the silence, it's also given my brain room to work things over.

Frowning, I glance over at him before turning my eyes back to the road. "What are you running from?"

With a groan, he bends forward, reaches under the seat and moves it back with a rumble from the components. He stretches out. "You know why clichés are so popular?"

"No."

"Because they're true. So, here's a cliché for you." He gestures with one strong, capable hand as if he's actually handing me something. "The less you know, the better."

Normally, that kind of dramatic statement would make me laugh, but his face is complicated with real emotion, and it feels anything but funny. "Is it… the police? Have you done something illegal?"

He snorts. "I'm not running from the authorities. Kind of the opposite of them."

"The opposite of the police? People outside the law?" And he didn't answer my question about doing something illegal. "Should you leave now?"

His lips tuck up at the edges in a forced smile. "Trying to get rid of me?"

"No. God, no. But I don't want to be the cause of you being caught. I need you to be safe."

He lifts up his glasses and stares at me for a long few seconds before swallowing and saying, "And I need *you* to be safe, so I guess we're going to have to compromise. We look into every lead this morning. If I find nothing, I can leave knowing you'll be okay. If I find something, you can go to the police with it. Agreed?"

I bite my lip and work it between my teeth because I'm uncertain and nervous. I say, "Promise that you'll leave after this morning no matter what." I wink awkwardly at him and I'm sure it's as bad as Ford's wink. "I can't let all my good work of saving your life go to waste."

He laughs, reaches over and brushes knuckles across my cheek, down my neck, and the swell of my breast. "Why now? Why couldn't I have met you years ago? When I had time? When I could make the choice to stay and really get to know you?"

I cringe. "That's not a promise."

He leans back. "You're killing me. You know that?"

"Promise."

His jawline tightens. "Promise me you'll hire security if we find anything suspicious but not suspicious enough to go to the police."

I can't afford to hire anyone. I can't afford to get my hair cut. I've poured every last dime into Loco for Cocoa. I say, "You promise first."

He bursts into disbelieving laughter as I pull up to Angelica's office.

Chapter 16
Honor

Angelica Torres's weather-worn home/business is pink, small, and well-tended with flowers on her square cement porch. Laz and I step up to the white door propped open by a box fan.

Angelica, a fiftyish woman with silver hair, square jaw, and brown skin, sits behind her desk under a hanging light that had likely once been set over a dinner table. She's always so stylish; today is no exception. She's wearing a sexy leopard-print dress, perfectly applied makeup, and long, painted nails, and yet she seems tired or maybe stressed.

Talking on her cell, she doesn't seem to see me. I knock on the open door. She looks up from her computer screen and waves us inside in a way that almost says, *why didn't you just walk in, the door's open?*

Laz and I step inside. Angelica hangs up a moment later and claps her hands together, a sound so loud, I startle.

"¡Maravillosa!" she says in a deep sultry voice. "You have changed your mind and are here to accept!"

For a moment, I can't even answer. She seems so genuine, as if she truly expects that I've come here today to hand over the business I've spent the last two years building.

Shifting on my feet, I shake my head. "No. I appreciate the offer, but, as I said before, I'm not interested in selling. I'm—"

"Let me come out to Loco for Cocoa. Let me explain to your abuelo that this is a foreign investor, stupid, and that you will never see this kind of offer again."

A foreign investor? "I don't need you to explain anything to Abuelito. This was my decision."

Not entirely true. Abuelito and I had discussed the offer thoroughly. In the end, he said he'd be happy no matter what I decided. If I had sold, he would've taken his share and gone back to San Juan with his brother, José. He's been considering going home since Wela's death.

Angelica's cell begins to ring. She ignores it and stands up. Nearly as tall as Laz, she towers over me. Her big, manicured hands wave away my words as if they're smoke. She purses her lips, then looks at Laz. "Why don't you tell her to take the money? You two can start a farm elsewhere or even open the chocolate store back in the States. You'd have much better luck there. Everyone here makes chocolate."

Laz nods like he's thinking about it, then puts his hands in his pockets, hunches a little as if to make himself less muscular, less intimidating, and says, "Maybe we could talk to the investor directly."

I bristle. What the hell? We're not a couple. This is not his decision.

Angelica shakes her head. "So you can cut me out of the deal? No."

"Wasn't thinkin' that," Laz says. "Just wanted to meet the guy. Can't be sure he's the decent sort."

Her cell rings again. She picks it up, looks at it, hits a button, then puts it back down. "I don't understand what the problem is here. This will make you wealthy. This will change your fortunes. You want hard work and uncertainty? Who knows when the next storm will arrive and knock out everything? Who knows if the trees will keep growing? Who knows if the ships will keep using your business?"

This last part, she delivers with a bit of warning in her voice, and it isn't lost on me that she is in charge of those deals.

I know I need to tread carefully, but this situation is annoying me beyond measure. How dare she suggest I need my

Abuelito to make the decision? And then talking to Laz instead of me? And he acts like he has some kind of power over me? No thanks.

As calmly as I can manage, I say, "I do understand your eagerness to make this lucrative deal work out, but I'm really not selling."

She *tsk*s and sits on the edge of her desk. "I'll let him know you require more money."

I'm so angry, I fist my hands at my side. She didn't hear a word I said. "There will be no need for that because, as I've repeatedly stated, the decision is made. I appreciate the work you've done already, but please, don't come back to me with any more offers on Loco for Cocoa."

With as much calm as I can manage, which honestly isn't much, I turn and stalk out. I'm halfway down the street before I realize that Laz hasn't followed me. Well, there's no way I'm going back in *there*. I lean against the already blazing hood of my car and wait for him. What is he doing?

Five minutes pass before he comes back out, and by that time I'm as hot under the collar as the hood of my car. I give Laz a what-took-you-so-long frown.

He smiles at me, then actually smiles wider when my mouth tightens. He comes over, puts his arm around my waist, and guides me around to my car door. Pulling it open, he says, "That could've gone better."

I slam the door shut and confront him. "That discussion was about *my* business. All decisions on *my* business are *mine* to make. You should have made that clear by following me out. I was making a dramatic exit."

He steps forward, loops his fingers through the belt buckle on my tan shorts, and kisses me lightly on the nose. "I noticed your dramatic exit, but, babe, dramatic exits don't help when your goal is information."

True. I feel myself blush.

He kisses me on the nose again, then he opens the door again.

I'm tempted to get inside, but I shut it again. "What did you discuss?"

He puts his hands into his pockets "Well, I asked about the offer on your business. Who made it. When it had come. Where the foreigner was from."

"Where?"

"America."

That doesn't mean much.

"I asked about her commission. And a bunch of stuff she wouldn't answer."

The hands on my waist dip lower, rest at the top of my butt. I like them there.

"So, you didn't get all that much information anyway."

"True, but I figured she wouldn't answer a lot of my questions. I was just stalling."

"Stalling, why?"

"I had a device in my pocket that collected data from her phone."

Oh. "Is that legal?"

His eyebrows go up and his deep hazel eyes seem a bit startled. "No."

I'm not sure what to say to that, so I step back, open my own car door, then climb inside. This time, I don't wait to turn on the air. I crank it up.

After Laz buckles into his own seat, I speed away, feeling like a thief. An illegal data thief. I've aided and abetted criminal activity. I am a thief.

"It was my choice to swipe her data," Laz says. "You're fine."

"How did you know what I was thinking?"

A lazy smile spreads across his mouth. "You got tells."

Tells? I want to ask what they are, but he opens his mouth first and asks, "What's your take on what went down in there?"

Annoyed probably isn't what he's looking for. "The woman made a lot of assumptions about me, my family, and our relationship."

"Go deeper."

I can't help but roll my eyes. Inhaling, I attempt to let go of the emotional for the clinical. "Well, she seemed genuinely happy about the idea that I was there to accept the offer."

"Genuine can be faked. What else?"

"She's busy. Her cell rang a lot."

"Super busy. Got three businesses there, right? The travel agency, the real estate, and business permits."

"Permits?" I make a left turn and head for our second stop.

"She had paperwork on her desk."

"Oh. I hadn't noticed."

He shrugs. "That's to be expected. There's lots of emotion for you there. She practically threatened your business, the tours."

"Exactly. And that's another reason I'm annoyed. She had no—"

"What else did you notice? Anything about her physically?"

I turn onto the street where one of my guides rents a room. "Why does her physical appearance matter at all? I'm not here to make judgments."

"No, you're not. Judgment is unnecessary. Observation is not judgment. Don't confuse the two. In observing, we notice things, even things that might make us uncomfortable. We don't judge. Don't add *this is good* or *this is bad*. That screws up objectivity."

"I'm not sure what you're suggesting."

"I noticed she's taller than average and has a deep voice. On a hot day at home in her office, she's dressed to the max. Hair. Nails. Makeup. Clothes. Jewelry."

"So?"

"Could be transgender. Could be she's happy to be in her skin, to be a woman. It's not a chore for her to dress up. She likes it."

"Or maybe she's just tall with a deep voice."

"Maybe. So we observe that. We observe she doesn't fit neatly into a gender box. And if the people Ponce are anything like the rest of the world, some people might put a value judgment on that. Judge her unkindly."

"Some would be *pendejos*."

"Some would. But we're not worried about them. We're thinking about her. She's got a lot she's dealing with, works three jobs, has no air-conditioning, and though her home is well-tended, it's rundown in ways that suggest lack of money. And did you notice the picture on her desk of the kid in the hospital gown? Maybe she's got a sick kid she helps."

I'm starting to feel ill about the way I'd stormed out. I hadn't picked up on any of that. If I had, I would've been less impatient. Instead, I was too busy listening to what she was saying, not why she might've been saying it.

I slide into an open parking spot along the road. "Sabotaging my business would ensure this deal and bring her money."

"She has motivation, sure. But if she knows how much the tours mean to you, why didn't she cancel the tours instead of sabotaging the business?"

I turn to him, letting the air-condition run so we can finish our conversation in comfort. "Cancelling without a solid reason would mean she'd have to deal with me, and she knows how hard I fought to get those tours. I wouldn't let it go."

"Okay. But couldn't cancelling the tours also lower the offer on the business? Assuming whoever made the offer sees its potential."

"Huh. So maybe it wasn't her?"

"Honestly, I don't see her as our culprit. She's desperate, but still playing by the rules. That makes her less likely to have done anything to harm you and your tours. But"—he holds up a slim black device—"this'll give us her recent contacts and email. So maybe we can learn more if we find out who made the offer."

"You mean before you leave?"

A long pause, a pause in which he looks out at the small colorful homes across from the apartment building we're parked in front of. "I'll make sure you get the information, even if I'm not here. Let's go see what your missing guides have to say."

Chapter 17
Tony

After spending most of the morning talking with Honor's missing guides, we're now at the last place on the list. Have to admit the first two men raised my suspicions. High.

We got the same response—sick, not feeling well—from both guides. The same *exact* responses and descriptions and stories. From what time they woke up in the morning—six a.m.—the medicine they'd taken that was an herbal concoction, and their symptoms. Headache. Fever. Chills.

Could be coincidence, but it seemed as if they were repeating a script someone had written for them. And, today, both are fine and dandy. Not only that, both guides quit on the spot. And one of them had a nice, new-looking moped parked in the driveway of his mother's house.

A bad feeling gnaws at me. How much money would Honor's uncle have to pay off the tour guides, sabotage the business, and force her to sell? I can't see it. And getting them to quit—that took a lot more money. So maybe the person who made the offer wants the property enough to mess with the business? If so, why do they want the property that badly? Seems like they have plenty of money to start their own place and in a more tourist-friendly location.

Things aren't making sense here. Time is ticking away, and I can't stand the idea of leaving Honor here to deal with whatever happens next. Because if this is some rich investor messing with her and her business, that person isn't going to give up and go away.

"You okay?" Honor asks, switching the car off, making me realize we've parked in underground parking beneath Tito's building.

I'm not okay. Someone has messed with her equipment. Someone likely paid off the guides and gave them enough money that they quit. Someone made a crazy high offer on her property. Does someone want her business? Does someone want her gone? Or worse? Questions I take as seriously as a man raised to imagine the worst.

"I'm worried about you, Honor. Worried that I won't be able to stick around and help you out."

She does that thing with her jaw, like she's tasting my words. "I guess we're even then, because I'm worried about you, too."

How the hell is she making me smile right now? I chuck her under the chin. "Stop worrying about me."

"You stop worrying about me. I'm a big girl. I've been doing this life thing for twenty-six years."

Damn, she's young. "Well, I've been doing it for thirty-four, so I've got seniority."

Her eyes run down my body in a way that has me paying hard attention. She licks her lips. Slowly. "Thirty-four... No wonder you're falling apart."

"Smart-ass," I say, as she maybe hearing the genuine affection in my voice, sticks her tongue out at me.

I really like this woman.

We get out of the car without another word and walk silently to the stairs at the end of the garage. The building's seashell-peach exterior and green trim reminds me of Momma. A woman who really likes color in her wardrobe and her decorations.

Even though I've spent the last two years astronomically pissed off at her for ignoring my opinions and for the casual way she let Justice bungle her operation, I still love and miss Momma. She saved my life in many ways.

Of course, I'm also scared shitless of her, considering she

wants to alter my brain, my memories, and neutralize any damage I've caused to The Guild.

I get it—the pressure she's under to keep unity among a group of misfits. The fact that I understand so well, understand so completely, the challenges in her situation, is why I'm so damn scared. She's spent forty years building up her secret society, forty years raising damaged kids, healing them, and sending them out as soldiers in her war. She's had to make a lot of tough calls in that time—calls that she believes always weigh toward the greater good. No matter how much it hurts her.

"Tito's apartment is on the second floor," Honor says. "I've been here a few times. He's a friend more than an employee, which is why him not calling or texting or letting us know he wasn't going to make the tour was such a shock."

"Well, money can make people do a lot of things they wouldn't normally do. He might've been to embarrassed or guilty to reach out."

She makes a sound that's meant to be noncommittal, but I take it for the disagreement it is. She seems to really care about this guy.

Two floors up, we head down a narrow cement hall. It's empty. I scan for cameras, but don't see any.

Honor knocks on the door. There's no answer. I'm not surprised. My guess is that, guilt-ridden, he'd bugged out of here after taking money… but he could also be at the store or taking a walk.

Honor knocks again, louder. "Tito, it's me, Honor." Still nothing. She shrugs. "I guess we can come back later."

My stomach rolls, and I try not to let my discomfort show.

She sees anyway. Somehow, she reads me like a book. A soft pink feathers her cheeks. "I meant I can come back."

No fucking way would I ever let her come back here on her own. I grind my teeth. There's nothing for it. I lean down enough to whisper in her ear. "I'm going in."

She pulls away, forehead wrinkling with unease. "That seems extreme."

God, we're so different. It honestly seems like I have no choice here. "Can you go down, move the car, take it a few blocks south, and wait for me?"

It's obvious what I'm doing. She has to live here, so I don't want her near anything illegal. I'll be gone tomorrow.

Her eyes dart around then back to my face. "Okay."

Pulling a baseball cap from one of the many functional pockets in my cargos, I approach the job. Now, if this had been my old life, I'd have done more recon and would have something other than a hat and sunglasses to obscure my face. Here's hoping the guy is out and not just taking a shit.

Pulling out my tools, it takes one-point-seven seconds to crack open the door and step inside. The smell hits me before I've even closed the door.

Retching, I cover my nose with my T-shirt, securing it with my sunglasses, remove my weapon from my hidden holster, and scan the apartment. Ransacked to hell and back. Broken TV and scattered glass—this wasn't quiet. Why didn't anyone call the cops?

The outer rooms are all clean. I pass the bathroom, toe open the door, and curse.

Tito.

The large man with chalky brown skin, shaved head, and black-painted nails has been beaten to hell and back. His head is in the toilet.

Sad as shit. Honor said this guy had been a friend.

I check the rest of the apartment before heading back to the bathroom and rummaging through the medicine cabinet—if this guy had a habit, it might explain what happened here. And right now, I want any reason for his death other than his connection to Honor.

Enough coconut oil to start a massage business, some vitamins, and a couple boxes of condoms, but nothing that indicates he was deep into drugs.

A knock on the front door ricochets down the hall and a deep voice calls out, "¡Policía, abre!"

Now someone calls the police? I definitely can't get caught in here. Having a murder charge put on me isn't exactly keeping below the radar. One thing my family will pick up on right away is my prints being pulled by authorities in Puerto Rico.

I can't get out the bathroom window. It's a portal the size of a toddler's head.

Another knock. Harder. "Abre o derribaremos la puerta."

I run on the balls of my feet into the bedroom. The bedroom window has a fucking crank on it. It squeaks as I quickly open it. There's a *slam, slam* from out front, followed by a splintering and crash as the door is kicked open.

I get the window as wide as I can, then begin to climb out. Halfway through, I hear, "Espera ahí."

A police officer comes into the room and orders me to stop. His gun is still in his holster.

Guy is kidding, right?

Forcing myself the rest of the way through, scraping my side, I catch the edge of the window, lower down, and drop into the alley below. I hit then roll and am up and running within seconds. The officer squeezes into the window and yells again for me to stop.

I run faster. When I turn the corner, I ditch the hat and glasses and inside-out my shirt—which is specially made with a light red lining.

Glad that I had the foresight to tell Honor to wait far enough away, I jog into the pharmacy parking lot and slide into her car. Good thing she left it running; I duck down and tell her, "Drive."

She pulls out of the spot and hits the road without a word. For a few moments, the only sounds are the air-conditioning and the tires *thwump, thwump*ing against the blacktop.

Her eyes dart over to me. "What happened? I saw the police."

Now that we're far enough away, I sit up and adjust the vent to my face. "Yeah. Someone called the police on me. Likely before we even got there. The guides must've alerted someone that we were snooping. They knew our next stop."

"Oh my God. I shouldn't have let you break in there. Did you even learn anything useful?"

Damn. Shit. "I did. Can you pull over up here?"

She pulls into a local eatery, a chicken joint, with—no lie—a live chicken running around in the lot. She parks next to a shiny new silver pickup truck and turns to me with eyes both frightened and concerned.

I take her hand in mine, lace my fingers with hers, and hold tight. "I'm so sorry, Honor. He's dead. Your friend Tito was murdered."

The skin around her eyes wrinkles. "I don't understand."

A lump forms in my throat. Christ, this sucks. "Someone killed Tito. Your friend is dead. I'm so sorry."

Her eyes widen. She starts to shake then to cry, and I take her into my arms, whisper to her, run my nose along her soft, wet cheek.

"He's the first guide we hired." Her voice is strained with tears and disbelief. "He encouraged me when I first started, helped me figure out how to organize the tours. He was a good man."

She lifts her head, rubs the tears from her face. "You think his death is related to the offer on Loco for Cocoa? My refusal to take the offer?"

Oh hell, she's had enough put on her. "Anything's possible. His death might be coincidence—"

She pulls away from me, puts her grieving head against the steering wheel. "You don't believe that."

"I think he was, as you said, the most loyal of your guides. The others were paid off not to show up, but it's likely he wouldn't be paid off. Someone murdered him to keep him quiet."

"My decision got him killed."

"No. His decision got him killed."

Her head jerks up and swings toward me. "Don't say that."

"I won't if you won't blame yourself for something that clearly wasn't your fault." I rub a hand down her arm. "Anyway, all of that is only a theory. There could be more here, something we don't know about, or it could even be a burglary. We can't rule anything out. We have to be methodical about this."

"We?" She shakes her head. "I can't allow you to stay. It's not right. I'm taking you to your boat." She puts the car into drive and exits the parking lot with a determined press of the gas pedal. "If this is true, if this happened because of my business, I'll figure it out. I'll work with the police. You can't stay here. I saved your life and that means something to me."

I wait for her to finish her pretty speech, wait for her to get curious, wait for her to glance over and look at me, then I say, "What kind of person would I be, Honor, if my comfort, my safety, my problems came before yours?"

Her brow furrows. "But I could ask you the same question."

And that blows me away. Her worrying about *me* blows me away. "You're…" I falter, because it's hard to walk this line, the one that says staying here will help her more than me going. Especially now, since The Guild knows I'm alive. If they find me, would they hurt her? I wouldn't let them. "When I was a kid, I learned about order of importance. It's a way of determining what to do first or who to protect first."

She cocks her head to the side. "How does it work?"

"Well, one of the ways is we ask ourselves, between the two of us, right now, who is in the most immediate danger?"

Her questioning gaze travels over my face before she looks back at the road. "I can't answer that because I don't know what kind of danger you're in, from whom, and how it all happened."

She's no shrinking violet. She's a ballbuster, and I have to say that's just my type. I can't afford a timid woman, not in my life.

"Can you trust me enough to allow me to determine the answer to the order of importance?"

"Can you trust me enough to tell me the details, so we can make a decision together?"

"Isn't a matter of trust. Remember the cliché: the less you

know, the better? If there comes a time when that's reversed, I'll tell you whatever you need to know to keep you safe. I promise."

"So, you think I'm in the most danger between the two of us?"

I put my hands together like I'm gripping a bat, swing like hitting a ball, and make a click sound then the roar of the crowd. "Homerun. You're in more trouble. For now. If there comes a time when the danger involves my shit, we'll act accordingly. Okay?"

She steers her car around a man riding a ten-speed bike, towing a two-wheeled trailer filled with unpainted pottery. "Are you sure, Laz? You barely know me. I mean, we haven't even slept together yet."

Yet.

Heat carouses through my blood like a giddy drunk veering all over the place. "I like the 'yet' part of that statement. And, honestly, that's a reason for staying, not going."

She laughs quietly, then goes silent. After a moment, she nods. "I'm going to accept your offer. Because, well, bluntly, I desperately want to find out what happened to Tito and don't trust the local police to figure it out. But, Laz, you have to promise, if you end up in more danger, you will go. No question. No looking back. Just take off. Promise?"

I stare out the window. Damn, I really like this woman. I say, "Can you drive me back to my boat to get my stuff? Oh, and are you good with me being your newest tour guide? I need a cover."

Honor grits her teeth. "You didn't promise." She sighs in a way that's part surrender and part frustration. "Hiring you for a day-gig is fine, but Abuelito and I always agree on any new hires, so you'll have to interview with him. Or I can tell him why—"

"Don't tell him why I'm here. I'll interview with him. It's best for what I need to do if only you know what I'm up to."

She shakes her head. "That makes no sense. Abuelito is family, someone I dearly trust. He gave me permission to accept or decline the offer. He is above suspicion."

"He's above *your* suspicion."

"You don't know him."

"Agreed. Which is why I'll have objectivity."

"Do you trust anyone?"

I used to trust a lot of people. "I've learned that family can sometimes betray you for reasons that have nothing to do with wanting to betray you."

I feel the shift in the car's momentum and realize she's taken her foot of the gas. We coast forward. "It's not fair," she says slowly, "You know everything about me. I'm allowing you to investigate my family, but you won't tell me a thing about you. That's not fair."

Not fair. Can't remember the last time I thought in terms of fair or unfair. Just and unjust, sure, because those terms deal in shades of gray, but fair and unfair seems so... innocent. Except, maybe it isn't.

Getting the words out is like slicing skin. It hurts that badly. "In my old life, I saw my sister doing something I knew was going to get her into trouble. I tried to warn her. Repeatedly. When that didn't work, I took matters into my own hands. I made a choice I thought I had to make to keep her safe. She saw it as a betrayal."

"Did you keep her safe?"

"Nope. She went full steam ahead, ignored me anyway, and paid the price. But, in the end, she went with my suggestion, and it turned out okay."

I don't say she had no choice but to use my suggestion or that turning out okay meant she and others lived while I lost everything, but to tell her that is to tell the whole story. And that would mean revealing The Guild and endangering her and her memories. That's a line I'll never cross.

"You're a good brother," she says softly.

I close my eyes as a lump rises into my throat. I fight back tears. In a choked voice I say, "She'll never forgive me."

Honor slams her foot on the gas, and we lurch forward. "Then she's a pendeja."

Chapter 18
Gracie

It's one a.m. on a Saturday, and instead of being downstairs helping Dusty, who is manning Club When?'s packed bar, I'm sitting before a wall of computer screens in my office on a video conference call with Momma, Leland, and my sisters, Justice and Dada.

There's only one person to blame for this situation: Tony. As if betraying our family wasn't bad enough, he's also screwing up my life and my work. No wonder I look so stressed and tired. I lean forward, examine my own image in one of five boxes on my screen, with bloodshot eyes and unkempt red hair.

Realizing I've lost the conversation, I lean away from the monitor and tune back in. Dada, her dark skin aglow, her face fuller from her pregnancy, says, "Living at the Mantua Home now with Sean, I've seen it myself. Tony is the unwitting leader of a mutiny among our youngest siblings."

"Basically," Justice says, the dim light in her room shadowing her Native American features, "Tony's betrayal has gotten us more betrayal."

Wearing a brown-and-gold niqab that covers her face and hair, Momma presses a button to adjust the camera to better include Leland, seated beside her. "I'm aware," she says, "that dissatisfied units in The Guild have formed their own faction, claiming their loyalty to Tony."

"Which units?" I say because I'd thought Tony's supporters stopped with Rome, Jules, and Cee, all of whom are part of the

Vampire Academy unit, the name given to the group of six adoptees currently aged thirteen to eighteen.

Leland and Momma begin to answer at the same, time then stop. The light in Momma's office plays off Leland's white hair as he shifts back, letting Momma take the lead. She continues, "All of Vampire Academy has gone over to the dark side, if you will, but we're also hearing rumbles from all three sisters in the Troublemakers Guild, two children in Lost in Translation, and even Bella of the Lollipop Guild."

"Bella's five," I say, rubbing my face. Twelve of my twenty-eight adopted siblings are siding with Tony—that we know about.

"There's another name to add," Leland says, and my heart sinks.

A mother knows, after all.

"Gracie, your son, Tyler, has been overheard with the kids in Vampire Academy talking about how Tony's betrayal is really a form of loyalty."

That stings, sharp and painful. I've only recently gained Ty's trust after years of not being in his life, and it hurts to think he would side with Tony on this. Especially after what Tony did to Dusty—altering his memory in a way that was largely untested.

"What are our options?" I say, sick with hurt at what Tony's actions are doing to the family, to my own son—dividing our loyalties—while he traipses all over the world on permanent vacation, leaving the rest of us deal with the implosion.

"We monitor," Leland says, "and try to address any rumblings."

"Finding Tony," Momma says, "getting him to admit he was wrong, getting him to agree to alter his memory as punishment, as Bridget has done, so that these rescued children can continue to depend on The Guild for structure is our ultimate solution."

"He'll never agree to that," I say.

"No shit," Justice says.

"I abhor this idea," Dada says.

"Yeah, it fucking sucks," Justice says. "But nothing and no one is worth losing The Guild over."

Dada shakes her head. "This is our brother."

"Which is why he knows better," Justice says. "We each made a choice to enter The Guild, to do the work of standing up and fighting when others can't or won't. We each swore to abide by the rules, our own fucking rules, in order to do that."

"She's right," I say, though it hurts like fire to say it. Tony faking his death, disregarding the rules, and leaving for parts unknown has blown The Guild structure—solid for forty years—out of the water. Especially for Vampire Academy. Three of their members already tried to organize their own black ops mission. It didn't go well.

"Then we are mostly agreed," Momma says. "Our secret society operates on a strict set of rules, and adherence to those rules is essential to keep order among a family filled with complicated personalities who have lived complex and often damaging lives."

"Amen," Justice says.

I let out a breath. Justice, who's, arguably, been hurt the most by Tony's betrayal, is now the most militant. She and her husband, Sandesh—whose sleeping outline I can see on the bed in the background of Justice's video feed—are stalking the globe looking for him.

"Okay," I say. "Let's get down to the real reason for this call. Justice, what do you have for us?"

Justice moves closer to her computer camera, so close her fierce, dark eyes fill the screen. "Turns out, our brother likes to sail."

Chapter 19
Honor

The raindrops fall slow and sporadic as I make my way up the mountain to Loco for Cocoa, but my wipers *chu-whoosh, chu-whoosh* against the windshield at the only speed they have: crazy fast.

A spin of my wheel directs us up the long road that cuts between the trees. Men with rain slickers tend the cocoa trees as Tío José works among the cocoa bean vats. As usual, I wave to him, and, as usual, he turns his back on me.

"What's his issue?" Laz asks.

"He resents me, a resentment I inherited. It passed from my mother to me." I roll my eyes. "He thinks I inherited part of what should've been his."

"You're gonna need to make that a little clearer."

I sigh. "Families are complicated."

"Ain't that the truth."

"This is going to sound harsh to your American ears."

He raises a *you're an American?* eyebrow at me.

Smiling, I flick my head to the side, conceding the point. "Honestly, it sounded harsh when I first heard it. My grandmother loved Tío, but because he's Abuelito's brother, she never considered him blood family. And Wela, my grandmother, was adamant that her half of Loco for Cocoa remain in the hands of a blood relative, so when she passed, she gave all of hers to my mother."

"José doesn't own any of the lodge? How would he benefit then from the sale?"

"He does. Abuelito sold, or, more accurately *gave*, half of his property to Tío José, but my uncle still has a chip on his shoulder because of what he sees as Wela's slight. Of course, it didn't help that when my mother inherited, she ignored the property for years."

"She wasn't interested?"

"She loved the idea of it, but Mom loved the idea of a lot of things. She was a huge romantic with a romance problem. She always picked the wrong guy. At thirty-eight, she finally decided enough was enough and went in vitro. She tried to manage her family, her inheritance, me, romances, and career, but she often fell short."

"Ah," Laz says, "Your uncle only sees his struggles."

He's so perceptive. "Exactly. And because Mom had money, he thought of her as the spoiled movie star who never really cared about anyone but herself."

"Your mom made movies?"

Turning into the employee parking lot, I cringe. This is the part I hate, the part where I become less myself and more the celebrity kid, defined by my mother, what people thought of her. I switch off the car and face him. "Natalie Silva is my mom's birth name. Her stage name was Kiki Hart."

"Your mom was Kiki Hart, the actress?"

I nod. He blinks, and I can see him reevaluating the situation. I wait for the questions—what was it like growing up with someone so famous? Did I visit any movie sets? Did I meet any famous people?

He squints as if he's recalling something. "She made two movies in Ponce, right? *Stranded* and the sequel, *Stranded Again*. I saw a commemorative plaque in town."

I'm so thrown off by the question that it takes me a moment to come up with the answer. "Yes. That's right. She made them about ten years apart. I wasn't around for the first, but I was here for the second. It was one of the best times of my life. I remember the lodge filled with the crew, staff, and movie people. She helped keep the lodge afloat with her movies, but after the last, it was a long time before she came back.

"Of course, José remembers. Now, I bring in guests, most of whom knew my mom and were old friends of hers, and he sees the whole thing playing out again. I think that's part of the reason he wants me to take the offer. He believes I'll abandon this place, too."

Laz says, "He doesn't see you for you."

"Verdad. It's strange, really, that he's so close with Abuelito because they are so different. Abuelito is more like you—very charming."

I look over and he smirks at me. The Big Bad Wolf has that kind of smile. The kind that seduces women stupid.

He brushes a curl of hair behind my ear. "How long do you think it'll take me to convince him to give me a job?"

"No time at all," I answer honestly. "And I can already tell the two of you together are going to be trouble. For me."

Chapter 20
Tony

Workers with poles topped with curved blades move through the surrounding cocoa trees, slicing the fruit from the branches and depositing them into baskets as Honor and I walk down the road from the employee parking lot to the hotel.

"What's in this bag?" she asks, leaning to one side as she carries it.

"I told you I could handle all four bags," I say.

She makes a frustrated sound. "Answer the question."

Because I can't help myself, I tease, "Top secret."

She full-stops, dropping the bag, putting her hands on her waist.

Laughing, I shuffle the bags I already hold and pick up the last one. I whisper, "The bag contains cameras, so we probably shouldn't randomly drop it."

"Cameras?"

We're close enough to the posada that I tilt my head toward the porch and the guests sitting outside.

"You're a very suspicious person."

"Gets the job done."

We make our way to the front in a silence that is heavy with awareness of each other. I like the newness of us, the fact that I learn something about her with every exchange. I can only hope that what's she's learning about me isn't making her nervous. She seems to see my training as being paranoid.

"Honora, you've brought a friend," Abuelito says, spreading

his hands wide as he descends the front steps. With his long, silver-white hair, white pants, and white shirt, he looks like the most honest man in the jungle. Or at least the most comfortable.

I carefully place the bags down and take his offered hand.

"Abuelito Ramone Silva," he says. "And you're the tour guide, Lazarus Graves, correct?"

"Sí, señor," I say, shocked he knows my name. We barely said a word to each other the one time I was here.

He claps me on both arms and says, "You've come for a job, no?"

The old guy is as smart as a tack. "Sí, I'm here for a job. I had a great time working with Honor and Junior, and I'd like to fill one of the vacant tour guide positions."

"Bueno. You have the job."

What? He accepted me without even looking at my faked resume. I'll have to double-check every single person working here. Not that I hadn't intended to do that anyway.

We shake hands, and Abuelito rakes knowing eyes over my bags. "I think you need a room."

"Pardoname?" I say because I'd kind of assumed I'd be staying with Honor. Half this equipment is meant to secure her room.

"Don't worry," he says. "The room is part of your salary."

Honor slides a longing look at me that sends a wave of heat smashing through my body like Godzilla through Tokyo.

"Abuelito," she says, pink dusting her cheeks. "He'll be staying with me."

Her grandfather's thick brows settle again over clever midnight eyes as his gaze darts from me to Honor. He adjusts fairly quickly to this news. "Claro. Of course. Let me help you with your bags."

"It's okay, Abuelito. I can help him."

"Oh no." He shakes his head. "Lanie has been in the shop all day without a break. I think you should relieve her. I've got the bags."

A hand flies to Honor's mouth, and she turns toward the walkway that leads out back to her chocolate store. "I forgot." She shakes her head in disbelief then bites her lip. "Is it okay if Abuelito helps you?"

She's really asking if I'm okay dealing with whatever Abuelito has planned because he did not bring up her needing to get to work for nothing. "Sure," I say. "I'll drop the bags and be right down."

Giving me a light kiss on my cheek and blushing deeper, she slips her room key—at least it feels like a key—into my pocket before flying down the walkway.

When she's gone, Abuelito rubs his hands together like a villain who just put the first step of his master plan in motion, and I know we are about to have a *talk*. He picks up two of my four bags. "Follow me."

Grabbing the other two, I follow.

Crossing into the foyer, he leads me up the beautiful hand-carved stairs and around a corner.

"There're two entrances to her room?" I ask like an idiot who wants this man to know I've already entered his granddaughter's bedroom through a different door.

He glances over his shoulder with eyebrows raised. "Sí," he says, frowning.

We walk the rest of the way in silence.

Abuelito lightly drops my bags at Honor's door. His eyes go to my pocket. "She gave you her key?"

I nod, not about to open the door and invite him inside. If he wants to chat with me, he can do it out here.

He waits a moment for me to open the door, but, when I don't, his thick eyebrows draw together and his stare goes cold. "You have a thing for my granddaughter."

He hits the exact right button. My shoulders rise. "*Thing* would be inaccurate description, señor." It feels disrespectful. "What's between us isn't a crush."

He dismisses that with a, "Pfft," and a shake of his head. "I may be old, but I haven't forgotten the lessons of my life. Before my granddaughter, it was my daughter in this room. I know that, to some, a gentle heart can seem like an invitation to take advantage."

He nods at the door, and all that Honor said about her mother comes into clearer focus. "After her mother's death, Honora came here to me, broken and shaken. I took her in, held her through her grief, and championed her when she found a way forward, a reason to get out of bed."

I see the situation clearly. A grieving father takes in his granddaughter after his daughter's tragic death. He welcomed Honor despite the years of neglect from her mother, welcomed her, and let her create a vision for this place.

I suddenly understand him. Maybe because, as Honor said, we are alike. Welcoming Honor and allowing her to transform this place was also his way of keeping her safe. He's been protecting her ever since and sees me as a threat.

I want to tell him that Honor's gentle heart is safe with me, but that's not true because, when I leave, we will both be hurt.

Swallowing a ball of genuine emotion, I say, "Did Honor tell you that she saved my life?"

He doesn't answer, but I can tell by the confusion on his face that he doesn't know.

"That's how we met," I say. "On the anniversary of her mother's death, she went to the beach in Ponce."

"During the storm?" He spreads his arms like he is objecting to something that might yet take place.

I barely hold back the smile. "Yes, and I have to thank God she did because I was kiteboarding in the storm and nearly drowned. She pulled me to safety."

He claps his hands together. "My granddaughter rescued you from the water on that day?"

"Yeah," I say, kind of loving his reactions. "When I got out of the hospital, I'd intended to set sail."

He waves his hands animatedly. "You have a sailboat. Are

on an adventure. And you didn't set sail because Honora needed you. She saved your life. It was destiny, you say?"

I think I know where Honor's mother got her romantic tendencies from. I try to dim his enthusiasm. "I'm telling you this so you understand my intentions. I don't want to hurt Honor. It's the opposite, in fact. I want to protect her for as long as I can."

He knocks his head to the side, suddenly serious. "Protect her from what?"

Shit. I'm losing my edge. Doesn't help that this guy doesn't miss a trick. I don't answer, but I see the wheels churning behind his clever brown eyes.

After a moment, he says, "It was odd, no, the accident on the tour?"

We stare at each other for a long, long moment. Honor trusts him. I feel that I can, too. I nod once, slowly, then say, "Your guide, Tito, is dead. I'm so sorry."

His eyebrows go up. "An accident?"

"No."

His face falls. Crestfallen, that's what that look is. He says, "He was a fine dominós player." He wipes at tearing eyes. "With a good laugh and many colorful stories." His voice lowers. "You will be missed, amigo. Rest now."

His lower lip curls down in a considering gesture. He grunts, then declares, "Honor wants you here. You are a good man so here you will stay. And we will each, as you say, protect her."

He claps me on the back, decides that's not enough, and draws me into a fierce hug that smells like cocoa butter and cigars.

I feel a stab of guilt. I can't imagine how he'd react if he knew I've got about a week I can give to his precious granddaughter before I have to run for my own life.

Chapter 21
Tony

After putting my bags in Honor's suite, I take a hot second to log onto the secure site I set up for Rome and me to use. I need to upload the information I took from Angelica's phone.

Shit. There's a message from Rome. My heart beats faster as I open it.

You sail?

I close my eyes. Shit. I've been secretly taking lessons since my mid-twenties. I was never sure why I didn't tell anyone—until the day I decided to run. As much as I love my family, trust goes both ways. Them not trusting me completely led to me not trusting them completely. A fact I hid even from myself until the end.

I open my eyes and continue.

They think you're in the Caribbean. You're not, right? That would be stupid and not like you.

Thick dread tightens my throat. Not even technically out of the US yet.

They've set up a special ops team, like a regular mission, so you better be far enough out to not even get this message.

Shit. I take in all the details Rome has shared with me. No doubt he broke into The Guild computers to get them. The Guild has great security against intrusion from outside forces, but not so much from insiders with mad computer skills like Rome.

He's reporting that Justice has discovered my boat name and my pseudonym. Thankfully, she doesn't seem to know I've changed boats and names since then.

Rome ends his message with: *If you still want your memory, sail on, wayward son.*

If I still want? I won't let them take my memories of the Brothers Grim operation in Mexico. What they label a betrayal was me rescuing Justice and keeping the family code—*no League member will ever allow another member to irresponsibly risk themselves, the security of a mission, or the secrecy of The Guild.*

I rub the *All for one* tattoo over my heart. If they took that information from me, they… take me. Essentially, it's who I am. The person who risked everything to keep my family safe.

But they wouldn't only take that now. They'd also take Honor and Ponce. My mouth goes dry with the thought. I want those memories, every one.

Who's on the ops team? Rome didn't say, but I ask in my reply and also let him know I need him to go through the files on Gray I'd uploaded.

No time to waste going to visit Honor's store. I'll explain it all to her later, but, right, now I have to unload this equipment and get started.

I work quickly, unpacking what I need and stacking it in a pile as I ponder how long I have before they find me. Not long. My sisters are surely already checking the Caribbean islands. But that isn't an easy check. Lots of places to hide, and they sure as shit won't start here. They know I'm smarter than that—uh, they *think* I'm smarter than that.

There are plenty of islands for them to check, but they won't start at tourist traps. They'll go for more secluded areas. They'll search mountains. Shit. I'd hoped to give Honor a week, but now… I need to find and eliminate this threat to Honor fast.

And if that doesn't work?

It *has* to work.

I gather up a pocketful of small, nearly invisible cameras, and leave Honor's room. It takes about forty-five minutes to place them in discreet and strategic locations around the inn.

When I'm done, I walk across the red, brick patio out back, past the outdoor firepit surrounded by tables, and over to the bar. The croaks of the noisiest frogs I've ever heard fill the air along with the smell of moss and trees and flowers as I take my seat next to the only other person at the bar.

We haven't been introduced, so I hold out my hand. "Lazarus Graves."

Dude stares at my outstretched hand, then, as if realizing his part of the social contract requires a response, startles and grabs my hand. He pumps once, then lets go. "Ford Fairchild." He begins to laugh. "Lazarus Graves. That's a great name. Are you a guest?"

"Nah. Newest tour guide."

"Really? Honor didn't mention they were hiring new guides."

Why would Honor mention that to a guest? "So are you a guest or..."

He puts up a single finger getting the bartender's attention.

The man, shockingly pale, who stands about five-three, comes over.

"Jorge, I'll take another whiskey, and Laz will take the Loco for Cocoa specialty brew." Ford turns my way. "I'm a guest," he says, giving me whiplash, as I'm still stuck on him ordering me a beer I didn't ask for. "I'm one of Honor's mother's old friends—old enough to butt in where I don't belong."

Butts in where he doesn't belong and picks drinks for absolute strangers. Guy looks like an actor. Fortysomething, in shape, with the kind of good looks that suggests an easy life. Or at least one of wealth.

"Were you one of Natalie's movie buddies?"

A flash of shock, maybe surprise, hits his face, then Ford's smile widens. "I'm a financial attorney, not an actor, but I did once wish to act. You can even spot me in minor roles on a few of Natalie's films. My Uncle Winthrop financed the films, so I was given a part. Nepotism at its best."

He laughs awkwardly. The bartender puts a bottle of beer and a glass in front of me, then whisks Ford's drink away and replaces it with a fresh one.

I take a sip from the bottle then lift it to read the label. "This is really good."

Ford smiles. "That's why I ordered it for you. I talked Honor into adding it to the bar, but no one ever orders it. It's expensive. I was starting to feel bad about her outlay, and, as good as the brew is, after three weeks here, I can only drink so many."

"Well, I'll do as much as I can to help you out." I take a long pull. "Three weeks, huh? That's a long vacation."

"I'm able to work remotely. Mostly." He spins his glass around on his coaster, but doesn't drink. "To be honest, I've loved the island since I first came here as a teenager."

"You've visited Puerto Rico before?"

"Years ago, for those films of Natalie's I mentioned—*Stranded* and *Stranded Again*." He smiles at the memory. "It was summer. I was fifteen and had a huge crush on Kiki Hart. So, when she spoke with me, befriended a kid with more connections than friends, I thought I'd died and gone to heaven." He laughs a little too sadly.

I say, "Sounds like you never got over that crush."

Ford finally sips his drink, stares at the ice bobbing in the amber liquid. "There are few people who you meet who genuinely change the course of your life. She was one of them. The world is a sadder, darker place without her."

Guy's really carrying a torch. Or is he? Natalie Silva had to have been twenty years older than this guy, and he does have a wedding ring on. "Your wife know about your crush?"

He laughs. "Oh, she knows everything. She's a wonderful person, as is my youngest child, my daughter."

"How many kids do you have?"

He squints at me as if trying to figure me out. "One."

This guy is a little offbeat.

"Lazarus."

I turn to see Abuelito carrying a box filled with climbing gear. "We have two new guides inside. Would you like to meet them?"

Guy should not be hiring that fast. "Sure would." I get up and shake Ford's hand. "Nice meeting you. I'm sure I'll see you around."

Ford shakes his head. "I don't go on the tours, but maybe we'll share a drink again before I leave next week."

Which is actually what I meant, but I don't explain that to him. "Sounds good." I pat him on the back and follow Abuelito into the lodge.

After meeting the newest guides and a few other guests, I'm back in Honor's room, checking the security feed. It's perfect. My laptop runs camera shots in a corner of my screen as I forward Rome the guest list Abuelito inadvertently shared with me. Okay, I stole it, but I don't have time to be respectful of privacy. I have to streamline my mission.

Streamlining means breaking rules and depending on Rome. There's no way I can protect Honor, interview people here, pretend to be a tour guide, and do all the cyber work too. Damn, I really miss The Guild's resources right now.

I send a quick explainer to Rome, letting him know to start with the most obvious security threats based on Guild criteria and work his way down.

I hear Honor come in and pause as I type to say hello, then ask her, "The names on your hotel registration for the next few weeks… there've been no changes? These have all been set up in advance?"

"Yes."

"And there's no one who'd made a reservation recently?"

"Nope. No one. Can we have sex now, or do you want to grill me more?"

I shoot to my feet, spin to her, and grin.

Chapter 22
Honor

I was surprised when I came inside my room and found Laz working. And, I have to admit, a little disappointed when he didn't jump right up and greet me, but thanks to him, I'm learning to ask for what I want.

And I do want. I need this man like sunshine, like air, like chocolate.

He strides over to me, pulls me to him, and lets his hungry, possessive kiss do the greeting for him.

In no time my head spins and my hands shake. I pull his shirt until he, smiling, flips it off over his head. My fingers instantly rush over swells of muscles.

Soft skin. Hard muscles. He pulls back from the kiss and his eyes dip to where my hands have roomed. My breathing loud, I unzip his pants, slide them and his boxer briefs down his body. Kneeling, I help him step out of his clothes, stand, and stare. He is so beautiful. The kind of man I've seen in magazines, and not one I'd ever thought to have my hot hands on.

"You okay?" he asks as I'm doing a statue imitation.

"*Okay?* This might be the best moment of my life."

He laughs softly and I kiss his chest, stroke him until a bit of moisture seeps from the slit of his cock.

He stops my caressing, placing his hands over mine with a whispered, "Slow down."

I do, but it's not easy. He tugs my shirt and lifts it over my head. Okay, slow isn't in my vocabulary right now. My hands drop back over him, down him, and in my groping need, he is there, kissing my neck, worshiping me, unclasping by bra. I shrug free.

"I can't…" His eyes devour me. "I don't have the words for how perfect you are."

"Really? I've always thought they were a little large."

"Bite your tongue," he says, then wickedly, "Better yet, let me."

His mouth descends on mine, possessing, while one of his hands caresses my breasts, pinches each of my nipples. His other hand undoes the button on my shorts. As I did for him, he helps me step out of my shorts and my panties. And like me, he stares, then stands slowly, tracing along my calves, my thighs, to…

Oh. He moves his fingers between my legs to where I throb and ache.

"Oh, yes," I say, as much moan as word.

He thrusts a finger deep inside, withdraws, then pushes it back inside.

And I am losing my mind. "No more slow," I say. "Please."

He chuckles like a most sinister version of himself. "You had your chance to be in charge. Now we do it my way."

His gaze hooded, he slips his finger out, brings it to his lips and tastes it over a low moan. "Not sure what I did right in my life… Not sure…"

Without warning, he scoops me up and carries me to the bed. As he lays me down, I catch a glimpse of myself naked in the ceiling mirror. I turn my head. The mirror was my mom's addition to this room, long before I came along. I kept it because, well, I always got a kick out of it as a child. As an adult, I see it had some other uses.

"Don't look away." His voice is husky, filled with demand and wonder. "Look at yourself."

Uncomfortable, I squirm, but he waits me out.

I look.

"See what I see. Soft, sleek legs. Round, full breasts.

Smooth, curvy hips. The V between your legs, warm and wet. I want you to watch, watch in the mirror as I take you and make this moment ours forever."

The sincerity in his voice… Tears fill my throat. I groan, arch, and spread my legs, inviting and desperate.

He crawls up the bed, brings his hot body over mine.

My body shakes as I welcome him with all that I am. My heart trembles as well.

He pushes inside and I cry out, rejoicing at the heat and pressure of him. We kiss and the world, every trouble and threat in it, becomes insignificant. Above us, his taut body, every thrust and withdrawal, every push and pull, reflects down upon us.

I writhe under the power, sweat, and muscle of him.

"So good," he says, and begins to increase the rhythm of his hips, the pounding pressure of his thrusts.

"Ay. Dios. Yes. So good. Yes."

My breasts bounce, my back rocks against the mattress with each pounding beat of his body. I watch him in the mirror, watch every muscular line as he drives inside me, watch as my nails rake his back, and my eyes go glassy with my impending orgasm.

His hypnotic, pulsing thrusts are a dance, a quickening rhythm that plays me, and I am barely able to keep up. He has taken control of me in every way. I don't call his name as the pleasure builds and builds. Laz isn't his name. I grab his strong biceps, kiss them, moan and whisper, "Querido, I'm so close. So close."

He thrusts impossibly fast, and I thrill with each intrusion of the hard and deep length of him. The pressure unbearably good, unbearably…

I cry out as I come. My core tightens and releases, vibrating with each tingling pulse.

I lose my mind as one orgasm recedes into another, so quickly it seems there is no pause. I'm shaking under the onslaught of electric tingles as he angles his hips, pumps and rides me, then breaks apart with liquid warmth and a long low groan of satisfaction.

In the mirror, I watch as his thrusts, the quick, deep movements, the long, demanding lines, the tight muscles in his back, his ass, slow and relax.

He kisses me, his tongue deep and penetrating, and I savor every bit of him.

He drops onto me, kissing my cheeks, and the moisture that rolls from my eyes. I don't know when I started to cry. All I know is I have never felt this much in my entire life. Sensations and emotions, warmth and bliss, ecstasy and a shattering, but none of those words comes close enough. I have no idea what has happened to me, but I am not the same person I was before this moment.

Laz shifts, and I wrap my legs behind his knees and hold him in place. "Stay. Stay in me. I've never felt this before. I don't want it to end. Not yet."

He drops back on top of me, lifting himself partly up onto his elbows. He curls his head down next to me, breathes heavily against my ear, and says, "You feel it, too?"

There is no question in my mind what he means. My body is thrumming, a live electrical pulse beating against my skin. "I feel everything," I say. The way his hips align against me, the hair on his legs against my smooth calves, the press of his arms against my ribs, the heat from his skin, the beat of his heart, his breath, his being. Everything.

There is only us in all the universe. Everything else has disappeared.

Moments pass in this ethereal place before life and sound slowly come back. Now his heartbeat *and* the croaking of frogs through the window, his heat *and* the feel of my sheets against my back, his breath growing quiet *and* my mind shutting down. Sleep.

I wake to the buzz from my cell phone and, for a moment, I can't understand the delicious warmth against me. Then I realize with a surge of joy that it's him. Laz.

I smile and elbow him, so he grunts and rolls off me, then I reach for my phone.

I bring it to my ear as moonlight streams through the window, revealing us in the mirror above, and I love it. "Hello."

For a moment, no one replies, then a mechanically altered voice says, "Do you think he'll protect you? He won't. You're fucking dead. Your body is already rotting. Just like Tito. Just like your mother. Did he like it? Did he like fucking a corpse?"

Bile rises in my throat along with horror. I toss the phone away, retching as I race to the bathroom just in time to spill the contents of my stomach into the toilet.

I'm shaking and vomiting when Laz rushes to my side, drops to his knees, and rubs my back. "It's okay, baby. I'm here. It's okay."

When I'm done, I lean against his chest, and he cradles me in his arms.

"Shh," he says over and over as I cry against him.

When I finally stop, my head is pounding.

He wipes tear-streaked hair from my face and asks quietly, deadly quiet, "Do you know who was on the phone?"

It's then that I realize he has my phone in his other hand. I'm not even sure—I may have tossed it in his direction.

I take the phone with shaking fingers, then open the call log. "Unknown number."

"Was there anything distinct about the voice?"

"It was disguised. Mechanical. The person threatened me. Said I was already dead."

He draws me closer, and, as if to reassure himself as much as me, pulls me into his lap. "Tell me exactly what the person said."

I shake my head. I can't. I won't repeat those things. I still have enough of my Wela in me to know words give the Devil power. Repeating them might make them real.

Wiping at my mouth, I tuck my head into his shoulder and ask, "Can you teach me self-defense?"

Chapter 23
Tony

Three hours after the phone call that woke me and Honor from a deep, satisfied sleep, I wake up, kissing her once, lightly. I'm so tempted to kiss her again that it hurts. But I don't because, if I do, I'm not getting out of bed.

Don't think. Just get the fuck up. Protecting her means getting your ass up.

With as much care as pulling a precarious piece in Jenga, I remove myself from her sleeping form. She shifts a little, makes a small sound of protest, then drifts back to sleep.

I set the bedside alarm clock for thirty minutes from now and dress in the fading moonlight, watching her breathe as I do.

I can't put words to what I'm feeling. Putting words to it, well, it sounds fuckin' ridiculous. Not for nothing, it's still there. I more than care for her. More than like her. I…

No. Hell no. That's impossible. Fairy-tale stuff.

Pivoting on my heel, I leave the room, securing the door behind me with the sensors that I'd set up. If anyone but Honor—who I'd taught to disarm it late last night—opens this door, they'll set off an alarm loud enough to wake the dead.

Walking through the hallway, noticing the creaks and cracks that the day seems to hide, I make my way down the back stairway and through the kitchen. Her chef is already here, bent at the wide steel oven, inserting tins of bread. I slip out before he sees me.

At the yoga center, I flick on lights, take off my shoes, then begin dragging out mats to set up a training area. When I'm done,

I check the secure site through my phone. No messages from Rome.

I begin to warm up with a few squats and basic Muay Thai kicks and hits. It feels great to be warming up with mixed martial arts. Like coming home.

Forty-five minutes later, fully warmed up, I check my watch.

She might not be coming. We were up late, and she has to be at work by eight. Wouldn't blame her if she stayed in bed.

"Hey."

Startling, I spin, grab her, and nearly put Honor into a choke hold.

"Sorry." I let her go. She's dressed in loose sweats and a black fitness top, with enough cleavage to put a smile on my lips. "How do you keep sneaking up on me?"

She slips off her shoes. "I perfected my sneaking skills during my homeschooling."

"You were homeschooled?"

"Yep. Which meant hanging out a lot with my mom on sets in her trailer. I'd get bored, so, being naturally quiet, I used to follow adults around, mimic their movements. If they turned, I turned. Honestly, I got so good at it, it wasn't fun anymore."

I gape at her. "That's incredible."

She pulls her hair back and ties it in a ponytail. "I was always good at hiding." Her face grows tense. Her jaw tightens. "But I'm done with that, so what can you teach me?"

She's so beautiful, so soft and warm, and all I want in the world is to protect her, but, to keep her safe, I need to teach her to protect herself.

"First, you have to trust your own instincts."

"What kind of instincts?"

"Your fear. Real fear—bone-deep intuition that something is wrong—is a gift. Don't ever ignore it, no matter how stupid it seems. Often times, our subconscious mind is picking up signals that our chattering mind is blind to."

"That I can do."

"Good. What do you know of situational awareness?"

"Nothing." She shrugs. "This is actually the first time I've heard the term."

Yikes. Okay. I quickly explain to her about paying attention to her surroundings, to people around her, to escape routes, and exits, then say, "Every human—no matter how much bigger, stronger, and meaner they are than you—has similar weak spots. Eyes, throat, nose, groin, and instep." I fake poke at her eyes, her groin, her neck.

She flinches. "That's it?"

I nod at her genuine interest. "Connection points are weak, too, as are certain organs, but let's get the basics down, okay?"

"Got it," she says. "So, which weak spot do I attack first?"

"That's the thing." I slide around her, acting as if I'm sizing her up. "The best place to attack is the spot you can easiest get at. Now, I'm going to come at you, and you go for my most exposed weak point."

I lurch forward as if intent on hurting her.

She stumbles back and falls on her ass.

"Whoa. Sorry." I pull her to standing and kiss her lightly on the nose. "You asked for this, remember?"

She scowls. "Fine. Let's start again."

"Okay. Pay attention and tell me where you should counter-attack."

I move slowly toward her. Telegraphing my intentions, I reach for her throat. "Groin," she says, and continues from there to call every line of defense correctly.

"Instep," she says on the last round, as I hold her by her neck from behind.

"Perfect," I say, demonstrating how to smash down on the correct spot. "You're doing great. Now, I'm going to demonstrate a few easy self-defense moves, so you have a couple things you can fall back on when you counterattack. You ready?"

She puts up her hands like a boxer, dances around like a lunatic, and pretend spits on the ground. "Ready."

We get to work, an air of playful focus about us. That lasts about forty minutes.

Holy shit. If someone had asked me three weeks ago when I was guiding my sailboat through a storm and responding to every crisis with detached and focused calm, I would've said I have a boatload of patience.

But that was Before Honor, before she shattered my self-control with her kisses and sighs, before she opened my heart with her strength and innocence, before my concern for her safety sent me racing to set up security, racing to imagine every danger, racing to research threats. Before someone had called and threatened her life while I held her secure in my embrace. And before I knew her, knew this time with her was precious, knew *she* was precious.

Now, my fear for her is testing every thread of patience I thought I had. I need her to get this stuff down yesterday, but trying to get her to perform the simplest self-defense move is like trying to teach the Tin Man in *The Wizard of Oz* how to do a spin kick.

I have no idea what to do with her. I've trained five-year-olds who are better at self-defense. She's so bad, I had to break it down to the simplest of moves, like, "Shove me." Who can't fucking shove someone? Honor, that's who.

And holy shit, I'm getting frustrated, as frustrated as her face says she is. It's hard to believe someone so fundamentally in touch with her body in bed and so surefooted on land can be so stiff and unsure, so wooden and unresponsive when it comes to fighting.

After another failed attempt in which I capture her hands and thrust them back at her, she unleashes a series of curses in Spanish, crosses the room, and fills a paper cup from the watercooler.

She's sweated through her top. Her body is shaking, and I can't say she isn't trying. She is. She's taking it seriously, putting in the effort, but also putting up her own barrier to that effort. She has a mental block on the physical actions of fighting. Honestly, I think it's the idea of causing harm to someone.

I need to try something else, try getting past her hesitation and self-consciousness. Maybe if I make her angry enough to stop overthinking everything. That's so not in my own best interest when I'm sleeping with her. And, just as importantly, I want to keep sleeping with her every chance I can.

She tosses the cup in a wicker wastebasket and meets me back on the mat. I go for cheerful. "Breaks over. Let's try again."

"What's the point? I suck."

"Not gonna make anything better if you put yourself down."

She wipes sweat from her brow. "Are you trying to tell me I don't suck? I thought we were being honest with each other. I'm hopeless. I can't be taught."

Her words catch me off guard, drag me back to the gym underground at the Mantua Home, back to the training mat with Leland. *Uncle* Leland. I said nearly the same thing to him during our first week of instruction, and he responded with nearly the exact thing I now say to Honor. "Fuck that. It's not true. Unless you want it to be true."

I move into her, lift up her chin, and kiss her. I let go of my fear and frustration and give in to the fairy-tale feeling, the stupid, impossible, racing, hot, full, and desperate feeling. All of it goes into the way my lips work against hers.

Then I stop, breathless and wanting. "Do you want it to be true?"

She shakes her head.

"Tell me what you want to be true."

She leans into me and rests her head on my chest. "I am Honor, fierce and capable and strong."

I kiss her atop her head. "That's just the start of the list, Honor. Just the fuckin' start."

Chapter 24
Tony

After our shower, I plop onto Honor's couch and check the camera feeds. All looks quiet.

"I have to run to the chocolate store," Honor says. "I'll meet you outside by the hiking trail."

I blow her kisses like an idiot. She smiles before leaving, and I don't feel so much like an idiot. After the tension of this morning's training, I worried there would be fallout, but things quickly returned to normal between us.

Well, as normal as hot sex in the shower that had me orgasming so hard I saw stars and nearly blacked out, but, then again, that's kind of our normal.

Clicking through to the secure site, I clench my teeth together so firmly, air can't slip past. Rome got back to me. I open the email. Nothing about my family's pursuit of me. I ease my lips apart. Rome curated the information from Angelica's phone.

I begin to read. So far, there doesn't seem to be anything on the origin of the offer, but Angelica is a busy lady. She's taking lots of calls, and... lookie here. Now why is José Silva calling Angelica, not once, but repeatedly?

Looks like I gotta go talk to José. This should be fun.

Stones crunch under my boots as I walk the dirt road to the fermenting station. Slim male workers, shirtless and sweating, harvest the cocoa plants. The now-familiar whisk of a blade proceeds the slice and crash as fruit drops into a basket. Above that noise, a thousand birds sing in the trees. I can understand why Honor loves it here so much. It's kind of paradise.

Passing a pathway that runs through the trees, I hear arguing. Shielding my eyes, I squint and spot José arguing with Abuelito. Abuelito places his hand on José's shoulder, but José knocks it off and storms away.

Abuelito tips back his hat, notices me and shrugs as if to say, *I just can't with this guy.*

That seems to be the consensus.

José doesn't even make eye contact as he passes me and stalks toward the fermenting station. He transmits exactly what he wants me to know. Basically, *you mean nothing to me and my life. All will be the same after you are gone.*

Well, that might be true. But if the wear and worry of José's body testifies to anything, that back-to-normal won't make him any happier.

He looks much older than Abuelito, who Honor said is the older brother. José's countenance says he works a lifetime in each and every day, and that each of those moments is an insult and a burden. One he never forgets or forgives.

A few strides and I catch up with him. I hold out my hand. "Lazarus Graves."

José stops, eyeballs the extended hand for a moment. "*No entiendo.*"

Really? Last I checked, names translated. Dropping my hand, I switch to Spanish. "*Soy el nuevo empleado.*"

"I meant I don't understand that name. Awful. Did your parents not realize you would have to go every day into the world with it?"

Honor's uncle is the opposite of Abuelito. No charm. "Yeah. Well, guess we all carry the burdens of someone else's decisions."

José's eyebrows rise. "Until we decide not to."

Guy doesn't look like he's decided anything but getting up, getting dressed, and doing the same exact thing for the last forty years. Or maybe he has.

"I met Angelica Torres the other day. Nice lady. She mentioned you two speak regularly. Friendship, romance, or business?"

José puts his hands into the frayed pockets of faded pants the color of limp celery. "I don't believe that she mentioned me." He squints at me. "Why are you talking to me?"

Seems certain Gray would protect him or at least keep secret the fact that he called a few times. Is that because they have a personal or business relationship? "Just trying to get to know my girlfriend's family a bit better."

With that, José shrugs. "Don't bother. You will not be here long. I know your type. Her mother had many men like you. And Honor, too, will have many men just like you."

The thought causes a fierceness in my chest, like an animal that bares its teeth and growls at the approach of a sensed-but-unseen threat. I fight to keep that animal back and down, because if I twitch or open my mouth, I'm going to do or say something I will regret.

When José spins and walks away, I let him go. I'll gain nothing by pressing him now.

After a minute more to cool off, I walk back up the road and find Honor dressed in her tour gear with tan cargo shorts and a backpack on, looking like this man's dream hiking guide. She's standing beside a series of long, rectangular wooden platforms, almost like a raised garden, but, instead of mulch and plants, they're topped with cocoa beans, being spread out by women using soft wooden rakes.

Honor waves me over. "These women are," she says, gesturing at the two women, "like familia. Ana,"—she points to the cherubic-faced woman with a friendly smile—"has worked here since my mother was a child. Now Maria, her granddaughter"—she points to the younger version of the first woman—"works here on weekends while making her way through college."

Maria waves, continues raking, and, without looking up, asks softly, "How did you two meet?"

Because I'm beginning to love telling this story, I quickly explain why Honor is my hero. I might exaggerate my ineptitude, but accurately portray her heroic deeds in a way I hope flashes as brilliantly to them as it does in my mind. And when I tell them the part where I looked up into Honor's eyes sure she was an angel, they clap.

Ana gestures at Honor and says, "And on that day? See? Your mother still looks out for you."

Maria nods, and Honor makes a polite noise of agreement before waving goodbye, then charging away as if flames nip at her feet.

I say my goodbyes and catch up with her, grabbing her hand. "You okay?"

"Did you understand what Ana suggested?"

"Yeah. Like your mother fixed us up from the grave."

Her hand is loose in mine, almost not responsive. The sun shines off her soft, dark curls. She pulls her hand away, and angles her head, her silver eyes flashing with the sun. "It's more than coincidence, right? *We* feel like more… like destiny. We feel like enough to face any danger, to face any secrets between us, right?"

I absolutely get what she's saying and asking. This thing between us is wildfire, a shooting star, a tsunami of feeling so deep that I've stopped worrying about Momma taking my memory of what happened in Mexico and have started to worry she'll take my memories of Honor. Would my family hurt Honor? A knife of alarm slices through me.

"I can't stay here, Honor. I can't."

She takes a whole step back, like I pushed her.

I rush to fix it, to be honest, because that pain in her eyes guts me. "Yeah, it's different. I feel it. If I had a choice, I'd stay." I add the word, the stupid word that feels true, but logic tells me *can't* be true. "Forever."

"Maybe you could stay," she says, "if you let me help you."

I close my eyes and fight the pain in my throat. "Order of importance, remember?"

For a long moment, she doesn't answer.

I open my eyes and see her eyes filled with tears. They spill down her cheeks.

I reach out and wipe them until they disappear.

Hands tense on the straps of her backpack, her focus drifts to Junior and the tourists surrounding him as he gives instructions. She heads off in their direction and very softly, almost inaudibly, whispers, "But that's not fair to you."

Chapter 25
Honor

Relationships change people, sometimes for the better and sometimes for the worse, and, sometimes, I'm learning, they make you do and say stupid things.

I'm mortified by my exchange with Laz moments ago. One night of great sex doesn't give me the right to ask him to change his whole life for me. And yet, that's exactly what I did.

As I reach the hiking tour group, Junior finishes collecting the paperwork. "Perfect timing," he says. "Waivers are signed, hiking gear, water, and food are all checked. Everyone here is good to go."

"Thanks," I say. "You're the best."

He nods. "Yeah. I know." He whistles to get people's attention. "Roll call." He reads each name out loud so that I know who's who. I frown when he introduces Don and his son, Cole. It's a long walk for a tween boy, but we have multiple warnings about the length of the tour, and I must assume this father knows his son's abilities. I've intervened before in these things, only to be shown kids are often better hikers than adults.

Junior puts his hand on my shoulder. "I'm leaving you all in my cousin's capable hands. Enjoy your hike, everyone."

"Have fun at the beach," I whisper to him.

He grins at me unapologetically, because he deserves the time off.

"Hi, everyone. My name is Honor, tour guide and chocolatier," I say, as I walk over to the ten people here for the hike. "And this goofy-looking guy is Laz."

Laz snorts unexpected laughter and does a funny kind of salute. Tension slides off of me. I want to make things okay between us. He's helping out a lot, and I appreciate that, even if I want more and want him to want more.

"We'll be your guides for this hike, so if you have any issues, questions, or need me to shield you while you take a pee break, just let us know."

There's awkward laughter, but I know from experience it's best to mention it now. I turn to Laz. "I'm going to take the lead, since I know the trail. You want to keep track of the people in the back of the line?"

"On it," he says, and falls back as I start down the trail.

The first two hours of the hike are near perfect. People are interested in the birds, insects, the tiny but loud frogs we call coquí, and plants of this region, so the conversation is free flowing. I love sharing what I know of Puerto Rico.

After a quick break and snack, we start off again. I tell them about how the cocoa and coffee trees were, at one time, forced out for sugar plantations, and how, after the coffee came back, my grandmother decided to do the same with cocoa tress.

I'm interrupted by Don, the man hiking with his twelve-year-old son. Completely off topic, he asks, "I bet your mom, Kiki Hart, would've hated this hike. She would've rather been in a bathtub sipping champagne."

He laughs at his own joke, and I'm taken aback. It's been a while since I've had to deal with people, often reporters, who come to Loco for Cocoa to get inside information on Mom, but I have no doubt he's fishing.

"Your mother was Kiki Hart?" another guest asks, and I hear someone else whisper that they should've known from the eyes.

Steadying myself, I say, "Mom and I took this hike many times."

There are more murmurs of surprise. As I keep walking, I fight to keep my cool and handle this as I've handled it in the past, by drawing a firm line between Kiki Hart and Natalie Silva. "But Kiki Hart wasn't my mother."

Now people are confused, and Don tries to protest, but I keep going.

"Kiki Hart was a media image, a persona who my mother, Natalie Silva, portrayed for many years. But, in person, she wasn't anything like Kiki, the party girl, the sex symbol with the lavish lifestyle. Natalie rarely wore makeup, jewelry or expensive clothes. She was an avid hiker, loved to be outdoors, and worked hard to promote conservation and support issues near and dear to her heart."

"I've seen a few of her documentaries," Don says, as if to soften his prior statement.

Well, at least he's trying, but I surely don't want to go there, so I keep walking, trying to figure a gentle way out of this.

"Is that a waterfall?" Laz says.

I almost sigh with relief. "You have good ears. There's a waterfall ahead through those trees."

Tension broken.

"Watch your step," Don warns Cole as we descend into the rock-strewn area at the base of the waterfall.

"This isn't the Fire Swamp, Dad," Cole says.

I have noticed a tendency for Don to warn his son off of simple things, but his father has a point here. "True. You won't find any rodents of unusual size, but Abuelito calls this a land of a thousand lands. He says that you can be happy on this island, but never comfortable. It will turn on you as surely as a storm."

I bend down and dip a finger into mud, then walk to Cole. "Do you mind?"

He shakes his head, and I put two dark streaks under his midnight eyes.

He smiles up at me all interest and innocence. "Do I look like a soldier?"

"Definitely," I say, and we take off our shoes to wade into the water.

Dropping my boots on the ground, I take in the misty waterfall that stretches above us over dark and jagged rocks like a beautiful threat. I turn to our guests. "Feel free to find a place to eat your lunch, but be careful—the rocks can get slippery."

"As you wish," Laz says.

I snort and bump him with my shoulder. I whisper, "I'm a little worried about how long it took us to arrive here—three hours."

"If need be," he says, "I can piggyback Don on the way back."

I shove him again, though it *was* Don who'd slowed us down. "He didn't complain once," I point out.

"You can't complain when you have your kid with you."

"He's a great kid. Don did that right."

Laz nods. "And he has good taste."

"Good taste?"

He winks at me. "He's got a crush on my favorite tour guide."

I smile, but don't deny it. It's not like I didn't notice. I thought it was sweet.

As everyone splits off with their closest companions, I take a seat next to Laz, extend my legs, and move as close as possible to him. He has that kind of pull on me, the kind where touching him is an absolute necessity.

I lean against his shoulder. "This is one of my most favorite places on the island. It reminds me of better days with my mother."

"You did a great job of dealing with the questions about her and with letting people know the truth of who she was."

I like hearing that. "Thanks. People often confuse her with her image. I once had someone call me out online after Mom died, saying I was concealing her true death because there was no way Kiki Hart was killed by a hit-and-run driver while walking in her neighborhood. The guy insisted I was covering up her drug overdose."

"That must've been a dark time. I'm sorry you went through that." He rubs a hand up and down my arm.

"That's why I came here, to get away from the mirror world."

"*Mirror* world?"

I swish my jaw around as I consider how best to explain it. "You know, I spent a lot of my life sheltered, homeschooled, surrounded by people who loved me and loved my mom, but, at a certain age, I became exposed to people who'd decided they knew who I was based on who they *thought* Mom was."

"Tell me about that," he says, and it feels like something a therapist would say until he puts his arm around me and draws me closer to his side.

"It was when I started dating. You know, guys who thought I'd sleep with them or do things with them because my mom showed her boobs in a movie. At sixteen, after two bad experiences, I stopped dating until my third year in college."

He frowns, squeezes me closer, as if protecting me from memories. "I have to admit," he says, "this wouldn't be the first time not knowing popular culture has bit me in the ass, but I remember Kiki as some kind of activist."

"Oh, later-years Kiki was. Yep." I let out a deep breath. "After Mom stopped making movies and started making documentaries calling out abuses and unfairness in the movie industry, the mirror world got really scary."

He shifts so he's looking directly at me. "In what way?"

"There were active campaigns to discredit her and her films. There were commentators and videos calling her the dopey sex goddess who'd lost her sex appeal and had gotten crabby and bitter. She was reviled and mocked to such a degree that whenever a new documentary came out, the mirror world went crazy. She'd have multiple death threats."

He scratches the back of his neck roughly, then shocks me with his next question. "What happened to the person who killed her?"

I tense. The wound of that still physically aches. "They never found her killer. Not even after I hired two different investigators. The lack of evidence was shocking, considering Mom lived in an affluent neighborhood so all the homes had security footage, but neither the police nor the investigators came up with any substantial leads."

He shakes his head. "With all that security footage, your average hit-and-run driver is gonna get caught. Have you seen the footage? Did they identify the car used?"

A chill runs the entire length of my body. "Are you suggesting... it *wasn't* an accident?"

His hand moves down my arm, his fingers intertwine with mine. "Not sayin' that. I'm asking questions because this is a lot of information, and I'm naturally suspicious."

Fists of anxiety begin to pound my chest. "If it wasn't an accident... You don't think it could be related to what's happening here, do you?"

He grimaces. "Can I see her documentaries?"

"Yes, of course. They're online. Mom put them out for free because she couldn't get anyone to carry them." A fly buzzes my head and I shoo it away. "There are files, too."

"Files?"

"At the hotel I have all my mom's files and notes about her films and the people who worked with her on them. Could that be relevant?"

"We'll find out, Honor." He moves forward and kisses me on the lips. "Fierce and beautiful and smart. Wish I could share more of my history with you."

My throat grows tight with emotion. "You share the truth of who you are in different ways, by action, by showing me you are a person willing to put himself in danger to protect me. No matter what our future holds, that truth will always be enough for me."

Chapter 26
Tony

The group that returns from the hike is a lot quieter than when we'd set out. Six hours of up and down with the weather turning on you, slipping and sliding through mud, will do that to you.

Truth is, I'm more tired from Don's helicopter-parenting Cole. *Watch it, Cole. Don't do touch that. You're going to fall. Stop bouncing.* There's going to be a problem there when Cole hits his teenage years. The kid is already eye-rolling like a champ.

I'd have preferred a bit of silence to think on what Honor had shared about her mom's death. It's not impossible that a celebrity is hit by a car in their wealthy neighborhood with all sorts of security camera footage around and all sorts of coverage on the event, but it would be one hell of an oddity.

Still, it's probably not related to what's happening here. At least I hope it's not, because this could be a lot messier than it appears.

I've got all these pieces and can't make them fit. And I'm not sure they belong in the same puzzle. How could someone making an outrageous offer on Honor's property be related to Natalie's death? Unless… Could the person who hit Honor's mother be trying to make up for his or her actions by offering an outrageous sum for the property?

Crap. I don't know. I've never felt more adrift, never missed the resources The Guild provides more. I need a team, not just my eighteen-year-old computer geek brother.

"Get ready to run," Honor says as the sky turns to dark. She calls it.

We're steps out of the woods and off the trail when a crack of thunder erupts nearly on top of us and the sky opens up, gushing rain.

As tired as we are, the rain and that clap of thunder are plenty motivation. We run.

Like Honor, I slow my roll and make sure all the guests are in front of us.

She turns to me as we jog behind them, grabs my slick-with-rain hand, and smiles. Her silver eyes pin me like steel, like a spike to my heart.

"Let's start a fire." She grins wider. "In my room."

This woman is full of good ideas.

I really like Honor's little suite. It doesn't have a full kitchen because she says she can go down a few steps for food, but it's got a living room with a fireplace, small office space, and a big California king. Lady knows the way to my heart.

Once the door closes behind us, she pulls me to her and brushes eager lips across mine. We kiss, open-mouthed and wild. Like everything about this, about us, we've shared a lifetime in a few hours, and it pours into this connection.

I can't get close enough, can't kiss her deep enough. We collide and explode with want. After several moments of hot kisses and heavy breathing, she pulls on my damp cargo pants. "Take these off. I want to give you head."

My eyebrows must shoot to the roof along with my body temperature. "That might be the nicest order anyone has ever given me."

There's never been a guy in the history of damp, stuck-on pants who's gotten out of them gracefully. I try. I really try to be cool in the face of my raging cock and shaking hands. Nearly make it, but just as I'm working my cargo pants over the tops of my feet, I get caught and crash to the floor.

Finished taking off her own clothes with no problems, Honor's hands fly to her mouth. She looks at me for a moment, sitting on the ground, pants around my ankles, hard-on at full attention, and bursts into laughter.

Most men—men who didn't grow up in a house full of women who regularly laughed at him—might be bothered or embarrassed by this situation, but not me. I see it for what it is. An opportunity.

I wink at her. "Looks like I'm going to need your help."

Smiling, she drops to her knees, pulls off my pants, and tosses them across the room. She positions herself between my legs, and I spread them to accommodate her as she bends, and, with a delicate flutter and flick of her soft tongue, licks up my inner thighs.

I practically jackknife in anticipation.

Her tongue runs over the swell of my balls. She sucks one into her mouth and a hiss a breath rushes from my mouth.

"Honor... that's..."

A moan chases words back down my throat as she sweeps her tongue to my other ball. Woman has the instinct of a goddess. If she'd been in my body, she couldn't know how to make me feel better.

With an audible pop, she releases me and slides her tongue up then down the length of my cock while cupping my now-thrumming balls. Thrusting toward her mouth, I beg her to take me fully.

She doesn't disappoint.

Her lips wrap their velvety warmth around me, and I nearly come.

I moan loud and long, watching the sway of her tits as she speeds up the rise and dip of her head.

"Slow..." Reaching down, I slow her by winding my hands through her hair. It's that or lose it.

Her eyelids lift so that she's locks her gaze directly on me while doing something with her tongue that brings on another wave of pleasure.

"Too good. Going to come."

She smiles around my cock. A wicked smile that says I'm in deep trouble.

Pulling against the hold I have on her hair, her mouth drops down, taking in nearly the whole of me.

Fuck.

She works the length with enthusiasm, a genuine moaning pleasure that kills my restraint. I'm so hard, it begins to hurt. She dips and sucks, building friction, driving me to the edge.

"Slow down," I gasp, trying to regain some control.

She runs her tongue along the seam of my cock, then begins to move that slick muscle with a speedy, fluttering vibration. What the hell is…

I lose it, buck into her mouth without control, and come like a flood, like it'll never end, like the orgasm will carry on for days.

When I'm done, she swallows and smiles at me like she's won some game we're playing.

And, man, I'm dead tired and so satisfied. But she obviously doesn't know she threw down a challenge. Or that I grew up in a family where a challenge is *never* not accepted.

Game on.

Chapter 27
Honor

Outside, thunder breaks in the sky and rain pelts the window as the storm continues. On the warm, dark floor of my bedroom, my skin slick from the heat between us, I curl against Laz's chest. "We never did start that fire," I say.

"I think we did," he says, and kisses me, then startles me by scooping me into his arms, standing, and carrying me to the bed. With a gentleness that makes me feel precious, he places me on the bed, leans over me, and kisses me. *Mmm.*

His warm hands trace down my body to sink between my legs. He strokes me, thrusting in and out with two fingers. In no time, I'm saturated and reaching for him.

Grabbing my hand, he leans far over and presses his forehead against mine. "What can I do for you, Honor? What can I do to show you... To make this moment last forever in your mind? Last for all the days that I won't be here?"

The thought of him leaving fills me with intense grief. I push it away. If all we have is this moment, then I want every second of it. Grief can wait.

As he stands in his perfection, every blessed inch, I realize exactly what I want. "Will you dance for me?"

A smile plays on his lips. He steps away, searches the floor, and finds his pants. Wrestling his phone from inside a deep pocket, he turns it to a soft song. Oh, I recognized the artist, Shawn Mendes and the song, "Mercy."

The acoustics fill the room. He lifts up one arm like a ballet dancer... I expect him to break into a teasing, joking *Magic Mike* dance, but his other arm floats up. He lifts his foot in perfect pirouette. Like the most graceful ballet dancer, he spins.

My breath catches as I watch him dance, like a heartbeat, like a prayer, like he's saying something with his movements that he hasn't said with his words.

Tears spring to my eyes. His body is an instrument that he is using to serenade me. It is graceful and heartbreaking and exquisite.

I'm stunned to silence as this flawless man spins and jumps and glides across my room. The curtains blow in on a rainy breeze scented with green and jasmine and cocoa, and the cut of him, the strength of his hard lines, the bunch and pull of muscles, sets me aflame.

He writes a poem to me with spins and fades, with his arms and legs, and I feel the truth of him. I don't need him to ever tell me another word about who he is. I see the truth.

The music stops and he bows to me with a delicious, sweat-slicked body. The room fills now with his soft breaths and my heavy ones.

"Come to bed," I say, feeling sentimental and emotional and overwhelmed.

He returns to me, so beautiful my breath catches. His lips and fingers dance over me, fierce and flowing. He slips a finger inside my already throbbing core.

I arch and encourage him deeper as his lips travel to my nipple. He bites lightly and I nearly break apart. He teases each nipple as one skilled finger curls inward and finds the bundle of nerves within my body. He strokes.

Oh. "Yes. There."

His finger strums inside. His mouth praises me, loves me, then, unexpectedly, descends and captures my clit. I toss my head and cry out.

He's everywhere, inside and out, sucking and playing. The tension grows so tight and high, I'm mindless with need.

With exacting pressure, he bites down on my clit, and I scream out and come so hard my body shakes.

For long moments after, I twitch with aftershocks.

He doesn't stop his exploration, though his fingers gentle, a tenderness that shows he knows the exact rhythm to play.

If he'd gone too hard and fast, the pleasure of those aftershocks might've been lost, but his softness lets every last shock of pleasure flash and whisper through me.

His fingers still inside me, he licks my clit then devours it. My hips shoot up. Holy… What is he…

The second orgasm slams into me, bows my spine, startles and shatters me.

"Yes. Oh. Yes!" I surrender to his strength, and he catches me, wringing every last ounce of pleasure from my body.

The orgasm slows and stops. Satiated, stunned, I can barely keep my eyes open when I hear him whisper, hot and gloating, "I liked the way *you* danced for *me*."

Hours after amazing sex, we're sitting up in my bed, my mom's old laptop open between us, and we watch her last completed documentary. A silhouetted figure is on the screen. In an altered voice, he's describing unwanted advances by a well-known director, along with blackmail and financial abuse.

Laz pauses it. "I'm often amazed by things like this, big truths about abuse on the fucking internet and no one does shit."

"It's the mirror world. People believe what they want to believe. Much easier to accept the lie and dismiss the truth."

"The lie?"

I close my eyes and blindly run a finger along the computer's edge. "Years before my mother got pregnant with me, she had a drug problem. She went into rehab. When she started making documentaries, someone put out this video of her, totally stoned…" I exhale the tension of years of dealing with the hurt and frustration of watching the video go viral. "She became Kiki the drug addict, the weirdo making all that crazy noise about the movie industry and abuse."

I wipe the tears that have slipped down my face. "I hate knowing that's how some people will always see Mom, even though she'd been clean for decades when it came out."

"You can't fight the mirror," Laz says.

"You can't," I agree. "There was so much hatred directed at my mom after that. People accused her of making stuff up, trying to revitalize her career by drawing attention to herself. They threatened her life. I was so afraid, I stopped telling people my mother was Kiki Hart." He doesn't say anything, and I wonder if he finally realizes. I say, "I told you: la Léon Cobarde."

He pushes the old laptop away, then draws me into his embrace. "Doesn't matter how many times you tell me that, Honor, I'm never gonna see you as a Cowardly Lion. Plus, I can see why you wouldn't want to claim that false image. To you, your mom was the woman posting the videos, trying to make a difference, Natalie Silva."

A chill of relief works down my body. "That's true, but I don't want to lie and pretend that some of it wasn't pure fear. Mom did a good job of protecting me. Homeschooled until high school—a private school. I even attended a small elite college, pursuing my passion for food and gastrological chemistry."

I curl into the warm reassurance of his steady presence, inhaling the spice of his body. I'm crying, but I can't stop talking. Until this moment, I didn't know all of this pain was inside me. "After Mom became so hated, I was shell-shocked. Part of me wanted her to shut up. It wasn't doing any good, speaking out. It's like people who hate are so loud and people who don't hate naturally aren't."

"I'm sorry, Honor. She deserved better."

"She did. And she didn't deserve to be murdered, because more and more, I'm becoming convinced she was."

He wipes a tear from my eyes and takes a long moment to answer. "The hatred from online kooks isn't usually deadly. It's more likely that, if she was murdered, it was someone with a personal reason. Are all her documentaries online?"

"Not all. She died before she could finish the last one."

He stills, as if this bit of information has fully captured his attention. He pulls the laptop back. Fingers working the keyboard, he opens some files. "I noticed before, the amount of money she spent here was crazy. Tens of millions on research. What was she working on?"

"I don't know specifics, but I know she had a big-name star willing to go on camera and admit to being lured into a multi-decade-long sexual cult tied to some huge movie financier. By necessity, she did all the filming in secret, kept everything under wraps, and I didn't press. Honestly, I didn't want to know. Until she died, I had no idea she'd basically spent her life's savings on that last film."

"Where can I find that film?"

I hold out my hands. "No idea. After she died, I toyed with the idea of releasing it, but…" I wave at the paper files, the thumb drive, external hard drive. "If there was ever any kind of completed film, I was never able to locate it."

Eyes laser focused on the computer screen as he searches through her files, he says, "These documents are extensive. Lots of passwords to online locations, and, look here, some indicate they're hidden on the Dark Web."

Rolling onto my side, I adjust my pillow, propping my head up. "How could we find something there?"

"Not easy, but I know a guy."

"A guy?"

"Yeah." He keeps clicking the keyboard.

I kick at the blankets, restless and frustrated and tired of exposing every little detail of my life to a person whose name I don't even know.

I watch him. Blankets partly covering one leg, blue boxer briefs on, muscled stomach creased as he bends over the laptop. I run a hand down his thigh almost to the scar. "How did you get that scar?"

He stills. "Doesn't matter."

No. Nope. I grab his thigh and squeeze. "I really *need* you to answer this."

Putting the laptop on the nightstand, he rolls onto his side, smooths my hair back. The night is cool and smells of the rain and all the deep, earthy scents churned up after a storm. He closes his eyes. "A dog bit me."

I tense, waiting for more, wanting to shake more out of him, some truth, but I *need* him to *want* to tell me. After many long, frustrating moments, he whispers, "I don't think he intended to kill her, just got carried away."

I have to force my hands to unclench and not to dig into his thigh. "Who didn't intend to kill who?"

"My mom. My dad was an abusive guy."

"Your father killed your mother." Pain for him grips me so hard I can't breathe. I swallow hard. "Did you see it?"

He looks toward the open window and the almost full moon. "No. Would've. But at one point..." He scrubs at his face with his hand. "I went after him. He dragged me out of the room, shoved me into the laundry room. We had this dog, trained to be vicious."

Oh, that's his scar. I sit up, reach down, and rub the length of it.

"Tore the shit out of my leg. I kicked it off, crawled into the dog kennel, and locked the door. So no, I didn't see him do it. But I heard. Even over the dog growling and barking, I heard. The cries, the crash, the thud. And, later, when he came into the laundry room and got some cleaning supplies, I saw her on the floor." His head lowers, as does his voice. "Pretended to be asleep in the cage."

"How old were you?"

"Six."

"Six? You were a baby." *Pobrecito.* I have to swallow twice, then clear my throat before I can speak again. "Did you have to testify? Did he go to jail?"

He jerks, jumps out of the bed, and stands there shaking in the moonlight, all taut muscles and wild beauty.

I couldn't have caused a greater reaction in him if I'd held a hot poker to his side.

He runs an agitated hand through his hair and begins to collect his clothes. "I need... space. I'll go to the yoga room. We'll talk tomorrow."

I'm stunned by his reaction. My entire body goes into a state of panic. I get out of bed. The pain is obvious on his face. Did I cause that? I can't let him leave. I need to make this better. I walk over and tear his damp pants from his hands before he can slip them on. "No."

The briefest hint of anger before he shakes it off and says, "Give me my pants."

Pulling them behind me, I stamp my foot. "No."

"Fine. Your guests will get an eyeful."

He moves to step around me, and, without thinking, I loop my leg around his to bring him down just like he taught me. Except I get caught up with him, and he begins to fall on me. I cry out.

He grabs me and twists in midair, so I somehow end up on top of him. He winds up with his back on the floor, his front to my front, and his hot breaths pushing against my lips. Anger lines his face, and I feel wrong and guilty for trying to force him to stay, for not respecting his need for space.

I swallow. "I'm sorry. It's painful to watch you go. It hurts me. How can I sleep, knowing you're out there in pain because of something I said?"

His face softens. He lets out a breath, brings his forehead to mine. "This isn't your fault. Nothing you caused. You changed everything, Honor. You don't even know. You changed *everything*."

He rolls, gathers me to his side, tucks me against his body, and whispers, "He didn't go to jail. I never told anyone what I saw. Not until now."

Oh.

I hear him swallow, and when he speaks again, his voice is

clouded with pain. "He pretended he didn't do it. And I pretended I didn't know he did it. It was a matter of survival."

"And you've lived with this the whole time? Never told anyone?"

"Until you, I didn't..." He swallows again. "No one ever asked."

"No one has ever asked about your childhood?"

"My therapist did, but I never told him about this. My adopted family... Nah, they've all got stories. Mine..." He shrugs. "Not that big of a deal."

It *is* a big deal. "You were adopted? What's your family like?"

Silence. A closing down. "It doesn't matter anymore. What's important is that I live my life in a way that makes up for not saying anything before. Or, I *did* live my life that way."

"It does matter. I want your story. I want your truth. Does this have anything to do with the meaning behind your tattoos?"

He kisses my ear, rests his cheek against mine. "Just lie here with me a minute. Okay?"

Ugh, so frustrating. I open my mouth to object when I feel a single tear slip from his face and work its way down mine.

"Okay," I say.

With my head pillowed on his bicep, I breathe deeply, swallow my questions, and pretend to sleep.

Chapter 28
Tony

I didn't plan on sleeping on the floor of Honor's room; it just kind of happened. But when her alarm sounds, I come fully awake, grateful she's still here, curled up with me. Last night was... a lot.

Sunlight streams through the windows, caressing the outline of her hips. She rolls and throws the nearest object—a shoe—at her clock, silencing it. A former archer, she has a good aim.

She makes a sound of deep regret and says, "I need to make the chocolates."

I don't want her to go. "How long do you have?"

She sighs, nuzzles my neck. "Now. I have orders to fill, and my self-defense instructor is a pain in the ass, expecting me there before the yoga class shows up."

"Okay, but if that's true, you definitely shouldn't be nuzzling my neck... uh, or my ear."

She shuts me up with a kiss.

Fine by me. I roll onto her, and begin to tease and stroke her body—a manipulation meant to get her too hot to leave.

She moans under me. This is headed in the right direction. But she pushes against my chest. "I can't. I have to make chocolate."

Damn. I roll off of her. "Your loss," I tease.

She slaps my chest, sits up, kisses me, once, twice, then sweeps her tongue into my mouth.

I kiss her back, waiting for her to make her escape. She climbs on top of me, her wet core throbbing against my hard-on.

Okay, I really hope she's not going to stop now. This is the best feeling in the world. This hot woman on top of me, soaked, and sliding against my cock.

She moans and again whispers, "I can't," before grabbing my cock, lifting up, and sliding down.

My eyes spring wide at the exact moment hers do.

"Honor, are you—"

I don't even care anymore. My eyes roll back in my head as she slowly slides down, then just as slowly back up.

All I can do is hold absolutely still, afraid she'll startle and bolt if I remind her she needs to get to work.

She kisses me, open-mouthed and desperate, and, with no more warning than that, begins to ride me. Fast.

Her body bouncing, hips pumping, ass thrusting up and down, with her making frantic, mounting sounds of need and want, all I can do is grab her waist and hold on for dear life. That and focus on something other than the heave of her tits, so full and ripe.

Focus on something other than her sighs, her moans, that building heat.

Focus. I'm two seconds from losing myself inside her.

She throws her head back and comes, even as she continues to pound me.

Wonderful, blessed moments later, she slows, bends down, and kisses me on the lips.

I start to roll, to get her under me, but she stops me with a push of her hand against my shoulder. I lie back down, and when she moves to dismount, I say, "Are you fucking with me?"

She snorts. "I definitely am, cowboy." She lifts off, holds my cock, and turns herself around so her ass is in my face.

She slides onto my cock, both feet under her, and proceeds to ride me into the ground.

I'm undone. Unfuckingdone.

She moves at a pace that is so excruciatingly good, impossibly fast, that she manages with her hands on her thighs and her ass bouncing.

I arch to meet her when she descends, and the sound of her labored sighs tightens my skin until there is only her slick, surrounding heat, and nothing for me to do but to release hard and hot into her soft, waiting body. With crazy, stupid gratitude on my lips, I say, "Gracias… gracias… gracias."

Dismounting, she falls back onto me and breathes hot and heavy against my chest.

I wait a minute before asking, but I gotta ask. "You said you can't, but went and did it anyway. Not that I'm complaining. I'm the happiest man on the planet right now, but just so we get this straight, no means no, right?"

She laughs, punches me in the shoulder. "Of course no means no. I wasn't saying I can't have sex with you. I was saying I can't leave you. I knew I should, but I just couldn't. You are irresistible."

"If I had known that was what you meant, I would've been a lot more participatory. I was afraid to move. Didn't want you to stop."

She rolls away with a playful, "It worked for me."

Chapter 29
Tony

I'm a desperate man. I have to keep Honor here and training, but it's all I can do to get her to stay in the yoga tree house.

Can't say I blame her. Though she did a good job of taking me down last night in her room, she's reverted to her usual stiffness in self-defense class. And these are slow, careful lessons. Lessons designed to imprint the movements, not mimic the speed of an actual fight.

"This is a waste of time," she says from her place flat on the mat.

"It isn't. I've never had a student I couldn't teach, and I'm damn sure not giving up on you."

She rolls her neck, wipes sweat from her eyes, then reaches for my hand.

I pull her to her feet. She smells of sweat and chocolate, and it's all I can do not to nuzzle into that scent. "Let's try to slip past your mental defenses."

"How?"

"We'll get you to do what you did last night. You probably don't even realize how much you startled me. You were damn quick and quiet. Try to remember how that felt to move and act."

"Last night I wasn't thinking. Now, I can't *stop* thinking."

Hmmm... Maybe I can slip past her mental block using the *now-whatcha-gonna-do* method that Justice taught me shortly after arriving at the Mantua Home.

I'd been walking around, getting a feel for the huge home,

when Justice had jumped out from around a corner and nailed me in the chest with a kick. I'd stumbled back and fell on my ass. She'd laughed and cocked a grin. "Now whatcha gonna do?"

Pissed, embarrassed, I'd charged at her.

She'd taken me down in one-point-five seconds. Being taken down by an eight-year-old when you were twelve was as hard to swallow as charred steak. But scrappy-and-angry failed against trained-and-focused every time. Right now, Honor is angry, but I can put her in a situation where she lets her instinct and training take over.

I let out a breath. "Try to get past me."

She grimaces, sighs, then relents. Dancing around a little, she dodges at the last minute. I bring her down to the mat and put a knee into her back. "Now what do you do?"

She tries to push up.

I press down.

"Okay, I get it," she says. "Get off."

This is killing me. "Whatcha gonna do?"

"I don't know. You haven't taught me that yet."

"Wrong. I have. I've taught you how to get out of this exact situation." And I don't have her right arm, am leaning close enough to let her put an elbow into my face, and am barely holding her. One shove and I'd back off. But she isn't willing to do it, to hurt me, to hurt anyone. She did it last night when she thought it meant saving me from pain.

Maybe that?

I get down closer. "When I was eleven years old, I ran away from my abusive father. This situation, the one you find yourself in right now, I found myself in with a stranger. And guess what? Saying 'get off' didn't fucking work." I swallow. Saying it out loud makes all those old feelings bubble up. "Fight for that kid, Honor. Defend him. Show me."

She moves like I lit a match under her, genuinely taking me by surprise. She slams her elbow into my face. Hard. For real.

Fuck.

She twists, knocks me off, and sits on my body, lifting her fist to punch me.

I hold up my hands. "Honor. You did it."

Her eyes open wide. She rolls off and begins to shake.

I sit on the mat next to her, rub at her arms and... she starts to cry. Shit. I made her cry.

She sniffs. "What did you do?"

"The first time? Someone came into the alley, and I used a distraction to get away. The second time? Well, that time, I had a knife and made sure when that same guy came after me, he saw it. Made sure he could see how hard I'd fight. He left. After that, I spent most nights sleeping behind a dumpster."

Her eyes go wide and shocked. "I can't get my head around your life."

Another tear traces down her face and I catch it with a finger. "I'm sorry, Honor. I shouldn't have told you—"

"No. It's okay. I want to know about you and your life. It's just different from how I lived and was raised. I told you before that I was kind of sheltered."

Maybe there's a clue there on why she hesitates so much in training. "When was your last fight?"

Her eyebrows go up. "My last fight?"

Okay. Maybe *fight* isn't the right word. "When was the last time someone physically threatened you? Got in your face?"

"The other day. My uncle José."

I ball my fists. "He threatened you?"

"Not really. You were there. He kind of blocked my way. He didn't touch me or make it seem like he'd hit me or anything."

I exhale. I thought I was going to have to go punch that old guy out. "How many fights have you been in? What's the most violence you've ever experienced?"

"Violence? Like me hitting someone or someone hitting me?"

"Either."

She looks down. "I've never hit anyone and never been hit."

"Tripped. Shoved. It doesn't have to be hit."

She looks up at me with her silver eyes wide and curious. "Where *are* you from?"

The real world. "Are you telling me you've never been hit? Not as a kid, not in school, not playing soccer, not shoved, not tripped, never?"

"I was pushed into a pool once, but as a joke, not with malice. As for sports, I danced and did swim team and of course did archery for sport. Not hunting. I would never. I didn't play sports that required aggression."

An archer who has never killed anything. "So you've never experienced any violence, not once?"

"Never, and up until this very moment, I thought that was normal." She leans closer, plucks a hair on her yoga pants. "What about you? When was your first time?"

"I guess I'm your polar opposite. Can't remember a day without violence."

The clink of silverware and glasses in the courtyard below drifts up through the windows, letting me know people are up and eating. I add, "But it's not something that requires your sympathy because here I am, unbroken."

I watch as Honor fumbles with her distress, opens her mouth to respond, then accepts what I told her with a nod.

She says, "Well, give me a chance to catch up. You have lived a *lot* longer than me, old man."

I laugh. "Whatever you say, *baaybee*."

She sticks out her tongue. "Nice, Tone."

My heart jumps into my throat and knees me in the Adam's apple. "What'd you call me?"

Chapter 30
Honor

On the floor in the yoga tree house, the sun working its way inside, sweat dripping down my back. Insects buzzing outside and the sound of utensils, of people talking and eating breakfast drift up, but my focus remains on Laz.

What did I call him?

"I didn't... I said nice tone. Your tone. You said *baby* in a mocking voice."

Understanding pinches his features for a beat before his face becomes completely blank and impassive. My heart starts to pound. What just happened? What did I say? Nice tone? Nice. Tone.

I work these words, chewed on them with a swish of my jaw as I flex my toes up and down against the squishy blue mat.

Still acting as if nothing happened, Laz begins to collect his things. Oh, something happened. What in those two words could mean anything to him? Nice?

"Tone?"

He flinches.

"Tony?"

He spins.

My hands fly to my mouth.

Of course. Of *course*. Goose bumps wash over me in such a fierce rush, I have to repress a full body shudder. Him. Tony is him. Tears rush to my eyes. "Tony? Is that your name?"

He stares at me with his own eyes growing moist with some

unnamed pain. It is. His name. For a moment, he is unmasked to me, and I cannot breathe.

As much as we've shared—and we've share something far deeper than anything I've known in my entire life—there's been a giant emptiness between us. The emptiness of him, of who he really is.

Knowing his name, saying his name aloud—Tony—counts. I hadn't expected it to be so important, but it is huge.

A lump of emotion rises and blocks my throat, but I swallow it and open my mouth to say it again, to taste his name on my tongue like I've tasted his body.

He shakes his head, closes his eyes, and puts up a hand up in a *stop* gesture, as if I'm causing him physical pain. "Don't call me that again, Honor. As much as... as good as it feels, it's not safe."

He opens his eyes, giving me as much of his truth as he dares.

It isn't enough. Suddenly, it isn't nearly enough. Now that I have a piece, a taste of his truth, I want it all.

"What had happened to you after you ran away? Where did you end up? What or who are you running from?"

He backs up with every question, but I am moving forward. The moment I said his name, a small bell in my heart rang. *Tony.*

I wrap my arms around his neck, kiss his cheek, and put my lips against his ear. "Anthony. Tony. Tone."

He shudders, groans, then wraps his arms around me. "Fuck. You shouldn't."

I whisper, "Kiss me, Tony."

He does, full on the mouth, wrapping me tight in his arms. Hot and wild and as needy a physical response as the looming threat against him, the barrier from his past that keeps and will continue to keep us apart.

My heart swells, batters against my chest.

I pull back and stare into his beautiful hazel eyes. "What is this feeling?"

"I... I don't know." He smiles, awed and a little sad. "Like something from a fairy tale."

The sound of someone whistling drifts into the room. We break apart, and, a moment later, the yoga teacher appears.

Lanie waves at us as she enters, wearing cream-colored yoga pants and a matching top. She begins turning on the tea-tree diffusers around the room.

"Hey, Lanie," Laz says, rubbing the back of his neck. "I'll clean up the mats. We're done here."

We start to clean up even though I want to run back to my room with him and whisper his name in his ear while he pours himself, his truth, into me.

On our way out, Laz smiles at Lanie in a way that's all charm. "Sorry if we delayed your class prep."

She shakes her head. "They won't be here for a few minutes. You two can stay if you want. It's a fun class."

I laugh. "I can barely use my arms right now."

Lanie shifts slightly, tilting her head to the side. "What are you guys practicing?"

Whoops.

Laz asks, "Is that a hint of a British accent I hear?"

Lanie smiles. "Yep. I'm an offshore financial expat. One of many on the island."

"What's that mean?" Laz asks, though I'm fairly sure he knows and is making conversation.

"The Caribbean has a lot of havens for business. It attracts people who use the lax laws to do things other countries outlaw. Years ago, before I embarked on my journey of rediscovery, I was not the most honest of people."

Laz's mouth drops open, and I almost laugh out loud. I'd had the same reaction to Lanie's openness the first time I met her. The woman has no secrets, including things she should probably keep to herself.

A few people arrive for her morning class and we make our exit. Outside, our hands entwine. Laz/Tony leans toward me.

"Awkward conversation with Lanie, but it sure makes searching for bad guys easy."

I laugh and realize that laughing and smiling, despite all the bad stuff happening, is now something I do regularly. I might only have a little bit of his truth, but it's enough. I know him. He's here fighting for me, helping me despite whatever danger he faces.

I lean against him as we walk. "Sorry about today's lesson. I'll be better tomorrow."

He snorts. "If you get any better, I might not survive it."

And that, right there—him reaching out to remind me of my one successes and not the multiple failures of today—is another reason my heart has followed my libido in throwing caution to the wind. Now, if my head will only get with the program and stop worrying.

Chapter 31
Tony

Hand-in-hand with Honor, I cross the courtyard to the hotel. My earlier thrill at having her speak my name has turned into regret and gnawing guilt.

What if knowing my name puts her in danger? Fuck. I should've played it cooler. Should've... But it felt so good having her say it, having her see me, the real me. And it's one name, a first name. How can Honor knowing my first name change anything?

Logic tells me it can't. After I figure out the threat to her, I can leave, knowing that, if they discover my connection to her, they'll leave her be. The only way they'd ever mess with her is if they suspected she knew about The Guild. She knows nothing, and it's going to stay that way.

"What's going on?" Honor says, bringing my attention to a group of anxious people, including her grandfather and Don, standing by the patio, talking and gesturing.

We angle our walk to pass by some tables and head in their direction.

Honor puts her hand on her grandfather's arm, taking his attention from the group. "Abuelito, what's going on?"

"Ah, mija, there you are. We could use your help. A boy is missing."

"What boy?" I ask. "A guest or one of the kids from the village?"

Abuelito's eyes switch to me. "He's a guest." He points to Don. "This man's son, Cole. He went on your hike, no?"

"Cole. Yeah. Great kid. I saw him this morning when I was on my way to the yoga center."

"Where? Where did you see him?" Don snaps, looking daggers at me.

"He was outside here, hanging out." I call up the mental image of him from this morning. "He had on red mesh shorts, a white Nike T-shirt with red stitching, tan hiking boots, and a backpack heavy enough to suggest he carried a good amount."

The group of people gape at me. Don's face sours. "You noticed all that and you didn't stop him? You didn't ask yourself what a boy of twelve was doing preparing for a hike?"

"I did actually, and I asked him. He said he was going on a hike with you to the waterfall."

"And you believed him? Left him out here by himself?"

"Yes, but I told him to wait inside because it was still a bit chilly out here. He went through the back door, and I went to where I needed to be."

"You should have brought him back to my room," he says. "You work here, right? Don't you care about your guests?"

I don't respond to Don's deflection. The guy is distraught, and the truth is, I'm getting there. This probably doesn't have anything to do with the threat to Honor. Then again, the kid could be in more danger than a kid hiking alone in a rainforest, which isn't exactly safe to begin with.

"The waterfall is a long walk from here," Honor says. "But if we run, we can catch up and have him back in no time."

"Run?" Don says, putting a hand on his round belly. "I'm not very fast."

"You know your son better than anyone," I tell him. "Let me and Honor run the trail. You think of all the places he might go, might be interested in, so you can search around here."

"Of course. Yes," Don says. He turns to Abuelito with red rising into his face. "Cole wanted to see how the cocoa is harvested."

Abuelito nods. "There are many paths through the trees. Follow me."

Cupping his hands around his mouth, Don calls his son's name as he follows Abuelito around the lodge.

Honor and I don't waste time. We put on rain jackets because of the darkening sky, gather some light packs, put in some water and first aid supplies, and start out.

After two hours with no luck, we stop and call the lodge to see if Cole has shown up.

He hasn't.

"We're going to have to backtrack," Honor says, pulling on the collar of her slicked rain jacket. "There's no way he could've beaten us here. I'm worried he went off the trail."

I hadn't even thought of that. "You're probably right. He had an hour lead on us, but he's a kid, and I can't imagine him going faster than us."

We turn and begin making our way back. We're no longer running, but moving at a decent clip. We're both looking for signs along the trail that indicate someone passed into the woods.

"I'm so worried about him." Her shoulders slump under her backpack. "I should've been tracking him. Honestly, I was so focused on looking ahead, hoping to spot, him that I could've missed signs that he went into the woods."

"We'll find him. It's most likely he left the woods somewhere back along the wooded trail."

We begin to move faster, thinking he might've left the trail much earlier than we thought. And, wouldn't you know it, it begins to drizzle.

Honor curses and begins hunching down as she walks, examining the ground for signs of his travel.

"Look," she says, bending to pick up a red-and-black Loco for Cocoa candy wrapper. She points at the footprint nearby, a child's footprint. She stands up and gazes into the trees. "It leads into the woods."

Stepping off the rocky, water-softened trail, she moves into the forest. At this point, I'm an observer because she is that good.

She mentioned that she was stealthy, but she never mentioned her tracking ability. Kind of like her not to toot her own horn.

"Oh, God," she whispers, and my heart starts to pound a thudding dread.

She reaches under some ferns and brings out a tween-sized boot with a stain of blood on the side. She holds it up. "Is this the boot he had on?"

I grab it, turn it. "Yeah."

No telling what happened to him. He could've stumbled in here to pee, lost his footing, hit his head, and is wandering the forest in shock. Or...

"As long as the rain doesn't get worse, I can track him," Honor says, whisking away deeper into the forest. Stomach dropping fast and heavy enough to dent earth, I follow, calling Cole's name.

Honor is a marvel. She makes her way through the woods as silent as a breeze, scanning the trees, waterlogged footprints, and broken ferns, then picking her way through them as if they've told her everything. I've got to get her to teach me these skills.

A crack of thunder. Shit. The sky opens up and pours. In no time, rain pounds the large-leafed trees loud enough that it seems a train's coming. Our pace slows.

After we crest a hill, Honor stops, puts up a hand.

I draw closer. "What's up?"

"Something is off here." She looks around. "The direction..."

She trails off and I try to figure out what she's getting at. We stand at the top of a rough hill. Below is an area that's thick, choked with vines and brush.

She claps rain-drenched hands together "We're headed back to the hotel."

"What? Are you sure?"

She pulls her rain slicker tight around her head. "Yes. But that's not all." She points at the ground to a man-sized shoe print. "Cole isn't alone."

I reach under my soaked rain jacket and pull my gun from the waistband of my cargo shorts.

"You have a gun?"

I nod and she pinches her mouth closed, takes me in for a second, then says, "You're different when you hold it. I can see the real you. I can see Tony."

I feel different, spring-loaded, expectant, and ready. I peer through the curtain of rain, and tell her, "Go on. I got your back."

Water rushes past our feet, soaks our boots as she begins to walk. At the bottom of the hill, thick vines hang from the enormous trees, creating hunter-green curtains.

Honor points at the center of these thick, hairy vines, and I see it—a dry place, a shelter of sorts by the trunk of the tree.

With a signal to me, she steps aside and lets me enter. I duck down and spot Cole on the ground. Scanning the cave-like space with my weapon, I make sure there are no other openings, no one else hidden somewhere behind the enormous tree trunk before I motion for Honor to come inside. She does, dropping to the ground and to Cole instantly. I let her tend to him, waiting for whoever might be hiding nearby.

"He's alive, but unconscious." She begins to examine his foot.

Still antsy, I strain to hear past the sound of the storm. I kneel beside her and Cole, put a hand on his head. "I'll carry him. Can you lead us back out?"

"Yes, but…" She bites her lip. "I don't think we should go back the way we came."

"You know another way?"

"We aren't too far from the hotel. There isn't a path, but I know I can get us there from here."

"Okay. Let's go."

Chapter 32
Tony

The rain has stopped, but the drip of water sliding off leaves continues. We're nearly out in the open, but it's still uneven and difficult terrain. I'm watching my step. Tying a ninety-pound kid to my back and carrying him through thick jungle over rocky stones slick with rain isn't easy, but I've got a good guide.

A moment ago, she'd finally gotten a signal and called to let everyone know we'd be coming in from the back of the inn, but, now, she's all business again. She picks the best path and motions me forward, warning me of dips and places I need to watch. I try to mimic her natural awareness, but fall far short.

"When I was a kid," I tell her, "my uncle told me stories of trackers with skills like yours, but seeing it real time is mind-blowing."

She considers this, but says nothing, motioning down at a rock instead.

I avoid the rock.

Her innate feel for the land, balance, and stealth—as silent a ghost over Bubble Wrap—could help her evade an enemy or sneak into a place. She'd be useful to The Guild.

Fuck. There it is. My upbringing. Analyzing those closest to me on what skills they can bring to The Guild. I've gotta let that shit go.

Although, right now, it's hard. It's serving me almost as a defense mechanism, a way I can see skills that might help Honor help herself. This experience with Cole has my every hackle raised.

Had Cole been going to meet someone? If so, who and why? And why would this person lead him back almost to the hotel? Why not just meet him closer to the hotel? Why would the kid keep going, stumbling forward though he'd lost a shoe?

"You okay?"

I lift my head from watching Honor's feet, the cat-like walk—proud and silent and graceful—and follow her into the clearing around the lodge. "Yeah. Why?"

"You look like you're chewing lemons."

Chewing something a lot sourer: fear for her.

I nod as a group of people rush our way. Honor had used her cell the moment we'd gotten a signal, so they are ready for Cole.

I pull on the line at my center chest, releasing the knot, and shifting forward, so that I can bring Cole from my back to my front, carrying him like the child he is. The kid utters a frightened noise that fades into murmurs.

With a cry half-grief and half-relief, Don rushes to us and takes his son into his own arms. "Cole." He kisses the boy on the cheek. "It's okay. Daddy's here."

"I think it's shock," Honor says. "I checked him out and he's uninjured except for a small cut on his hand."

Tears slide down Don's face as he talks to his son, basically doing what any frantic father would do after his kid went missing. He places his son on the gurney and emergency services takes over for him. Don walks beside the stretcher now, holding his son's hand as they head to the waiting ambulance.

Abuelito comes over, kisses Honor's cheek, and puts a hand, damp with sweat and rain, on my shoulder. "You are both heroes. Now, if you are recovered enough, can you please turn off that alarm? Some of our guests are threatening to leave."

I hear it then, the alarm I'd set on Honor's room. *Fuck.*

By the time I clear Honor's room and turn off the alarm, my ears are ringing. The room's been ransacked.

"I hate that someone was in here," Honor says, searching the room, picking up papers.

"Don't clean up just yet," I tell her. Sitting on the chair by her desk, I use my cell to access the security cameras and check the footage. The guy in the video has some situational awareness. He approaches the room hunched, wearing a hat and glasses to shield his face, maybe a wig, and he keeps his head down.

I pause the playback. Something there, some familiarity, but nothing I can put my finger on.

Honor comes over and sits on the arm of my chair.

I hold up my cell, so we can both see the screen. "This guy look familiar?"

"He's bent over—maybe older?"

"Nah. Look at the way he moves otherwise. He's bending over to hide his face."

She nods. "That makes sense. How did he have time to make this mess with the alarm going off?"

"He knew something about security, enough to disable the first alarm."

Her eyes widen. "You had another alarm?"

"Sort of. I put a backup on your mom's laptop. If someone opens it without entering the password for the original alarm, the secondary alarm goes off."

"That's clever."

"Human nature. You find one alarm, you think it's all good, so you go about your business."

She points to the floor and the papers scattered there. "Whoever he was, he was looking for something of my mom's. He went through her files before opening her computer. Do you think he got what he wanted?"

"That's the question, isn't it?" I pick up a paper closest to the laptop. Someone highlighted part of a sentence halfway down the page. "What's this about?" I point to the highlighted phrase, *TomCaneIsDEAD1972.*

"I don't know what it means, but I know that Tom Cane was the name of a male lead character in a movie Mom starred in."

"Did the character die?"

She squints at the page. "No. But it could be a password of some kind. All her passwords are pretty random. She gave me my first computer a password and I still remember it, 101bluecoquísseatingsugar."

"What was the name of the movie they were in together?"

She closes her eyes as if trying to remember. "*Built to Last*?"

I open the laptop and do a quick search on the movie. I read Lenox "Lex" Walker's bio, and my stomach sinks. "It's not the character who's dead. It's the actor who played him. Lex Walker. Did you know him?"

"Yes." She puts a hand to her forehead. "I met him a few times casually."

"He died three months after your mother."

Her eyes narrow. "You don't think… Could he be the star, the one she said was willing to talk on camera about the rumored sex cult?"

"I'm leaning toward yes. And this looks like more than a rumor. It looks like something big enough to get them both killed."

"But he died on set in a stunt accident. It was a big deal. There were accusations against the industry, production company, and producer. There was a lawsuit, multiple lawsuits, and a police investigation."

"Good. That means there will be details. Clues other than what your mom left here."

"Are you saying Mom left this password or whatever it is here on purpose? Left this clue for the police or me, in case…" She lets out a small, pained cry. "In case she died, or was killed or hurt?"

"Maybe."

She puts her head in her hands. "I let her down. I… was so stupid. I…"

I pull her from the arm of the chair into my lap. "Don't. It's not your fault. And we're on it now, right? We'll figure it out."

She lifts her head with a sudden jolt, looks at me with tears running down her face. "We?"

I wipe the tears away, swallow, and nod. "We."

Chapter 33
Honor

It seems like forever since I've had a moment to do what I love best: make chocolate. I'm happiest here in the kitchen in the back of the Cocoa Casa, among the tools of my craft—stainless-steel appliances, molds, whisks, carving tools, and measuring bowls.

It's not yet four a.m., but I am filled with the energy of creating art for the tourists who will be coming in on the ships today.

Because everything in my life has changed, it feels weird to be back in my regular routine, making chocolate, preparing to go down to the satellite store by the pier, while Laz, Junior, and our two new guides run today's tour.

Doing the soothing work of creating sugary art is about the only thing that could've gotten me out of bed with Laz.

Under the bright lights of the specially crafted kitchen, I pull out ingredients and tools with a clanking of pots and clinking of containers. Yesterday was an awful day.

I'm glad Cole wasn't seriously injured, but the whole incident has left me shaken, and then, to come back and find that someone had broken into my room, and, worse, that Mom might have feared for her life enough to leave clues in case something happened to her... It was just too much.

Releasing the tight hold I have on the jar of cocoa nibs, I pour half of it into the large drum of my steel blender, then add sugar and some orange liqueur. While it blends, I turn on the chocolate-tempering machine and adjust the temperature before breaking up chocolate squares.

Sometime later, I startle when the sound of someone moving into the small kitchen breaks into my awareness.

"You seem so happy making chocolates."

His deep voice shivers its way down my body. A wave of joy and heat rush through me. I smile at him. "You and chocolate are my two favorite things."

His eyes light at my words, and I go further. "I love making chocolate."

"Love, huh?"

I ignore my heating face and say, "What's not to love?" I dip a spoon into the heated well, draw out a creamy, dark spoonful, then feed it to him.

"Mmm." He closes his eyes around the bite. "You're right." He opens his eyes and locks onto me. "There's nothing here not to love."

For a moment, all the playfulness fades away and chills rush down my body. It is too big, this moment. Too real.

I turn away and start to clean up. "What did you think of the chocolate?"

As if disappointed in the turn in our conversation, he lets out a breath before answering. "Never tasted anything like it. Nutty and orange, with a hint of liqueur."

I take off my apron. "Yes. But the trick is to get it to stabilize. I need to pour it into molds, but I'm finished decorating all the other pieces." I point to the coolers, stacked and ready.

"Mind if I load them into the car and let you finish up here?"

"Of course not," I say and smile. "I appreciate the help. I usually have to do all the heavy lifting myself."

He kisses me on the cheek. "That's what I'm here for."

I watch him gather the coolers and can't help but wonder what it would be like to have him here always. I could make chocolate. He could do the tours. And we'd share this place, us together. It would be a dream life.

The door chimes as he exits and, sighing, I turn off the tempering machine.

Hot wind blows in through the open windows as I drive with Laz down the mountain.

"I might not work the tour today," he says. "I don't like leaving you alone."

"Don't you dare. I'll be fine in town. The police are right around the corner. Go and help Junior. He's totally freaked out after what happened with Cole."

"Can you blame him? Don couldn't leave the island fast enough."

"I know. He cancelled the rest of his reservation last night." Over the objection of his doctors, Don took Cole on a flight home this morning so he could have his son examined back in New York.

He twists in his seat. "You hear something?"

I take my foot of the gas and listen. I do hear something. We drift for a moment, down the narrow, winding road. "Oh no," I say, "We might have an unwanted passenger. I've had mice crawl into my car before."

"I got it." He undoes his seat belt and looks into the back. "Holy shit."

There's blur of movement, and Laz crashes back against the dash while lifting his foot. A snake shoots between the seats and latches onto his boot.

Heart racing, I pull over to the side of the road and get out to race around the back. I grab the first thing I see, a steel scraper.

I open the back door and find Laz pinning the snake into the floorboards by the heel of his boat.

"Here," I say.

Calm and serious, he takes it and looks around as if just realizing we've stopped. Using the sharp, flat edge like a guillotine, he pushes down with all his weight.

I look away as the steel bites into the snake's neck.

"It's done," he says.

I look back and see the severed head still attached to the heel of his boot and the snake body gyrating on the floor of my car.

"It's deadly, a viper," he says. "A fer-de-lance. I saw one on a mission in Costa Rica once."

I shake my head. "We don't have deadly snakes on the island. The racer snake has venom, but not enough to kill."

But the evidence is there, right in front of me. Someone put a venomous snake in my car. It had to be on purpose because there aren't any here.

Laz pries the snake head from his boot and flicks it onto the side of the road. "As soon as it stops moving," he says, "I'll put it away."

"You want to keep it?"

"Evidence. This isn't the action of a career criminal or someone who has enough money to pay a career criminal."

I break into a full-body shudder. I try to control it, but quickly realize I have no control. "I can't stop shaking."

"Adrenaline backlash. It's okay. I got you." He puts his arms around me and holds me tight.

I hold him back, anchoring myself with his body. "Someone tried to kill us with a snake. Where did they even get one? I've heard of snakes accidentally coming in with freight at the pier, but the authorities are so strict about finding and eliminating them."

Laz whispers, "How well do you get along with your cousin?"

Horrified, I push away from him with a startled shove to his chest. "Junior?" Sour moisture rolls across my tongue. "You think Junior did this?"

"He was the one who put the faulty carabiner on Bud. He had access or at least connections at the pier. Not everyone does. And he wasn't there when we went looking for Cole."

Could Junior have been the one to break into my room? Could he have something to do with those who'd killed my mother? And what did any of this have to do with the offer on the property?

"No!" I shout at him. "If I can't trust Junior, I can't trust anyone."

"It might not be him," he says, but it feels like he doesn't believe that. "Angelina has access to the pier, and we know she's spoken with José a few times."

"José and Junior? You don't want me to trust anyone." I step away from him. I start shaking so hard my lips chatter. "What did you mean, your mission in Costa Rica? Who are you really?"

He curses, runs a hand through his hair. "I know you're confused. Questioning everything. Take a breath here. Remember our first training session when I told you fear can be a gift, a way to discern trouble?"

I nod and watch how he moves, where his hands go. Does he have the gun?

"Well, there's also a kind of fear that holds us back, lies to us, and robs us of safety when we are safe. The trick is to learn the difference between the two. The imposter fear and the instinctive gut-level-warning fear. So, let me ask you—right now, without thinking too hard on it, what does your gut say about me?"

The truth comes instantly to my gut, heart, head, and lips. "It says I can trust you."

Something like relief or gratitude crosses his face. He rubs the heels of his hands hard against his eyes. When he lifts them off, his hazel eyes are glossy with moisture. "Hundred percent. Never in doubt. Got it?"

I begin to sob. "I don't know who to trust."

He steps toward me, but I step back.

"Honor." His voice cracks on my name. "Please let me hold you."

I shake my head. "I need to know who you are. I can't take this anymore. I feel like I've lost everything. Like I have no safe place to land. Give me a safe place to land. Give me some truth that I can hold onto, that I can believe in. Give me you. Please."

His face a mask of pain, he nods, and I reach for him. He sweeps me into his arms, wrapping me tight, tethering me in the reality of his strong embrace.

I bury my face in his chest, breathing in soap and salt.

Chapter 34
Tony

We're standing on the side of a winding road, a snake head three feet away, a snake body in the back of her car, and Honor is shaking in my arms.

And I'm panicking. It wasn't the near-miss of the snake, not the break-in last night, and not discovering Natalie's co-star died months after her that's causing this panic. It's Honor asking to know who I really am.

I've never felt fear like this, a battering against my chest, a wood splitter piercing my throat. It's not about betraying the family, though there's a little of that. It's about what they might do to her if they were to discover she knows about The Guild.

How can I deny her? How can I deny her when she is losing so much of what she's trusted in her life? When she's gone from being sheltered to being attacked? When she's putting her faith in me?

I can't.

Looking into her eyes, I brush hair from her face. "After—"

My phone buzzes in my pocket. A Taser to my abdomen would've caused less of a shock. Only one person has this number. That person knows never to text. Never.

Already calculating where to ditch the burner, I pull it out and read the one-word text: *RUN!*

Cold washes down my body. My already hammering heart picks up to double time. My brain goes still, blank. They know I'm on the island. There is no other way he would send that text. Or... could they be here?

A car whooshes down the road, passing by harmlessly. "We can't stand out here. We have to go."

"What's going on?" She grabs at my shirt. "Tell me."

Shit. Order of importance. Stay calm. Break it down. "You need to start carrying a gun. And I need to check your car before we get back inside."

Her face falls. Her pain and confusion give a sharp kick to my heart. And then it all drops away and she stares at me with suspicion.

Shit.

"What did the text message say?"

"Leave it, Honor."

"No. You agreed to tell me about yourself, then you read a text and now everything is changing."

"It was a warning. The people after me are close."

Her eyes widen. "I'll take you to your boat."

"I'm not leaving."

"You promised if you were ever in more danger—"

I rub at my face. What would she think if I told her she's trying to protect me from my own family? "I promised we would do this. *We.* And as for who is in more danger, right now, that's still you."

"I have enough information now that I can go to the police. The snake is evidence."

"That's an exaggeration, but you can't know how much it means to me that you're trying to protect me."

She growls at me. "You are"—she stomps her foot—"so frustrating!" She moves her hand rapidly between the two of us. "I'm not playing this game where you get to make the decisions. You want your secrets, but *we* need to come up with a plan that works for both of us."

"Okay, okay! Let me think."

Stay or leave, protect her or protect myself isn't working here. She's not going to let it go. I need a third option.

Maybe…

It's crazy, but if I collect all the information—including Natalie's laptop and files—then get Junior to tell me what he knows, I could present the case to Momma. She'd take it, I know she would. The documentary against Winthrop alone is a huge incentive, but the rest of it? She'd take it.

Every cell in my body wants to stay here and protect Honor, but I'm not an idiot. I'm endangering her in a different way, compounding her danger. The Guild has the resources to take on the case, and they're on their way here. If I do my job right, they'll protect Honor with everything they've got. That's how they work.

Who else could I trust to take care of someone I... uh, care for a whole hell of a lot?

"I think I have an option that'll work for both of us, and it will only mean a couple more days." A couple of really paranoid and super careful days. "If I can get the mystery of this sorted enough to present this case to extremely reliable and intelligent people who will help and protect you, would you trust me enough to trust them?"

"Who?"

"If this all works out, you'll know who."

"And you'd be safe? You'd go?"

The thought of sailing away from her... brutal. "Yes."

"Promise?"

I can't even choke the word *promise* out. I nod.

"Okay," she says.

We get back to work in silence, a silence in which I think we both feel cheated—might be the definition of compromise there.

After checking the car for bugs, tracking devices, or any other nasty surprises, I put the snake body and head into a leather pouch from my backpack.

I hold up the pouch. "Can I store this in a cool place?"

Honor steps back and shakes her head. "You can't mean with my chocolate?"

Biting back the smile at the absolute horror on her face, I clarify. "Can you shift the chocolate into the two containers so I can have the third? I want to ship this to someone. I think we need to get more people on this team."

She considers me for a minute. Considers me with eyes that deliver the same jolt to my body as a bolt of lightning from the sky—pure, silver-hot energy.

"Who?"

Oh, hell. "My brother."

"In addition to the sister you mentioned, you have a brother?"

"Yeah."

"Just one?"

"Brother?"

She nods.

I shrug. "Last I checked."

For a moment, I'm sure she's going to press me more, and I hate the idea of us spending our last day together fighting, but she lets out a breath. Her face softens.

"You know, Tony, I... I really lo—" She bites her lip. Tears well in her eyes. "I really appreciate your help."

My throat fills with the words that suddenly want to jump out and rush forward, but that wouldn't be fair to her. Not when I'll be gone soon. "I really appreciate your help too, Honor. From the bottom of my heart. I appreciate it."

Chapter 35
Justice

Lapping waves rock my brother's boat within the makeshift pier as I storm around his deck. If someone had told me eight months ago that I'd be in Puerto Rico hunting down one of my own siblings—my very best friend, my brother—I would've gently explained the dire error in their prediction. With a fist to their head.

And yet, here I am, searching storage compartments, wearing all black under a broiling sun, all because my not-dead brother chose to hide out on a Caribbean island.

I kick closed another storage lid. It's a nice-looking boat, sleek and white and expensive. Looks like Tony is living the good life. Fucker. I want to punch him in his alive face, watch blood flow out of his alive nose.

After jumping from the boat with my sack full of stolen loot, I march down the pier. Now that I've searched the boat top to bottom, I realize I need to calm down. This anger is worse than useless. It's clouding my judgment.

Now why does that thought sound familiar?

Oh, right. Tony would repeatedly accuse me of letting my anger get in the way of my judgment during the Brothers Grim op.

Waving off a dive-bombing seagull—nothing in here for you, bird—I step from the pier and walk toward my rental car. The bag bounces against my shoulder. Not sure how much of this was necessary to take. Except for the gun, which I tucked into my waistband in case Tony does show up.

Here's hoping Gracie and Dusty have had more luck. The good thing about having a team is you can split up and split the work.

A good-looking blond, hot enough to turn coal to diamonds, with broad shoulders and a slim waist, walks toward me. My heart does a little dance in my chest. *Well, hello there, handsome.*

A wide, appreciative grin breaks across Sandesh's face. "Whatever you're thinking, the answer is yes."

I smile back. "I was thinking I've got someone to carry my bag."

I toss it at him, and he snatches it from the air, slinging it over his shoulder with a "Happy to help in *any* way."

His tone is teasing, but he's proven time and again that he means it. My partner in all things, he's been trying to make things easier on me since the moment we found out Tony was alive.

"Thanks," I say. "Want to steal my brother's boat and get out of here?"

He gives me a sidelong glance. "You're still conflicted?"

"Yes. Dammit. As much as he hurt me and the family, part of me wants Tony to get away." Sandesh makes a noise of objection, and I explain before he bursts a blood vessel. "The childish part, the *that's my big brother* part. The part of me that wept for him every night for three months wants it."

"I know *that* part because I held her every one of those nights." His tone says he hasn't forgotten or forgiven.

"Then there's the other part, the adult part, the *fucker-how-dare-you-screw-with-me-and-our-family* part that wants to kick his nuts into his throat."

Sandesh sets my ill-gotten gains by the dark blue sedan. "Got to say, I hope that's the part that wins."

I pop the trunk. "Probably will. She's so damn determined."

He laughs, and I check out his ass as he puts the bag into the trunk. Because it is so fine, I pat said ass. He slams the trunk and turns to me with a grin.

"Sorry," I say, "you're hard to resist."

He draws me into his arms. "No one says you have to resist." He kisses me soundly, deeply, then lets me go, issuing a longing growl I feel in my soul. Not for the first time, I wish we were doing something, anything, other than hunting down my traitor brother.

Wish in one hand... "Do you think he's abandoned the boat, gotten another one, or has taken a different way off the island?"

Sandesh considers, eyes narrowing. "Maybe. But abandoning a boat can get you unwanted attention and is a lot riskier than selling. According to the guy running this place, Lazarus Graves still owns the boat and is still paying the slip rental fee."

I snort on hearing *that* name again. "Lazarus Graves. So, funny."

Sandesh shakes his head. "It's funny if you've been sailing footloose and fancy-free for months while your siblings grieve and your family falls apart. All because you couldn't take letting someone make their own decisions or face the consequences for your own actions."

"You're right," I say. "Fuck that noise. He shouldn't be out here still being funny, being anything but miserable after what he did. He's an asshole."

"Couldn't agree more. Anyone who causes you that kind of pain doesn't deserve your conflict or your sympathy."

The absolute onslaught of grief after losing Tony had been... physical. A deep hurt as real as if my brother had punched a knife into my chest.

"Talk about role reversal," I tell him. "I'm usually the hothead you're trying to calm down."

After putting his hand against the small of my back and escorting me to my side of the car—he drives so my gun hand is free—he opens my door. "No one messes with my Justice."

I roll my eyes because it's too male of him. "It isn't about me," I say, slipping into my seat. "It's about the family and the unraveling of the unity that's been unbreakable for forty years."

"For me, it's about you," he says, leaning down so the smell of him, woodsy and clean, invades my nostrils.

I fist his shirt.

His cell rings.

Standing, he two-finger fishes it from the pocket of his black cargo pants, then looks at the screen. "It's Dusty." He hits the *Answe*r button. "One sec."

After shutting my door, he goes around and gets in on the driver side. He puts his cell on speaker and turns the engine and air on. "You're on speaker."

"We got him," Dusty says. "He's at the pier, getting into some kind of touring truck that belongs to a place called Loco for Cocoa."

My heart jumps double-Dutch in my chest. He's here? We have him. Finally.

But why hasn't he run? What's he doing with a tour company? I'll have The Guild run a check on the company. I exchange a look with Sandesh that tells me he has the same questions.

He nods to let me know I have the lead.

Good. Means I won't have to talk over him. "Is he armed?"

"Yes, ma'am," Dusty says before Gracie adds quietly, "He looks good—tan and healthy."

I avoid looking at Sandesh's narrowing gaze. I don't want him to see how much that matters to me. "What do you think, G?" I ask. "Should you follow?"

"No. He'll spot us. Besides, after making a stop at the Loco for Cocoa inn, the tour ends up back here. Dusty and I are going to make all the arrangements to grab him tonight."

I swallow into the sudden dryness that is my throat. "Okay. Sandesh and I—"

"There's more. A woman dropped Tony off. I'm sending you her deets. Can you find out what she knows? We can't afford to leave loose ends."

Woman? "Are you saying Tony has a girlfriend?"

Chapter 36
Honor

I park in front of the Loco for Cocoa pier store feeling jittery and anxious. I wonder if Tony—I can't think of him as Laz anymore—can do what he's trying to in the limited time he has or should I have insisted he leave?

I don't know. I *do* know that insisting he leave probably wouldn't have worked, but his plan does seem to have merit. Assuming that whoever he gets to help with this case is as reliable as he says.

I get out of my car, then carry the chocolate coolers inside. This is a normal routine that feels anything but. I'm more anxious than I've been in forever. Everything in me wants to race back and grab Tony and run.

Coolers in hand, I struggle past a pyramid display of bright-green boxes tied with yellow, black, and white ribbon, then past a glass case filled with bars and truffles.

Behind the glass cases, there are multiple countertops and boxes and shipping materials. Stacks of printed-out orders and shipping labels wait in the printer tray. Darn. I've let a lot of things go since the last time I was here.

I move some boxes off the wrapping station to create a space for the new chocolate on the counter. Something wriggles across the table. Oh no.

I pull back the green wrapping paper. Insects and tiny white ant larva writhe across the counter. Screaming, I jump back. The entire top of my workstation is covered in ants and ant larva.

What the hell? How did they get in and do all this in three days? Is that possible? This place is so tight, I need a special vent system to bring in fresh air.

My front door jingles and I look up from the mess to see two men have entered the store. They're dressed in short-sleeved, button-down shirts and khakis. I don't recognize either of them, but I do recognize the health inspector logo on their lanyards.

I step closer to the counter, hoping to block their line of sight. "Can I help you, gentlemen?"

One of the men laughs, a sluggish sound that borders on drunk. The other holds up the identification roped around his neck. "Somos parte de la inspectoría de salud. Hemos tenido una queja."

My heart sinks to my feet. They've had a complaint? I've been set up.

The health inspectors leave a large a neon orange sign taped to the storefront window, covering the beautiful and empty display boxes. Humiliating. I want to hide or scream. Instead, I turn the Closed sign, lock the door, and begin to clean up.

I become so focused on the task, removing all the ants, and bringing out the cleaner to make sure there is no trace of them left behind, that the knock on the door startles me. I turn, wondering what person would knock on a closed and locked door with a big orange Inspection Failure sign in the window.

A dark-haired woman stands there, wearing all black—on a hot day. In addition to being beautiful, she looks… dangerous.

Before we parted Tony had said, *Keep your situational awareness. Store your chocolate, do your orders, don't open your store, don't talk to anyone you don't know. Call me if someone shows up who makes you nervous.*

And all of that was simple enough when I wasn't face-to-face with an actual human knocking on my door. Sighing, I move to the door, and though it feels unforgivably rude, I call through, "Sorry. We're closed."

She leans closer to the door. "What?"

Darn it. I unlock and open the door a crack, point to the glaring orange side, and tell her, "I'm sorry. We're closed. We've had a bit of technical difficulty."

Is that what you call sabotage and threats to your life? The woman's earthy complexion and pin-straight black hair suggests Native American heritage. She wears expensive aviator glasses that reflect the mess that's now my hair.

"Oh. But can't I pop in real quick? I'm hungry, have lots of money to spend, and always leave an online review."

I try not to let my annoyance show. I'm so not interested in dealing with someone who thinks the entire world can be wrapped around their money and opinions.

"Yes, well, I'm sorry." I wave again at the sign. "We're both out of luck."

The woman's mouth twitches like she's trying not to smile. How incredibly annoying. I begin to shut the door and the rude woman slips her foot inside, blocking it.

My heart begins to pound, my shoulders tense, but then she smiles apologetically. "Sorry. I'm naturally curious." She points at the sign. "What happened?"

I think about telling her it's none of her business, but the last thing I need is this woman posting a bad review. "Someone sabotaged my store by putting ants inside it."

The woman tilts her head in a way that seems to indicate her doubt. My annoyance flares again. She says, "But ants like sugar, so maybe they just climbed in?"

"And created a whole colony, including larva, on my wrapping table in a matter of days? No. It was sabotage. Trust me. Not everyone around here wants me to be a success."

The woman removes her glasses, unmasking the kind of mysterious dark eyes that seem to know much and give away little.

Again, the danger warning flashes through me.

She presses against the door, and I realize if I try to press it close, she has a leverage advantage. One that she pushed on me before I even understood what was happening.

"That sucks," she says. "People can be such assholes. What's your name again?"

"It's Honor Silva. You can read about me, my store, and even order chocolate online." I reach into my pocket, pull out my wallet—I stopped wearing a purse after becoming a tour guide—and hand her one of my business cards. "I promise it is much better than this experience would lead you to believe."

The woman takes it, reads the card, slips it into her front pocket. "One more question—I'm looking to rent a room, preferably someplace in the mountains, near some hiking."

The last thing I want is this intimidating woman at the hotel, but since the door has a sign that reads *Ask about a room at Loco for Cocoa outside Bosque Estatal Toro Negro!* I can't exactly lie. I motion toward her pocket and the card she put away. "If you go online, you can learn about our lodge. Sorry, we're currently booked."

Not even close to booked. Actually, the opposite. With Don and Cole gone and Ford soon to be gone, we only have two rooms occupied. But, hopefully, this pushy woman won't go online to check for vacancies.

"That's too bad," she says, pumping her eyebrows at me. "I was just married, and my husband and I are touring the islands."

Oh, touring the islands on her honeymoon. That's so sweet. It's also something I will never get to do with Tony. My throat grows tight with regret. "That's a beautiful bracelet. I hope you enjoy your honeymoon and your stay on the island."

I try to smile at her and realize to my horror that I'm about to cry. My lips twitch. Tears flood my eyes. Ay. Dios.

The woman's sharp gaze softens. "Boy trouble?"

Paranoid or not, I'm not about to share that with this woman, but I have to tell her something since I am nearly in tears. I lie. Not like she'll ever know the difference. "Not anymore—we've split up—but it is absolutely for the best."

She crosses her arms and actually takes up more space in the doorway. "We all have dating horror stories, but that's how we find the good ones. You're better off without him."

"Thanks," I say, and the sadness in my voice is unmistakable and out of my control. Two tears spill down my cheeks. I look down at the woman's intruding foot, desperate to end this conversation. "I have to get back to work."

She pulls her foot out. "Nice meeting you, Honor. Good luck with your shop. I hope it all works out for you."

I say goodbye, willing myself not to shed another tear as I push the door firmly closed. I turn back to the shop and decide I've done enough. The ants are gone, so I'm going home to wait for the tour to show up.

Standing on the side of the mountain road that leads to Loco for Cocoa, I watch black smoke pour from the hood of my car. The tow truck company said it would be at least three hours until they could come and get my car.

This day has been the absolute worst.

I take out my cell again and call Abuelito. He answers his cell right away. "*Mija?*"

And now my phone is beeping that it's running out of battery. Because that's what happens when you have an argument with your boyfriend and end up sleeping on the floor of your room, then have a snake in your car, then have your business sabotaged. You forget things like plugging in your cell phone. Perfect.

"Abuelito, my car broke down about three miles outside of the city, on the road back home. Can you come get me?" I can't stand the whine in my own voice.

"Claro. Get the fire extinguisher."

"What?" I press the phone closer to my ear. I can hear people talking loudly in the background. Is the tour already there?

"Esta bien, niña. I'll send someone right away, don't you worry."

"Is the tour there?"

"Sí. The guests are here, but don't you worry, someone will be there shortly."

Don't worry? I'm worried. "Thanks, Abuelito. Appreciate it."

"Te amo."

He hangs up. I have no idea why the tour returned early, but I didn't have the battery to ask. I wonder who he's going to send. Actually, I know who he is going to send. The only person who isn't working the tour: José. This day officially sucks.

No sooner do I hang up then my phone winks off. Well, José will see me on his way down, so that shouldn't be a problem.

Only one thing to do now. Tying up my hair, I open my trunk and break into the stash of chocolate I'd been hauling back to the hotel. I grab a four-box of truffles.

Plopping into the front seat, door open, legs out, useless phone tossed aside, I pull the ribbon off, lift out a precious morsel, and bite into the smooth, dark piece of heaven.

Mmm. This is why I make chocolate. It truly is a mood changer, a day maker, a bite of happiness.

Head back, eyes closed, I let the chocolate trigger my endorphins and work on my serotonin. The magic of all that secret goodness makes everything better. But why stop at one? I reach for another truffle.

Not for nothing—as Tony would say—better than letting it melt out here, along with me.

Fifteen minutes later, I'm a lot happier and a lot fuller, and am pleasantly surprised when Abuelito's orange-and-white Chevy comes lurching up the road toward me—the opposite direction it should be coming. That hardly took any time. I stand up and wave.

More good news, José isn't driving. Ford is in the front seat. He must've borrowed the truck again to go into town.

He pulls over behind my car and waves energetically as he gets out. He's wearing preppy pink shorts, a white button-down, and boat shoes sans socks.

"Let me get that, Honor," he says, picking up one of the coolers from the open trunk, then hustling it back to the truck.

"Thanks, Ford. You're a life saver. Just when I thought this day couldn't find a bright spot, you showed up."

He smiles and proclaims loudly, "Always happy to brighten your day!"

Laughing, I grab the last container and put it into the back seat of the truck. "I appreciate it. I hope you didn't have to cut your shopping short to come get me."

"No, no." Ford brushes off my concern. "I was on my way back from the post office when Abuelito called." He looks back at my car. "Should we call someone?"

"I already did. They said it would be a while, but I left the keys, and they know what to do, so we can go. If you don't mind."

"Of course not! I'm happy to help. Actually, I was hoping we'd have a chance to talk before I headed home."

We climb into the truck, which he has thankfully left on with the air going. I adjust the nearest vent to blow into my face. "Me too, Ford. I'm actually happy after being so unlucky today."

He puts the car into drive. "Unlucky? Oh, do tell."

Chapter 37
Tony

It starts as a niggling of awareness in my spine when the tour truck pulls out of the pier. I'm looking around, scanning for what is causing this creeping feeling, but I don't spot anything unusual.

Still, the feeling can't be ignored. It's my bone-deep, tried-and-true warning system and it is hitting me full in the gut.

Handing the mic to the newest tour guide, I lean sideways out of the truck to look behind us. No one is following, and yet I need to get out of this vehicle.

I hit the top of the truck three times—the signal for something's wrong. Junior pulls over as the guests look around in confusion. I climb over the slat sides and drop next to the door a moment before Junior opens it.

"Que paso?" he asks, climbing out.

"I'm still freaked about the snake we found today. I'm going to walk into town and get a ride back to the lodge with Honor so I can make sure she's okay."

"What? No, you can't do that." He flushes, puts his hands into his pockets. "I mean, I need you. These guys are new."

"One of them is new but smart as a whip, the other one is a lateral hire. He worked for a rival company for three years before jumping ship to come here. He's great."

Junior shakes his head. "Don't go, man. Please."

This is not the kind of reaction I expected from him. He seems close to tears. Odd since he has three tour guides and only eight guests.

I lean in close. "Are you afraid because of the snake Honor found?"

He takes a full step back from me, shaking his head. "I told you. I don't know anything about it."

Yes, he did tell me. I didn't believe it then and I don't believe it now. He's hiding something, and I'd really hoped to find out more on this trip, but that involves ignoring my inner knowing. The last time I did that was the night my mom died. Everything in me wanted to beg Mom to leave that house before my old man got home. If I had? I don't know what might've changed, but I do know that I no longer ignore that warning system.

"I'll see you at the lodge," I tell Junior, and walk the hell away.

"You can't be relied on," he says, "I knew it the first time I saw you."

I could ask him to clarify that, but the buzz of warning has grown so loud I can barely hear anything right now, so I start to run.

Inside the cheerful though ragtag blue-and-yellow café, I listen as Bob Marley flows through the speakers, promising every little thing is going to be all right. I seriously doubt that. I came here to this place because everything is *not* all right.

I set up the laptop I purchased twenty minutes ago. The Wi-Fi here is as slow and relaxed as this damn optimistic song. This anonymizer will take twenty minutes to download.

As the computer continues to slow walk the download, I make a list of things I'll have to get together for Momma. Even as I write the list, my mind keeps returning to Junior.

Sure, a snake at the pier isn't exactly solid evidence, but there's also his reaction this morning. He was too upset about me bailing on him.

That itch on the back of my neck has increased. Which is why, instead of returning to my boat, I'd gone straight to the closest electronics store and cash-purchased a laptop and a no-frills, cheap-ass burner phone.

Download complete. Finally. I slide the computer across the blue tablecloth so the server has room to put the basket of eggs, ham, and toast on the table. I thank the guy, push away the food I ordered so I wouldn't feel bad about taking up a seat, and access the secure site.

There's an email from Rome, sent before the text. Kid wasn't taking any chances on getting me this message.

I open the email. *"They're in Puerto Rico. Run."*

Fuck. But where? Here? In San Juan? Arecibo? Ponce? Rome didn't say.

But I'm a hundred percent certain I wasn't followed today. I'd gotten off the truck miles from the pier and had run back.

Nothing else in the message, but there's an earlier message he sent as important. I open that one.

Holy shit. Rome found out who made the offer on the farm. *Ford Fairchild?*

And not just that, Ford has a police record. Twenty years ago, he'd broken into Natalie Silva's house in California. After calling the police, Natalie had later refused to press charges, saying it was a mistake.

As I read, my heart presses the throttle on my blood pressure. Ford has a family connection to a mega-wealthy movie financier named Carson Winthrop. Now that Rome has keyed me in on the name, I focus on it. Damn. I've heard of this guy Winthrop from Momma, and nothing good. Years ago... can't remember. Too much stress. Too much fear right now to think clearly.

Thankfully, Rome, gotta love that kid, went the extra mile and investigated Winthrop. Winthrop financed all of Natalie's movies in Puerto Rico and four of the films done by Lex Walker, including the one whose set he died on.

Could Winthrop be the man Natalie Silva had been trying to bring down? Magic 8-Ball said chances are good. That means Winthrop could be responsible for her death and the death of Lex Walker. Does Ford know this? Is he in on it? And what does any of this have to do with Ford offering Honor an outrageous amount of money for her place?

Unless the film, Natalie's last film, or details on how to find the film, is somewhere at the hotel. Could Ford be trying to protect his uncle by buying the property and finding the film? Maybe he doesn't even want to find the film. Maybe he'll buy the property and burn the whole thing down.

No. That's a stretch. Something isn't fitting here. I've got to settle down. Dammit. It'd help if the hair on the back of my neck would let me.

Fuck it. None of this matters right now. The important thing is Honor. I've got to get her and take her someplace safe until I can figure out what's going on with Ford.

Which means I've got to get Momma to recall the team that's after me. Which means, I need to make a deal with Momma.

My fingers fly over the keyboard as I type the message. *Momma, please call off your dogs. I'm coming in. I've got a case. A big-name case: Carson Winthrop.* Got to drop a juicy detail if I want her to bite. *This could be one of the biggest cases The Guild has ever taken on.* If Winthrop is involved in a decades-long scheme, that isn't an exaggeration. *I'm willing to make a deal and share the information if you're willing to stand down and help someone here, an innocent, who's caught up in this.*

Innocent. Honor is that. Is it too late? Will Momma accept a deal with me that doesn't involve fucking with my head? Am I screwing over Rome by sending this email?

No. If they haven't discovered him yet, he should be in the clear.

I've never asked anything from you. I'm asking for this. Please.

Exhaling as my heart pounds and the hair on my neck tries to flee, I send the email and close my laptop. After tossing a big tip onto the table by the untouched food, I stow my stuff, slip on my backpack, and head out.

On the street, I text Honor to wait for me, to stay in her store, and not to open the doors. I start a drawn-out surveillance detection route to make sure I'm not being followed.

I need to get Honor, tell her about Ford, and convince her to leave with me. I'll get Momma to take on this case once we've docked somewhere safe. We just need some time and some space. Wait. My head is spinning. I'm not thinking straight. I can't take Honor to the boat. Justice has surely found it. I need another boat.

I check my phone. No answer from Honor.

Taking a deep breath, trying to calm down the fight-or-flight mechanism in my brain that wants me to start running, I call her. Each ring is like an electric shock to my heart.

No answer. Could they have her? Could they know about her?

I recheck the gun secured at my back, then pull a slim, tan cylinder with a matching band from my pocket. Using my teeth, I tug the strap and Velcro it down, so the pepper spray lays tight, nearly invisible, against my palm.

My mind a raging bull, a wild animal in need of a red target, I throw caution to the wind, out the window, and over the bridge, and run toward Honor's store.

Cutting through a parking lot behind a service station, I see her shop. Never been so happy to see a cocoa bean-shaped building in my life.

I slow to a walk. Nearly there. *Please let her be okay.*

"Nice tan, Tone, Gracie says. "Very non-corpse like."

"The afterlife agrees with you," Justice adds.

Fuck. My sisters are behind me.

Chapter 38
Honor

Ford drives so slowly up the mountain we're practically at a standstill. Instead of finding it endearing or even annoying, it makes me nervous. Is he doing this on purpose?

I don't normally judge close family friends this way, but I'm feeling paranoid lately, and for good reasons. Someone sabotaged my store. Someone persuaded my guides to quit. Someone planted a snake in my car. And someone, maybe even someone I know, killed Tito.

Could someone have messed with my car so that it broke down? Could Ford have done that, then arranged to be available to pick me up?

Anything seems possible these days. Plus, after saying he wanted to chat, being so enthusiastic about it, he's shut down completely. He's gripping the steering wheel tightly, peering intently out the front window, and leaning forward, almost hunched.

Laz, uh Tony, taught me to pay attention to body language. Right now, Ford's body language screams at me. He's anxious, and now that I'm paying attention, I realize he is driving slowly on purpose. Could this have anything to do with what's happening at the hotel, the reason Abuelito couldn't pick me up?

I'd reach for my cell phone, but I have no charge, no way to contact anyone, and no weapon. I left the gun Tony gave me in my glove compartment. I forgot about it. So foolish. But wait, I have mace in my backpack.

I reach for my backpack and Ford lets out a burst of air, unexpected and intense.

I snatch my bag from the floor and he says, "I fell in love with your mother when I was fifteen."

I freeze with my backpack in my lap. "What?"

"I fell in love with your mother when I was fifteen."

A moment passes before I can speak. "I had no idea." Not the best response, but my head is spinning right now.

"I wouldn't want anyone to know." His face flushes with splotches of red. "Not that there's anything wrong with falling in love, I should say. But I'm not proud of the way I obsessed over her."

Obsessed? That word strikes a chord of warning that has me reaching into my bag. Mom had many stalkers over the years, some even dangerous. Though I didn't learn about any of that until I was grown. Mom could've done better giving me the truth, instead of always trying to shield me. "I'm sorry, Ford. If it helps, you weren't the only young man to fall in love with my mother."

Like the tic of a muscle, annoyance flashes then is gone from his face. "This wasn't some distant infatuation. I knew her."

I slide my hand into the side pocket and the pepper spray I put there. "I didn't mean to suggest your feelings weren't real." I swallow growing fear. I knew he'd had a crush on mom during the filming of *Stranded*. "You fell in love with Mom during *Stranded*?"

He slows the car and pulls over, allowing another car behind us to pass.

I reach for the door handle, ready to run. Taking a deep breath, I wrap my hand around the mace. I want to hear what he has to say, but I'm ready to jump out.

"Yes, during the filming of *Stranded*. Shy, awkward, and quiet, I was away from home for the first time. She was the only one who treated me with respect and kindness. She asked my opinion. She was genuinely interested in me. It took me a very long time, a lot of therapy, and, if I'm honest, almost two decades to get completely over her."

I grip the mace. That's a long time.

His throat works with some unnamed emotion. "It's not something we talk about, a young teen getting laid by a star. I mean, that's considered every boy's dream, but I wasn't emotionally equipped. It led me down a dark, decades-long road."

"But…" I feel nausea rising. He has invested an awful lot in this delusion. "You said you were fifteen. My mother would never—"

"She thought I was nineteen. Everyone did. I was big for my age, and because my uncle didn't want any *child actors* on set, he had papers made up that showed I was older."

He hits the gas, and we lurch forward.

I can't begin to know what to say. I know Mom could be impulsive, so I can't deny she could've made that dreadful mistake.

I try imagining how he must've felt. A child in so many ways, he'd followed his sexual instinct to sleep with a woman, and, after, thought he'd found the secret to the universe. Love and lust and all things Hollywood in one package. Of course he didn't just move on. Of course he didn't just put a notch on his belt. "Did she ever know you loved her, know your age?"

A wild bark of laughter. "She found out during the filming of the second movie, when I fell on my knees and begged her to give us a chance."

The second movie. He must have been twenty-five. "What did she say?"

"She was filled with grief and remorse, empathetic but honest. She told me that could never work for her. She asked me to get therapy, then offered to pay for it and even go with me. She followed through on both things."

"The second movie," I say, thinking back to that film and remembering spending time with Ford. "That's when I first met you." He'd doted on me. "I thought you were wonderful. Now, I see it was probably in the hopes of impressing Mom."

"Not just that," he says, looking over at me for a beat before returning his gaze to the winding mountain road. "I wanted to spend time with you, my daughter."

The mace rolls from my hand and hits the floor. Chills of disbelief roll down my body. "You're my... my father?"

He nods. A tear slides down the side of his face. "Your mother never reached out to me after becoming pregnant. I was only nineteen—or so she thought—and she'd wanted a child. But when I told her the truth during the second movie, she admitted what I already knew, what I'd known from the moment I saw your photograph in a tabloid."

Ay. Dios. My life feels like an awful lie. She lied to me—sheltered me with her lies.

I say, "She quit making movies after that sequel. Is that because of what you told her?"

He nods. "After she quit, while we were in therapy, she began to question how I got a false identification. That's what sent her on her quest to uncover abuses in the industry. I think she was trying to make things right as much as she could."

"Ford, I don't know what to say. I feel..." Sick to my stomach. "I'm so sorry. Even though I know it's not my fault, I feel guilty and ashamed."

He winces. "Oh, please don't. No. I don't want that for you." His mouth thins into a firm, determined line. "I'm not telling you to hurt you. I've worked through all of that, so I don't need sympathy. I'm telling you so that we can get to know each other, and so that you'll see I have your best interests at heart when I tell you that you need to take the offer on your property and go."

I don't bother asking how he knows about the offer. It's common knowledge around Loco for Cocoa, but I am curious about why he's insisting on this. "Why?"

"I don't want you to waste time on a dream that isn't yours, Honora, and you seem to enjoy the tours and the lodge, but not as much as making your chocolate."

"You've been paying attention to me." I reach out, tentative and shy. I grip his hand, and he squeezes mine. *My father?* "But I've made my choice to stay, stick it out despite the financial issues."

He turns up the dirt road that leads to the lodge. "Please take the offer on the property. I can put through all the paperwork for you. Tonight. The moment we arrive."

"Ford, I'm not even sure the offer is still available."

"It is. And trust me when I tell you if you don't take it, you're seriously going to regret it. You don't know what you're up against."

My hackles rise. "Is that a threat?"

"What? No." Ford sits up straighter, then peers through the windshield intently. "What's going on at the lodge?"

Mind whirling, it takes me a moment to register what he's talking about. Then I see it. There are three police cars in front of Loco for Cocoa.

Chapter 39
Tony

My legs shake and my gut turns liquid as I turn and face my sisters. On first sight of them, an unexpected surge of joy leaps through my body. I nearly smile with the unbelievable relief of seeing them again. Dammit. I've missed them.

Dressed for an op, black tactical pants and a T-shirt loose over her concealed carry, Justice no doubt has a second weapon in her hiking boot.

Beside her is Gracie, also in ops attire, with her pale skin growing red in the sun and her long red hair down below her shoulders. She's also carrying. They stand feet apart, hands by their sides, and lips set into firm, disappointed lines.

I want to ask if they're okay. I want to ask about the family. I want to tell them about Honor, about the situation, but the hardness of their eyes is a brick wall to anything I might want to say. Their eyes are telling me that I'm the enemy.

My heart puts both fists up and pounds the heavy bag of my ribs. Nerves, a deep sense of rejection, and a growing sense of unease flood me.

Justice and Gracie didn't follow me. They were waiting for me near Loco for Cocoa. Which means they know about Honor. And enough about her that they pegged here, not my boat, as the best ambush spot.

A throat full of run-while-you-can choking me, I walk toward them as if I've got nothing to hide or lose. Both things are a lie. I've been less terrified in my life, but, right now, it's hard to remember when.

They don't reach for weapons, tell me to stop, or assess the area or me for a possible hidden threat. Which means they have backup, likely Sandesh and Dusty.

Ambush. They came up from behind me, got me to turn around, then had the others sneak up on my exposed flank, trapping me. All of that makes things more difficult, but it can also be an advantage.

I stop five feet from my angry-eyed, tight-mouthed sisters. "Tell your boys to back off. We need to talk."

Justice's lips twitch in a half smile, well, grimace, before she speaks into a hidden mic. "Give me a sec before you shoot the fucker."

My shoulder blades begin to itch because I know my sister. She isn't joking. There are guns close at hand or already drawn on me.

Justice takes the first careful step toward me, closing the distance to four feet.

I draw in a breath deep enough to absorb the blow, because I have no doubt she's going to slug me.

Her eyes are filled with equal parts hurt and rage. As are Gracie's, but she's more likely to knee my balls, and, as an expert Muay Thai fighter, she has the skill to do permanent damage.

Three feet. It takes everything in me not to fall into a defensive posture, to keep my hands down, and to wait for the blows. But I'm willing to take the hits if it means she'll listen to me and hear me out.

No cost is too great for Honor. Once Justice and maybe Gracie take their revenge, I'll ask for their help with Honor, ask them to take her someplace safe, then find a way to escape.

Two feet.

One.

With a guttural cry, Justice fists my shirt, drags me close enough to headbutt, then lowers her head into my shoulder, and bursts into tears. She flat out bawls, her breath hitching and her tears soaking my shirt as she clings to me for dear life.

My heart breaks. My throat fills with emotion and regret. I can't move. Can't breathe, really. Why couldn't she have hit me? Despite my feet being rooted to the spot, my arms start to come up to hold her.

A calm, furious voice speaks from behind me. "Don't. Fucking. Move."

Sandesh. And he is not messing around. I let my arms drop back to my side, cupping the pepper spray, as my hands grow sweaty and my throat grows tight with grief and fear, and my heart abuses my chest. I can't settle on any one feeling—guilt, fear, regret, pain, terror. They cycle like a kaleidoscope of sharp, vivid emotions.

J smells so familiar, the lavender and vanilla scent, the salt of her tears soaking into my T-shirt, that I'm flooded with memories of us and our childhood.

Justice and I hanging out, talking shit in the campus garden. Gracie finding us, pelting us with crab apples and running away while we chased after. Gracie was always so fast. Justice, Gracie, and the rest of our unit playing seek-and-find—different from hide-and-seek in complexity and the ground covered. Running the campus, leaving clues meant to lead as much as mislead. That's my adopted family—no game is ever simple. What *was* simple is this" us. Love.

It'd gotten blurry when J looked to be headed toward her doom. I want to tell her this, to tell her why I did what I did, but she's sobbing into my shoulder like she will never stop, like I've broken her, and it is tearing me apart.

I have to say something even though I know, like I know her, that it'll break the spell, but anything is better than her crying. "I'm sorry, J. I'm so fucking sorry."

Her head flies up. She pushes against me, shoves me back, then slaps me across my face. The sting of her open palm is heat and pain and relief.

"Do it again. Anything. As long as it makes you feel better."

She balls up her fists, looks like she'll take a good and

proper swing, but doesn't. Her lip curls with anger. "It's not okay. It's not. You killed us. You did this."

Her grief guts me, brings me back to that first day, that first week at the Mantua Home when I'd arrived to meet my new family, a bunch of women and girls who, like my mother, had been hurt, abused, and abandoned by their families. I'd instantly known which side of that equation I'd belonged on. I'd let my mother die; that made me the problem.

From the moment I'd stepped into that home, the moment I'd learned what The Guild was about, I'd known, deep down, I wasn't worthy of being rescued. I'd tried to make up for it by meeting every challenge, training my hardest even when I had nothing left to give, by teaching my siblings, giving them the best of me, by speaking up when I saw one of our own in real danger, and by working to keep her safe instead of keeping quiet like I had with my mom.

But it hadn't worked, and I'm not even sure how things got so royally fucked.

"I didn't want to hurt you, J. Not you either, G. I love you. You have to know I love you."

Gracie's eyes are slick with tears, her fists clenched, face red with anger and maybe sadness.

Guilt grips my throat, squeezes. She looks so fuckin' vulnerable, so hurt.

"Security footage spotted you outside my club," she says. "Why come back? Why risk it?"

I can hear what she's really asking, and I rush to reassure her. "I was worried about you. I knew you'd replay your last words to me, knew it would matter to you." She'd called me a traitor. "I wanted to see if you were okay."

She makes a soft, choking sound before whispering, "You can't see that kind of broken from the outside."

And I have to close my eyes, because I'm so clearly on the side with the people who'd hurt them, and I can't take it.

There's only one person in this world who I'm not on the

other side of that line from. Honor. I have to get to her. "I wish I had time to convince you. I wish I could..." *Make you listen.* "There's a case here. Maybe the biggest The Guild has seen." I shift a little, try to get a feel for how boxed in they have me. "The woman who owns this shop—"

"Honor?" Justice says. "Your girlfriend. I met her. She's sweet, not a convincing liar, and gone. She left a few hours ago."

Sweat works its way down my spine. "I don't believe you. She would've texted." *I told her not to leave. I told her to text me if she left.*

"She did, but we intercepted her communication. I mean, if you knew she wasn't here, what are the chances you'd come back?"

She's really gone. Justice isn't lying. I need to keep it simple. I need them on my team. "Honor is in deadly trouble."

"*You're* in trouble," Dusty says from somewhere behind and to my right. "Or don't you realize what's about to happen to you?"

Saliva floods my mouth, and my stomach turns at the tone in his voice. The usual easygoing FBI agent with the Southern charm sounds angry enough to chew nails.

Licking suddenly dry lips, I say, "I know. M-erase. But, for the record, that isn't what I did to you, Dusty."

"Oh, I know that. You gave me an experimental drug, something you'd need permission to give a field mouse."

I gotta get out of here. "Look, I get that you're pissed. And if after what I have to tell you all, if Momma still wants to take my memories—"

"No need for *if*," Sandesh says. "Although I'd like you to keep the ones of Justice's tears, the ones where you felt, and you fucking had to feel it, how much you hurt her."

I can't swallow over the growing panic. "Listen to me."

"No," Dusty says. "You can talk all you want to Momma. We're here to take you back."

They aren't going to listen to anything I have to say. My only chance to get away is to inflict pain. Quick.

Aggressive. Determined. Shouldn't have let them surround me. Trying to get a sense of where Dusty stands, I adjust my shoulders.

Dusty says, "What's that in your hand?"

Ready or not. Here's hoping Sandesh won't shoot me. I listen intently for any movement from Dusty.

I think I have a beat on him when he says, "Ease your hand open."

Fear skitters across my stomach like a crab. Slowly, I raise my arms in surrender. "It's…"

I kick back, fast and hard, and my heel connects with Dusty's groin.

The big man hits the ground. I pivot, fire pepper spray into Sandesh's eyes. He curses, lowers his gun hand, and covers his eyes with his free one.

I spin to run, but Justice tags me with a punch to my throat. I roll out, choking, trying to catch my breath, and Gracie slams a roundhouse into my lower back. I lurch forward, nearly fall, but, saving myself, I spin and wave my pepper spray between Gracie and Justice.

Justice takes a step away. Gracie says, "You won't shoot," and leans into another kick.

I lightly press the button with a short burst aimed away from Gracie's head, and she turns into it, then screams—likely more from shock—loud enough to raise the hair on my arms. Dusty jumps from the ground like the Terminator. Big. Hard as steel. No stopping him.

Peddling backward, aware of the big guy closing in, I use what I know of Justice's fighting style and lurch at her.

As expected, she charges to meet me.

Using Aikido, I sidestep and trip her to the asphalt, setting her up as a roadblock of sorts to slow Dusty.

I run.

Dusty jumps over Justice, catches me around the middle and tosses me to down. Umph. Pepper spray arm slams into the ground with a crack and zing that shoots into my elbow. My arm goes numb.

Dusty drops on me like a pro wrestler. His fists slam, one, two, three times into my head.

Fully panicking now, I swing back, getting in a few solid hits, but he's in a better position and is seeing red, a total madman.

The hits come hard and fast until everything goes black.

When I open my eyes again, I'm still on the ground, feet all around me.

I groan and roll to my stomach. Warm blood pours from my nose. One eye is swollen shut. *Have to warn Honor about Ford.* Swinging my arms forward, dragging myself a few feet, I inch away.

I sense more than see my four attackers—catching their breaths—trailing me. They're talking to each other about me, about my useless struggle, like giving a play-by-play of a sports team.

"Is he running away?" Sandesh.

"I've seen faster turtles." Dusty.

I swing my right arm, haul myself forward again.

"I'd feel bad for him," Justice says, "Except soon he won't remember any of this."

"Give me the needle." Gracie says.

There's a sting, right in my ass cheek, then the world dims and goes black.

Chapter 40
Honor

I throw open the truck door, forcing Ford to jerk to a stop. I jump out and race over to the scene of the accident. Even if I hadn't just had that disturbing conversation with Ford, I would've had a hard time making sense of what's happening.

Someone crashed the tour truck into the lodge, taking out part of the front porch, and the front doors.

Material has fallen on the truck so I can't see inside, but it seems the truck made it far enough in that it might've damaged the front stairs and front desk.

A police cruiser and an ambulance are here, and guests from the tour mill about, though some are being tended by EMTs.

I rush over to one of the medical professionals. "Is anyone hurt?"

"Mostly shock," he says. "At least the kid waited until everyone was out of the way before he crashed it into the lodge."

Kid? I startle on seeing Junior in the back of a police cruiser. Abuelito is talking with a police officer.

I rush over to them, looking around for Tony.

"Have a heart, Lonny," Abuelito says, addressing the officer. "He wasn't under the influence and is so very young."

Though it prickles against my manners, I interrupt. "What's going?"

The officer Abuelito addressed as Lonny, a dark-skinned man with sympathetic eyes, takes me in. He sighs dramatically. "The driver of your tour truck, a Jesús Clemente, also known as

Junior, went off the rails. After taking the guests on an abbreviated tour, he drove them here, had them disembark, then crashed into the front of the lodge."

"Two of the lodge guests were mildly injured by debris," Abuelito adds.

My stomach pitches with dread. This is so bad.

"We've interviewed the rest," Lonny says, "and are making arrangements to drive the cruisers back to their ship and the remaining lodge guests into town."

I turn to Abuelito. "We can offer those guests free rooms."

"I did," he says. "I'm sorry, Honora. They do not wish to stay."

A lump the size of my confusion rises into my throat. "But why arrest Junior? It was an accident, right?"

Abuelito looks down and away. "I'm not sure, mija."

The officer shakes his head. "According to the guests, he had them get off down the road, then drove directly into it. You know how much these tours mean to island business. This is very serious."

I know how much it means, and how much it means to my business, and so does Junior. Why would he do this? "Is it okay if I speak with my cousin?"

Writing in his notebook, Lonny flicks his head noncommittally.

Squeezing Abuelito's hand, I head to the cruiser. The door is closed, but the windows are open. Junior sits with his hands cuffed behind him, looking down at the floor.

I bend to the window. "Junior. Are you okay?"

His eyes stayed glued to the rubber floor mat. "I drove into the lodge."

"On accident?"

He sniffs, sucks in mucus.

"Jesús?" I use his real name to get his attention.

He lets out a breath, looks up. "I did it on purpose, but I had to."

My heart skids to an abrupt halt. "Why? What reason could you have?"

"Don't you get it? The world is bad. People are bad. Even people you think are good, like your boyfriend. He abandoned me at the beginning of the tour." He kicks the seat in front of him. "If he would've stayed, it would've been fine."

Tony left? Cold washes down my body. "Is this about my mother? Her last documentary?"

Junior's head shoots up. "You should go too, prima. Things are not what they seem. Run, Honora. Get out."

The terror in his voice transfers to me, freezes my mind and vocal cords.

"No talking to the suspect," a second officer says, coming up behind me.

I shift as if leaving and whisper, "Did you put a snake in my car?"

A cloud of grief, a tangible darkness bows Junior's head. He nods.

My stomach sinks to me feet. *He had?* "Why?"

"Step away from the vehicle." The officer grabs my arm, but I barely register him there.

Junior's pain is so sharp, so tangible, that even after he told me about the snake, I tell him, "I'll bring bail. It'll be okay, Junior."

"Don't!" Tears fall onto his cargo pants, and Junior shakes his head emphatically. "Don't do that. Don't. Please. I need to be in jail."

He looks up at me with such terror that I simply nod.

Chapter 41
Tony

I wake up with a spasm, and I jerk against the straps tying me down. My head throbs, and I can barely see through one eye, but I take in the leather chairs across from me and the dark portal window.

The *thwump, thwump* of blades, though muted in the luxury copter, is unmistakable. They're flying me home. Honor is alone.

I work moisture into my dry mouth before I try to speak. "Hey." It still comes out as a rasp. I try again, louder. "Hey. J? G? Turn the fuck around. I need to get back."

Dusty and Sandesh walk over and stand in the aisle to my right. They're both scowling. Dusty has a cut on one eye and a swollen lip.

At least I got in a couple of good punches.

Sandesh says, "You're in no position to be giving orders."

Dusty gives me an evaluative look. "That eye's got to hurt, son."

Hurts like hell, and so does my neck. "Let me talk to Justice. Let me talk to Gracie. This isn't your business. Let me talk to my family."

Sandesh moves forward and squeezes my jaw hard. "Justice is *my* wife, *my* business, and *my* family."

"Sandesh, just... let him go."

Justice. Her voice, usually strong and sure, sounds remarkably small and tired.

After using his viselike grip to nearly shatter my jaw, Sandesh does let go.

I swish my jaw around, wishing I could massage it with my hands, but both of them are duct-taped to the chair, along with my torso and legs.

Justice sits in the seat across from me. She has a scrape along her jaw. "What do you want?"

Before I can answer, Gracie pushes past Dusty and Sandesh and takes the other seat.

My courage shatters when I see Gracie's eyes ringed in red. "I tried to miss you, G," I say.

She shakes her head. "I didn't know you were going to do that, so I turned into the spray."

Fuck. "Sorry."

Dusty hits me on the back of my head. When I glare over at him, he looks at me with all innocence. "You just turned right into that."

"Guess I deserved that," I say. "I've made a few mistakes—a monument of mistakes." I close my eyes. How long have we been in the air? How long was I out?

Focus. I can do this, but not by arguing my case, not by explaining why I did what I did. I can't drag up a freaking court case and all the emotions attached to that. I need to get them to want to help Honor.

That means appealing to them as operatives. I swallow. "I believe Natalie Silva, AKA Kiki Hart—yes, the famous actress—was murdered by none other than Carson Winthrop after she uncovered information about a sexual cult."

Justice inhales a sharp breath. "Carson Winthrop? You're sure?"

I nod, even though facts are still missing. "Yes."

Gracie shifts forward in her seat, leaning against her knees. "You're telling us that you have a case against Momma's arch nemesis? *That* Carson Winthrop?"

"Arch nemesis?" Sandesh asks.

"I heard of him," Dusty says. "When I was doing research into the family, I saw a video of Momma and Winthrop online.

They had a few words at a gala years ago that was recorded and reported on by a big YouTuber."

"A few words." Justice snorts. "After a speech Momma gave on systemic misogyny in Hollywood, Winthrop sauntered up to her and declared misogyny isn't really a thing, that it's made up."

Gracie takes up the narrative, "Cool as a cucumber, Momma turned to him and said, 'I always suspected you made your movies purposefully misogynistic, but now I see it's merely ignorance on your part.'"

"I remember it," I say. "That was the one time I can recall when my... Leland got physically involved on Momma's behalf."

"How?" Sandesh asks.

"In the video," Dusty says. "Winthrop sputtered for a moment before reaching for Mukta's niqab, saying, 'Maybe if you remove your mask, you'll see more clearly.'"

"Leland took him out in two-point=five seconds," Justice finishes. "And the guy later tried to sue him for it."

She eyes me, and I know she knows about Leland, about the fact that he's my uncle and Momma kept it from me my whole life.

I don't go there. I can't. I need to get them to turn this thing around.

"Yeah, the guy's a douche. Worse than. He's a murderer. *Multi*-murderer. Before her death, Natalie made a documentary with a big-name star, Lenox 'Lex' Walker"—no reason to tell them this part is a well-informed hypothesis—"who provided testimony that Winthrop uses the movies he finances to recruit actors into some kind of sexualized cult."

Grace pulls out her cell and starts typing. She says, "He's dead, this guy Lex."

Dusty sits on the arm of a chair across the aisle, his big feet braced against my seat. "You saying Winthrop killed Lex, too?"

I have them now. "Yeah, I am."

Sandesh makes a sound in his throat.

Justice looks up at him, then nods.

Sandesh pulls out a knife and cuts the binds holding my arms, then sits on the arm of Justice's chair. "Keep talking," he says.

I massage my jaw while talking. "Natalie's daughter, Honor Silva, is in danger. She—"

"The woman from the chocolate store," Justice said. "Your girlfriend is the daughter of Kiki Hart?"

Shit. I ignore that question and avoid the details I don't understand, like why someone offered Honor so much money for her property. "Recently, she's had her life and her business threatened. I believe it's because the documentary is on her property."

"Does she have it?" Sandesh asks.

"She has all her mom's old files. I believe it's hidden in them somewhere. Or maybe there's information or clues in the files as to where it's hidden."

"Winthrop is after her?" Gracie says.

Fuck yes. Where is Honor? How far am I from her? Quieting my panic, I keep trying to lure them in. "His nephew, Ford Fairchild, is on the island. I believe he poses an imminent threat to Honor. Her life is in danger."

Justice crosses her legs, right foot on left knee. "You really like this chick, huh?"

That question, the way she asks… It has nothing to do with if she'll take the case or not, or if she'll call Momma. It's her asking me as my sister, and it hurts like hell to be this grateful for that question.

I count my breaths, one, two, three before answering. "Before Honor, I'd never been in love, J. Never had that moment where I looked into someone's eyes and saw…"

Tears. Fucking tears. Goddamn it. I wipe them away.

Sandesh shifts. Yeah, it's fucking awkward for everyone.

How long will it take to turn this bird around?

Justice reaches into her boot, pulls out her own knife, and, with a few quick slices, frees my torso and feet, tossing aside strips of rope.

I moan with relief, sit forward, flex calves and shrug my shoulders. I rock my head around on my neck. "Thanks."

Rising, Gracie goes over and gets a water bottle from the fridge and offers it to me.

I drink it down in two seconds.

She hands me another.

I crack it open and drink half before asking, "How long will it take you to turn us around?"

Gracie sits back down. "We can't turn around. The pilot is internal security and has strict orders from Leland and Momma. He can't turn around, not without approval from Momma."

Justice says, "Best bet for getting Momma's approval would be to agree to M-erasure."

Fuck that. I don't have time to argue with them. "Then let me call Honor. Please. I'm begging. Her life is in danger. And she's sitting out there fucking waiting on me."

Gracie and Justice exchange a look. With a nod from Justice, Gracie hands me her cell.

"On speakerphone," she says.

Chapter 42
Honor

After dropping the last of our guests in town—Loco for Cocoa is officially closed until it can be repaired—I drive with Ford to the police station in comfortable silence. Oddly enough, the revelation that he's my father hasn't changed much about how I feel about Ford. I've loved him since I was a child. The only difference now is that I feel a need to make up for his pain, the hurt my mother caused him. No matter what he says, I can't let that go. He's a good person.

"I appreciate you, as a lawyer, going in to represent my cousin," I say.

"I agreed to help Junior," Ford says, "but you have to keep your end of the bargain, too. You shouldn't be at the lodge until it's been cleared."

I let out a breath. Even if Ford hadn't insisted I spend the night with *"Laz"* on his boat, I'd have headed there after this. I need to see him, ask him why he left the tour, and find out why he hasn't come back to the lodge. Of course, there might be an obvious reason for all of that—he'd had to run.

I don't explain to Ford that *Laz* and his boat might not be there. I can't yet accept that myself. "Where will you stay?"

"Don't worry about me. I'll call you in the morning after I get a better handle on what the rules are for attorneys here."

"I appreciate it. I really, really do."

He leans over and kisses my check so quickly I almost startle. "I love you, kiddo."

Chills ride my body. For a second, my throat refuses to work as it tries to absorb all the emotion. "I love you, too..." I can't say it. I've never said this to anyone in my life. I take a breath, like diving into deep waters. "Dad."

He makes a choked sound, squeezes my hand. "Sleep well. I'll see you in the morning."

He gets out of the car, and I watch him go into the station, wondering at all that was left unsaid between us. I have a sister. I can't...

There's always tomorrow. That's enough for one day. It's more than enough. I need to get to Tony

The area where Tony's boat is moored is quiet and eerie and dark this late at night, but not so dark that I can't see his boat is still here. He hasn't left.

I park Abuelito's truck and get out, using my now charged cell phone to guide my way down the planks.

I climb onto the boat, noticing for the first time, his boat is named *Another Brick in the Wall*.

I move to the doorway that leads below deck. It's open and there's a blinking panel with the words *System breached. Reset?*

I call down, "Hello?" I almost say *Tony*, but stop myself. "Laz?"

There's no answer, so I swallow a ball of fear as solid as lard and climb down. The boat rocks and I clutch the handle for support.

The flashlight on my phone does little for the dense darkness down here. I grope the wall, press, slap, and sweep my hands until something clicks and the lights flick on.

I gasp. The small galley and sitting area have been ransacked. My heart pounds so thickly that it feels like I no longer have room in my chest for it.

There's a small hallway with two doors. My breathing is audible as I walk in that direction. Is he down here, hurt and needing me?

As stiff and wooden as in any of my self-defense classes, I

peek into the first doorway. A bathroom, and it's empty. I walk across the hall to the other door that leads to a cabin with shiny mahogany wood paneling and shelving.

The room has also been searched. The cabinets under the bed are all open and things are strewn about.

They found him. I know they have. Junior said he left, but I know Tony wouldn't have gone, not even if he were in danger. They found him, and I have no idea what's happening right now.

My cell buzzes and I see an unknown number. My heart leaps. It could be Tony. He told me he was going to get another burner phone. I accept the call.

"Honor?"

I drop to the bed and sob, "Where are you? Are you okay? I've been so worried."

"Honor. Listen. You need to hide. Go someplace safe."

"Why? What's going on?" The boat rocks hard, and I realize people have come onboard. "Wait. Hold on."

He goes deadly silent. Someone or some*ones* move across the deck. Two men start talking and… mention my mom, Kiki Hart.

My heart in my throat, my hands shaking, I whisper, "Two men came onto your boat. I'm downstairs in your cabin."

His voice changes instantly. Gone is the sweet, caring, concerned man and present is the cold, calculated, listen-to-me-and-don't-fuck-around man. Present is Tony. "Honor, are you armed?"

"No."

"There's a gun under—"

Someone speaks near him, a woman. "We took all the weapons off your boat."

He curses. He has me on speakerphone? Who is that woman?

"Okay. Listen. Grab the bilge pump off the wall. Stand on the footlocker by the door. The pump is heavy. Steel. Hit the first fucker through with all your worth, slam him in the head. You don't hit to defend yourself. You hit to kill. Got it?"

Oh God. *Kill?* "They're coming down."
"Go after the next guy. Quick. Brutal. Find his weak spot. Use what I taught you."
"I... I—"
"You got this, Honor. You got it. Now, drop the phone. Leave it on. And go get 'em."

The instructions are delivered with a calm surety that almost makes me think I *can* do what he's asking.

Dropping the phone, I reach for the bilge pump.

My fingers feel as limp and padded as corn dogs. My palms are sweaty and my heart is surging, but I grip the pump, which looks remarkably like a bike pump, and climb atop the footlocker by the doorway.

I lift both arms. My mouth becomes so dry I can no longer swallow.

A man comes into the room holding a knife. Terror grips me, and, for a moment, I can't move. Seeing or sensing me, he spins toward me with his knife.

With a scream, I drive the bilge pump down and into his skull. There's a loud crack as the solid resistance of his skull gives way. The man drops to the ground.

My stomach flips, twists, and turns sour. I feel vomit threatening to work its way up my throat when arms grab me and drag me backward through the doorway.

I cry out in denial, in fear, in rage. Spreading my arms out, I braced myself in the doorjamb, struggle against his hold.

He wraps an arm around my neck and puts me in a chokehold, a situation I know very well because it's one of the ones Tony taught me to escape.

He hisses into my ear, "Your family asked for this."

Without even thinking about it, my right hand strikes back and my fingers jam into his eye. He curses, arches back, and we fall together through the doorway.

I roll, reach down, grab his balls, and yank like I'm pulling taffy.

His scream is iconic. A scream that makes every hair on my neck rise. He releases me and I run, slamming against the hallway's walls as I go.

Heart shrieking like a banshee, sweat soaking into my eyes every movement seeming slow and thick, I lunge through the cabin, up the steps, and jump from the boat.

I sprint down the pier, certain that, at any moment, someone is going to give chase.

No one does, and I make it to Abuelito's truck, start the engine, and take off.

Chapter 43
Tony

Honor's scream hits me like a fastball to the ribs. A crack of awareness, a sharp stab of pain in my side, and a floundering, groping struggle for air.

Dusty uses another cell to place a call to the police in Ponce, and I stand inside the luxury jet, stone still on the outside, heart racing and blood boiling on the inside. My ears tune in to the sounds coming through cell's speakers, but I can't tell what the hell is happening.

A *thunk*. Something breaking? A fierce and aggressive yell—that, I know is Honor—then a threatening male voice, then a bloodcurdling scream. Also male.

"That's my Daring Honor," I whisper. There are minutes of distant movement and garbled moaning. It's impossible to tell who's making those noises.

A shocking amount of anguish fills my body, like a thousand volts of electric current tear through me. Painful. Pitiless. Paralyzing.

The hot and heavy pressure transports me back in time, back to that terrified and helpless kid in a cage, unable to do anything while the person he loved most was hurt.

The Ponce police department is patched through, and Dusty tells them where the boat is moored and that a woman is being attacked.

He hangs up and everyone goes quiet, staring at me with a knowing pity. What was it Justice said to me when Sandesh had been kidnapped? *"Sorry is for someone who has no choice but to learn to deal with something. I have a choice."*

Do *I* have a choice? My only option can't be to leave Honor to fight through her own troubles. Even if she... Even *when* she makes it to safety, what then? Will she go back to the hotel and into the waiting arms of whoever sent those men. Ford?

I've got one thing to offer. One. And it's a no-brainer.

I turn to Justice. "Call Momma and tell her I'll do it. I'll agree to M-erasure. Just turn this fucking thing around. Now."

The pilot refuses to turn around until he hears word from Momma, but the moment Gracie gets approval, he reverses course. By then, we're gathered around a conference table in the back and my guts are in turmoil. This thing can't fly fast enough.

Walking the aisle, Dusty has a cell pressed to his ear. He's talking with the authorities in Ponce. He hangs up. "According to the police there's no one on board, but there are signs of a struggle."

She got away. She had to. Or could they have taken her? Killed her?

Gently, J says, "It sounds to me like she got away, so we should make a plan for when we get there, right?"

I rub the ache in my chest. I'd feel it. If Honor weren't on this planet anymore, fairy-tale stuff or no, I'd fucking feel it.

"Where is she likely to go after escaping?" Sandesh asks.

Where? Would she go to the inn or to Ponce or the store by the pier? Time's ticking. Choosing wrong could damn Honor. Which one. Which fucking one? "It's likely she went back to Loco for Cocoa."

"I'm on cyber," Gracie says, connecting her laptop to a station embedded in the table.

"Get me a layout for the inn," Justice says.

"I've got that," Dusty says, pulling out his cell. "We looked it up earlier. I'll send it to the air screen."

He pushes a few buttons and the layout appears floating over the table.

"Any cameras in there?" Gracie asks, twisting the layout with a flick of her hand in the air, almost like a magician.

"Yes," I say, realization dawning and giving me the first real sign of hope. "A bunch, mine. They're well-hidden. I doubt anyone has found them."

"Guild equipment?" Gracie asks, and I nod.

She begins to type into her keyboard. "Good. That will make my job a little easier. Give me the passcode for the Wi-Fi you used."

I do.

Sandesh reaches down and brings a duffel out. He holds it out to me, "Stuff from your boat. I think there are clothes in here."

"There are," Justice says.

I take the bag, find black pants and shirt. I change right there, shoving my dirty and bloodied stuff back into the bag while Gracie's fingers fly over her keyboard.

The tension in the group rises as we wait on her. I can't take it. "You got a connection?"

Twirling a Jolly Rancher with her tongue, Gracie shakes her head. "I… The password isn't working…" She trails off, continues typing. "You sure that's the one?"

"That's it," I say. My throat is so filled with tension it feels like steel rods have replaced the muscles in my neck and jaw. I'm two seconds from tearing shit apart. I hate being this… fucking helpless.

"Got in," Gracie says. She continues to type. "Dusty, I'm sending out the feed. Can you accept and project from the source?"

"Yes, ma'am." Beside her, Dusty hits a series of buttons on the control panel embedded in the table. The air screen shifts from the inn's layout to a series of camera images.

Justice lets out a, "Holy shit."

I sit forward in my seat to get a closer look at the first images, but have to move back because of the wonkiness of the technology.

"You covered ground," Sandesh says. "Good. Can we get this streamed live to our NVGs, Gracie?"

"Sure. If we need to go in there, images of blind spots will appear in the corner of our night vision goggles, so that we'll be able to see what we're walking into."

Images, taken from the cameras I'd hidden, cycle in midair, giving an incredible insight into the layout.

I laser-focus on every scene, taking in minute details in a flash. "What the hell?" I say as something disturbing floats past. "Grab it, G."

"Got it," she says.

The cycling camera shots stop. The front of Loco for Cocoa, doors and porch, has a gaping hole through it.

No one asks the questions—what happened here, where's Honor, is everyone okay? No one asks, because there are no answers.

Sandesh waves a finger in a circle. "Keep going. Slowly this time."

The images start cycling again but slower. Except for the front of the lodge, everything looks normal—

Wait.

"Oh God," Gracie says, stopping the feed on the back of the patio.

I can't even process this shit right now.

Abuelito and José are tied up and being held by three armed assailants. One is Bud, from the tour. One is the bartender, and the last is Lanie, the yoga instructor. I think of all the time Rome spent researching Winthrop and realize we needed to do a deeper dive into the employees. This is why you need a team.

"We need to call the police," Dusty says.

I shake my head, swallow the sick in my throat. "The inn is an hour from the closest station. We're thirty minutes out, and we're better equipped to deal with this without getting innocents killed."

"Where's Honor?" Sandesh asks.

"Maybe inside," Justice says. "Let's get more visuals."

The image winks out. Panic grips me by the throat. "Gracie?"

Shaking her head, she types furiously into her computer. "It's dropped. I can't find it or even one of the cameras."

I hit the intercom on the table and tell the pilot, "Fucking fly faster."

Chapter 44
Honor

I take the final turn up the road to the lodge with my body still trembling. It's taken me too long to get back. I had to pull over because I'd started to shake so intensely that I couldn't control the car.

I have no idea how long I sat by the side of the road in a fog of shock with worries and indecision gripping me. Should I go to the police? Should I try to find Tony? Should I call around to hospitals to see if the man I hit is okay?

Finally, I'd realized I needed to do an order of importance. First thing, warn Abuelito and José.

I'd tried calling but no one had answered, and since I was already halfway home, I made getting here my priority.

I pull into the employee parking lot, stunned by the darkness of the inn. Did they turn off the electricity? That's odd. We were told it was all right to keep it on.

A tremor of fear slides into my unsettled stomach. It's unbelievable how much my perspective has changed after the attacks of today—first snake, then men.

Fear is now a living thing inside me. It's like it's lying in wait, sensitive to the slightest brush of my thoughts. I'm trying not to let it overtake me, trying not to give it energy, but it's no use. What was it Tony said about instinctive fear?

Using my phone as a flashlight, I get out of the car and head into the hotel. I focus my light down, so I can enter through the gaping hole that, not too long ago, contained a truck.

I step over splintered wood, glass, and metal. Islanders are used to rebuilding, but I grew up in California. I'll have to dig for my sturdier roots.

My heart sinks at all there is to do when I shine my light up and over Wela's desk. I close my eyes in gratitude and relief. It's still intact, and, behind it, my trophies are fine. Maybe things can be rebuilt. Maybe I can do this.

A sharp cry issues from the back of the lodge and electric gooseflesh flashes over my skin. Not a bird or any kind of night creature—that was a human cry of terrible pain.

I turn out my light. I don't need it to move here, not in my own home.

I move through the dining area and toward the patio with a burst of adrenaline clearing my foggy mind.

At the window, I peer through. A fire casts a ghastly orange glow around a ghastly sight. My blood runs cold as I swallow the cry of outrage.

A bloodied José is tied to a one of the wrought-iron chairs. His swollen eyes stare blankly ahead. Whatever his fate, that blank look says he's already accepted it.

Two men are taking turns hitting him. I recognize one—Bud from the tour. The other, Jorge, our bartender, is wearing a red hat. They're both stronger and younger than José.

In the chair before José, Abuelito is tied up. He's twisting, trying to get free. I can't see his whole face, but he has a bruise on his right cheek.

Supervising all of them, with an impassive face and lips pressed tightly together, stands Lanie. Her mask is off, and I see her for who she is. A monster. Someone easily able to hide the cruelty lurking inside.

Is there someone hidden by one of the taller punching men? I strain to see into the darkness.

A man walks around from behind the other man, and I cover my mouth to squelch my gasp. Ford. His hands shake as he interlocks his fingers as if to pray. "Please, Abuelito," he begs my grandfather, "tell them where the film is so they'll leave José alone."

"He knows nothing," José says between bloodied lips.

Abuelito spits on the ground. "Even if I knew, I wouldn't tell you. My daughter died for that film."

Abuelito knows Mom was murdered? And he knows about the film? This whole time, I'd thought *I* was protecting *him* from those truths, not wanting to share them until I knew for sure what was going on.

Ford gets to his knees before Abuelito, fingers still intertwined. "Please, what I did to help has endangered my wife and daughter. He's now threatening them. There's nothing more we can do. Give my uncle the film. He'll never turn himself in, and he'll never be convicted in a court of law. He'll always win. You know it's true, otherwise you'd have turned the film over to the authorities."

Abuelito shakes his head weakly, looking his age for the first time since I've known him. "You tried your best to help, Ford. I'm sorry you and your family were dragged into this, but I don't know where the film is."

"Stop lying," Lanie says, as serene as if at a yoga practice. She leans toward Abuelito. "You and José and Honor contacted Don Stoltz, a newspaper reporter, to give him the film so he could put it out for you. You thought it clever having Tito serve as your middleman. Look how that worked out. Now, tell us how to access the original film online, and we'll leave you to clean up the mess you've made of this place."

They think I had a part in this? I'm playing catchup to my uncle and my grandfather, who'd obviously known a lot more than they'd let on.

Heart pounding, stomach turning, I ease my feet back and run through the dining room into the front hall.

I have to call the police. Wait. I can't. The electricity is out. Of *course* it's out; this was planned. No electricity means no internet, means no extender, means no cell or phone service.

A series of thick, meaty strikes and José's cries break into the front hall. My heart hurts as if I were hit in the chest. The hair on my neck rises. Dear God, they're killing him.

Sweat slicks my hand. It's only me now. I have to take what Tony taught me, my skills, and rescue the people I love.

My decision quickly made, I sneak behind the desk, open the trophy case, and remove the compound bow with the strongest power stroke, along with the quiver filled with arrows that decorate the case. They're competition arrows, not the thicker ones meant for hunting, but if I strike a weak spot just right, they'll disable or kill. And I never miss.

Throat dry, heart hammering, I take the safety off my weapon, step past debris, and exit though the hole in the front of the posada.

As silent as the moon across the sky, weaving through the trees that line the path, I move until I can see the whole of the patio. *Order of importance.* The two men holding José are the biggest threats.

"I told you she'd come back here." A voice carries into the woods from the front of the posada.

Fear skitters like an insect over my body. Carrying flashlights, the men from the boat pass by my position and cross onto the patio. The one I hit with the bilge pump has a bandage over his head. *He's alive.*

"Where the fuck is that bitch?" Bandaged Head says as he comes onto the patio. Neither man reacts to the beaten and bloodied men tied up before them. They look over their heads to Bud and Jorge.

Lanie removes a weapon from a holster at her side. I hadn't even seen the gun. She says, "Where's who?"

"The girl," Bandaged Head says. "She came back here. The truck is out front."

A stunned and worried look flashes across Abuelito's face. "Leave Honora out of this."

No time left to plan. I have to jump into these waters, ready or not. Drawing back on the string, the weight of the bow's powerful tension reassuring. My hand brushes my cheek before I aim and release.

The arrow slices cleanly into the neck of Bandaged Head. He goes down without a word. I nock and let fly another arrow. It tears fabric as it slips through Bud's legs.

"Fuck me!" he shouts, diving to the ground. Lanie ducks for cover. People scatter.

I shouldn't have let spite dictate that last shot. I need to be smarter. I have three arrows left. There are four people between me and rescuing my family.

A still and focused calm covers me as I glide through the trees. Given a moment with no attack, and hidden behind a table, Lanie fires into the area where I'd been.

A shout that's almost rage and almost panic breaks from Ford's mouth as he tackles Lanie, pinning her down.

I freeze in my tracks.

They struggle. A muffled shot rings out.

I hold my breath.

Lanie rolls Ford off.

Groaning, he clutches at his side. *Ford!*

Blood pools onto the ground under him.

Jorge takes a gun from his waistband. Cupping his flashlight along the top, he starts to scan close to where I'm actually standing.

As light and sure-footed as a cat, I stalk through the last bit of trees that break at a path before the Cocoa Casa.

I let loose another shot, taking out the flashlight and the gun, which clatter to the ground. Cupping his hand to his chest, Jorge falls to the ground, losing his hat in the process.

"Where the hell is she?" Bud says, pulling out his own gun.

I nock another arrow, but Bud is wise now, taking cover behind trees or furniture as he moves.

He signals one of the men from the boat to enter the woods where my first shot came from. They split up. That man zigzags into the woods as Bud heads into the tree line closer to me.

As Bud enters, I step out, raise my weapon and aim at Lanie. The last man, the one with a bandaged head, sees me and lifts his gun. I turn my weapon on him. My arrow punches through his stomach, knocking him to the ground.

"No!" José screams, and I turn as he launches himself at Lanie, who has her gun aimed at me. Bent from the weight of the cast-iron chair he's still strapped to, he's slow, but she isn't expecting him.

She turns and José slams into her. They clatter to the stones.

"Honor, look out!" Abuelito shouts.

Bud's shot hits me in the arm.

The force turns me, knocks me off my feet.

Bud rushes out from the trees, kicks my crossbow away, then drags me across the patio by my shot arm.

The pain is blinding. I lose track of where I am and what's happening, as slick blood slides down my arm.

Bud drags me in front of Abuelito and puts his gun to my head. "Tell me now, old man. I'm not fucking around."

Tears falling from his eyes, Abuelito says, "Junior took all of the information and hid it. He was supposed to slip from the tour today, leaving Laz to handle the group while he ran. When Laz left, Junior panicked and crashed the truck. He is safe now with the police. There's nothing you can do."

"Asshole," Lanie says, getting to her feet. She slams the butt of her gun against José's head. She has a scrape along her forehead and shoulder. She tells Bud, "If it's not here, we torch the place with them tied up inside."

"Agreed," Bud says.

Lanie sighs and looks at me. "You're proving much harder to kill than your mo—"

Her words are cut off by a loud, sudden wind, but I heard enough, and Bud hasn't learned his lesson about me. He's so sure I'm taken down that he's looking into the sky with his weapon by his side.

I grab his gun.

He tries to pull back, but I yank it free and aim at him.

"Don't," Lanie says. Her weapon is pointed at Abuelito.

The wind whips around me, along with a thrumming that tells me, as clearly as Bud's head tilting back toward the sky, a helicopter is overhead.

They've brought more men! I scream in rage and agony and disbelief.

Suddenly, the patio is filled with ropes. People start sliding down them.

Hands trembling, I wobble to my feet and shoot, one-handed, up at the sky.

Distantly, I'm aware of Bud and Lanie running.

A man with a green helmet kicks my weapon away before landing in front of me. He reaches for me.

I jump back. Sweat pours from my skin as I search for the gun. I spot it, but Green Helmet kicks it farther out of the way. I turn on him, using the only weapons I have, my hands. I beat on his chest.

"Stop," he says, grabbing me, he draws me close, shakes me. "For fuck's sake, stop. You're hurt."

Eyes watering, head pounding, I flinch at the familiar voice and stare at the face under the helmet.

"Fuck. She's been shot," Tony says. "Beam me up, Sandesh. She needs medical attention."

"La… Tony?"

"Yeah. It's me." He holds me close. "You've lost blood. Are you woozy?"

"Ford is worse," I say.

He nods, presses me closer. "We got him. All of them. I got you. Relax." He secures something around me. "Hold on. We're headed up."

My feet leave the ground. Darkness begins to wash over me. I fight it, trying to cling to awareness and to him. *He's here. He came back for me.*

I lean into his chest and, closing my eyes against the wind and vibrations, I whisper, "I love you, Tony."

Chapter 45
Tony

Honor finally looks at me. She finally sees me. I secure her in the harness and radio Sandesh to bring me up so she can get medical care.

The line pulls taught, and we begin our ascent. My team begins evacuating the injured as the bad guys have fled into the woods.

Honor clings to me, rests her head against my chest. She lifts her head and I look down to see her lips mouth, *I love you, Tony.*

A lump the size of California blocking my throat, I cradle her to my chest.

It's worth it. Whatever they do to my memory is worth her life and the lives of her family. Worth it.

If we'd been a minute slower. If she'd been an ounce less fierce, less determined. But we made it. We fucking made it in time.

My heart tears open as the impact of her words really hits me. She loves me. This woman. That shouldn't make my stomach hurt, but it does. Her love is one more sacrifice The Guild will ask of me.

I wish I could've told her I love her, too, all the fairytale love one heart can feel, but maybe it's best she doesn't know that.

It's better that I don't give her something that's going to be torn brutally away. Better if this ache is only mine to carry.

Chapter 46
Tony

I wasn't allowed to be part of the crew that dropped off Honor and her family at the hospital. Nope. The moment the op is over, I'm told to sit down and shut up. Once the woman I love and her family are seen to, I'm flown home as a prisoner of The Guild.

The whole ride home, I remember her, focus on remembering her, the feel of her, the feelings I have when I'm with her, every detail of her face, the flounce of her hair, the upward tilt of dark nipples, the soft sighs. I go over every painful and aching detail because I know Honor, the island, hot nights, and long days are a dream I soon won't remember.

We touch down at my family's private airport in Bucks County, PA. I'm not handcuffed, but as Justice, Sandesh, Gracie, and Dusty deboard, I'm told to stay seated for clearance from Internal. Basically, I'm treated like the prisoner I am.

"Hi, Tony," says Eugie, an Internal agent, climbing into the copter. She sits opposite of me and places a black bag next to her. "I'm here to do some routine examinations, okay?"

Since I was twelve years old, I've thought of Internal Security—the systems, personal, and technology that secures our underground and illegal operations—as a kind of a police force under Leland's command. So, even though Eugie is a few years younger than me, I squirm in my seat.

"Go for it," I say.

She removes a handheld finger scanner, presses my thumb onto it, capturing and confirming my identity. She then reaches in and takes out a retinal scanner, because why confirm someone's identity once? Even if you've known that person for five years and can tell who they are on sight.

I lean into the device without complaint because this is all part of the show. Momma wants me to know I'm no longer in the inner circle.

"You took out your chip?" Eugie asks in a soft voice that lets me know this bugs her and is probably something Internal has been wondering about.

I've got nothing to hide. I flip my right arm over so she can see the small misshapen lump on the inside of my forearm. "I took a pair of plyers and crushed it on our way to Mexico."

She inhales sharply, as if she knows exactly how badly that had to have hurt. "That explains a lot." She presses her fingers to the flesh around the device. "We've had the chips damaged before. I can remove this, if you'd like."

I nod and she takes out a device that looks like a gun with a tiny metal tip that reminds me of a calligraphy pen. She inserts the canula. There's pressure, then a pulling, and the small lump moves out and into the tube. She clears the device into a sterilized beaker. I see the bloodied and dented mint-sized device slide down the side and get stuck there.

"You need a new chip," she says, and I hold out the other arm. She fiddles with the insertion tool, adds a new tip, then shoots a tracker into my arm. "You won't have access to any sensitive areas without supervision until after your procedure. At that point, your clearances will be updated. Understood?"

"Yep, basically the chip will act only as a GPS, but won't be like my old chip, allowing me to roam the underground levels of the Mantua Home, until I've been made into a satisfactory puppet for The Guild. At which point, you'll updated my clearances."

She blanches at my statement. "Well, you check out. Ready to go home?"

My throat slams shut because my home is with someone else and I can never go home again.

"Eug." I use her nickname, because I want this information, and I need to make it personal. "Do you have any word on the people we dropped off at the hospital?"

She grimaces. "I'm not—"

"Alive or dead?" I say. "Healthy or in intensive care? Please. The basics."

She lets out a long breath, then leans close. "They're all alive and healthy. No one is in the ICU. We have someone on scene. They're going to take your people to a safehouse."

I let out a breath. I did it. I got Momma to take Honor's case. Thank God.

"Ready," I say, dropping my hands and standing up.

We walk out into a bright, sunny day. There's a limo waiting for me. There was a time when I took this for granted or took it as irrelevant, a means to get from one place to another.

Now that I've tasted freedom, going from one place to the next without all the bells and whistles, without people knowing where you are every step of the way, I see the limo differently—a golden cage that you pay for with your life of service.

I'd never minded before because I'd had a lot to make up for and my family was my life. Now, The Guild and all their wealth is asking me for Honor. I'd rather walk, swim, ride a bike the rest of my life than get in that fucking limo, but to do that is to cancel my deal and leave Honor and her family to the wolves.

I slide onto the cool leather seat across from Sandesh, Justice, Gracie, and Dusty. I stretch out, lean back, and close my eyes, feeling like a dead man walking.

I don't drift off. I'm aware of their conversation, aware of every turn, including when the limo pulls up to the Mantua Academy gates.

I open my eyes and get my first glimpse of the forty-year-old elite boarding school and cover for our secret society. Large iron fencing with advanced technologies encircles the one-hundred-and-sixty-acres of historic white and brick buildings. She looks good… but not like home anymore.

Still, I missed this place, missed the life. I take it in as if it'll be my last, and in some ways, it will be. Without the knowledge of why I'd betrayed my family, without the knowledge of Honor, I won't be the same man.

After the vehicle is checked by Security, we enter. Fall foliage fills the trees that line hills, walkways, and the numerous brick-and-white buildings. I see only a few cars in the large lot by the main school.

"It's still empty," I say, not really to anyone, but Justice answers.

"Yeah, thanks for that. Turns out when you send multiple drones onto campus armed with small explosive devices, the FBI shows up and parents get a little testy and insist on added security before they let their kids come back. Go figure."

I grind my teeth. "I was trying to save your life, and I made sure no one was hurt. I wanted to get your attention."

Justice springs at me like a lion after an impala, and slams a hand to my chest. "You saved nothing. You have no idea how my mission would've gone if you hadn't been playing games with me."

Like hell. "You were out of control. You needed to be taken off that operation. You made one stupid mistake after another. Everyone knew it. You think I was the only one who thought it was fucked up allowing you on a mission that involved such deep trauma?"

"Bridget doesn't count. She hates all violence."

"She counts. And so does Gracie. And so does Dada."

"Don't drag Gracie into the mud," Dusty says.

Justice moves her hand from my chest and sits next to me. She looks directly at Gracie. "G?"

Gracie exhales. "Yeah, okay. Fine. Dada and I asked Momma if it was the wisest thing to follow your plan to take out both brothers at the same time."

A moment of doubt flashes across Justice's face, but she's never one to doubt herself for long. "I guess I proved you wrong."

"You proved us right," I say. "That mission was fucked from the get-go. No way the Brothers Grim needed to be taken out by you in the same place at the same time."

"If you took out one—"

"The other would be notified. Bullshit. We had enough intel and agents to do them simultaneously."

"No."

"Yes, J. You wanted to kill them both to get revenge for what they did to you and your sister. We all knew it, and we all knew it was a bad idea. But, for some reason, Momma went along with it, even though the plan was fucked. The execution was fucked. And it was my job to run around, trying to put my finger in every fucking hole you put in the dam."

"That's your read," Justice says. "Mine is that if you hadn't warned the targets, hadn't gotten them to change their meeting location to Jordan, I wouldn't have had to embed with Sandesh or his charity. I wouldn't have had to scramble to put together a whole new mission. I would've succeeded."

"Were you scrambling during our recon op on that sex-trafficking center when you killed two guys? Oh, wait, killed one guy and let Cee, a teenager, kill the second."

"I didn't let her, and I was reacting to the situation on the ground. That guy was chasing her." She pushes a finger into my chest. "And I'm not the one who did this. You not trusting Momma, not trusting me, not keeping your vows to The Guild—"

"Fuck that. I kept my vow. No Guild member will ever allow another member to irresponsibly risk themselves, the security of a mission, or the secrecy of The Guild."

"Our job is a risk. Doing the work is a risk. That rule is meant to be applied to people like you, someone who is betraying The Guild, so don't even start with me with that bullshit."

The limo pulls to a stop in front of the Mantua Home, and I bite off my next sentence. Justice and I are both breathing heavily. Sandesh looks like he's minutes away from slugging me across the face. Dusty looks like he'd like to do the same thing on principle, and Gracie's face is pinched into a frown.

Avoiding eye contact with them, I turn and stare out the window. It's always a shock pulling up to the house, seeing how big it is. And a kind of pride, knowing that, beneath these sprawling grounds, are expansive secret levels filled with the technology and the training center for The Guild.

The chauffeur opens the limo door, and the others get out first. I wait for them all to file up the front steps and inside before I climb out. "Thanks for the ride," I tell the driver, realizing I don't know his name. He's new, young, early twenties, messy blond hair under a too-big cap. I make a note to chat with him later. Will I remember?

Wiping my sweaty palms on my pants, I cross the cobbled drive, past the fountain, and walk slowly up the stone stairs.

The large front doors swing open to reveal a grand staircase and a grander family. My heart does a backflip in my chest. Just like Dorothy in *The Wizard of Oz*, I realize I have missed them most of all.

Momma and Leland stand by the enormous front stairs. Her scarred face is covered in a gray silk veil, an irony that isn't lost on me, because The Guild doesn't see gray, not in this matter. Uncle Leland—nah, I can't do that—*Leland* wears a matching tie.

And everywhere else—in the doorways to the gym, on the steps leading upstairs, and in the hall—stands my family. I meet the eyes of all of them, one at a time, because I want them to see I'm not sorry. I'm not going down as the guy who did wrong. Sure, I was reckless and stupid, but for the right reasons.

When I meet the eyes of my sister Veta—black hair with a blue stripe and the leader of the Troublemakers Guild—she mouths, *Welcome home*, and starts clapping.

It takes a moment, but the clapping is picked up by Rome, Jules, Cee, and their unit, Vampire Academy, then spreads to others in the hall. All the younger groups are clapping. Even

Bella, who's only five and can't really know what's going on, starts to clap.

I spread my arms wide and spin around, because I love and appreciate them, and they clap louder with some starting to hoot.

The older units, including Justice and Gracie, seethe in quiet anger.

Momma spins on those cheering. The room quiets in a flash.

For a moment, it's like there's two parts of our family. Our once cohesive family organization is clearly divided into two sides now—those who support me and those who think I need to have my head messed with.

No wonder Momma's so pissed at me; I'm an unintentional leader of the rebellion. Unity has been the driving force for her entire life. Because, if you don't have group cohesion centered around a core values, you've got a lot of highly-trained individuals capable of going out on their own, creating problems, and endangering everything The Guild has kept a lid on for forty years.

Shit. My chances of walking out of here with my memories… zero.

Wait. Who the hell is that tall, black-haired kid? I stare at him. He looks familiar. It's the green eyes and the fact that he's standing next to Gracie that finally clues me in. My heart stops. Dead. Crushed.

No way. "Tyler? Ty, is that you?"

The kid smirks and nods enthusiastically, a little goofily. Joy rushes over me like a freakin' storm. Gracie's son is here. She got him back. *We* got him back. The kid had been a toddler when his father found out about The Guild and left Gracie, taking the kid with him.

My smile can't quit. "Do you remember me, Ty?"

What am I saying? There's no way—

He tilts his head. "Did you used to hold me upside down by my feet?"

That does it. That fucking does it. I walk over and grab him in a bear hug. Kid is tall. Taller than me, but skinny and wiry. Oh, he can be trained. Yeah. Definitely.

I let go, step away, but the smile is still there. I grin at Gracie. "He's back."

Tears spring to her eyes, and she makes a choking sound and whispers, "Where he belongs," and it sounds like she isn't *only* talking about Tyler.

"Well, that's just great," Leland says. His gravel voice sounds like it's been dipped in ice water and chilled overnight. At the North Pole. "Now that you've said your hellos, would you care to follow us downstairs for a debrief on how you nearly got your sister killed, brought the FBI to our front door, and ruined the Mantua Academy's spotless forty-year reputation?"

Chapter 47
Tony

Everything looks the same and feels completely different as Leland, Momma, and I step off of Elevator X into the underground levels of The Guild's operations center.

We walk wordlessly as our footfalls echo down sterile corridors. We come to Momma's colorful and kitschy office. The moment her door shuts behind us, Momma turns unexpectedly and wraps me in a hug.

I tense and battle to keep my arms by my side, taking in the scent of her perfume and the warmth of an embrace that helped heal the broken child in me.

She lets go with a softly whispered, "You made your choices, too."

She moves around her desk and sits down, wiping at the corner of her eyes where tears have soaked her veil. "Sit down," she says, and her voice tells me the tears and sentiment are gone.

I don't sit. I stand in front of her desk, hands clasped behind my back, feeling like an errant student hauled before the disapproving principal.

Through the slit that shows her eyes, brown and observant, there's no sense of Momma's emotions now. Standing behind her like a consigliere, Leland's face is blank. They'd both make excellent poker players. Except they never bluff.

Momma grasps the many bracelets along her forearm. "I read your letter about Justice's mission, considered it fully, and must admit that, perhaps, I should've explained my reasoning more fully to you. I forget, sometimes, that you are not only my children but Guild field agents who need to be brought into the operations and deliberations usually contained within Internal Security."

Is she apologizing to me? I don't respond—can't really think of how to respond.

She clears her throat. "Unbeknownst to you, Justice's mission did not have a singular goal—taking out the Brothers Grim and their organization."

I unclasp my hands and take a seat in front of her desk. "What other goal was there?"

"I understood and perceived that the Brothers Grim case was the one and only time—the one and only opportunity—where the children, grown and young, of this family would be able to mark a clear win against those who had harmed one of ours. Not even I had had that chance." She touches her veil and her jewelry jangles. "The man who scarred me never paid for his crime."

"What about my dad?" I say, biting when I should be tucking tail. "Seems like someone took some pretty good revenge on him." I look at Leland. "Right, *Uncle* Leland?"

Leland's shoulders rise. His jaw tightens. He clears his throat. It does nothing to change the gravel in his voice. "Your father killed my sister, your mother, and ran with you. By the time we'd found him under his assumed identity, you had already run away from home. His death wasn't something I set out to do." He rubs his knuckles. "It was a tragic overreach. One I paid for every day that I had you in front of me, unable to tell you who I was, unable to let you know…" He swallows. "I see her in you."

The room goes quiet. I'd suspected that Leland had beaten my dad to death and hidden his identity from me in order to keep quiet any connection between us that the authorities might've tied to my father's death. It still stings to have it confirmed.

"We are both sorry about the necessity of keeping that truth from you," Momma says, "but you must understand that the choices we make involve a complex series of circumstances. As was the case with Justice. Allowing her revenge wasn't only about healing her, allowing her that retribution, but about healing all of us. Do you not see that?"

"I get it. You wanted Justice to stand over the dead bodies of the men who'd hurt her and her biological sister, but that didn't make her plan better than mine or less risky. And isn't that why we have rules—rules that say safety supersedes revenge—to prevent us from making choices that needlessly risk our family?"

Momma exhales a whistle, slow and loud, that flutters her veil. "Perhaps my desire to see Justice prevail, to have her nightmare end with the destruction of her oppressors, giving a victory to all our girls, clouded my judgment."

She's admitting she was wrong? It's like the world shifts under me. I wait, disbelief and hope warring for control of my spinning thoughts.

"But there are no circumstances in which risking The Guild, betraying our family, attacking our school, and causing mental anguish to every child here with that drone stunt, were warranted. And no rule will allow you absolution for those sins. Surely you recognize that."

When she says it like that, it's hard to argue, but I do. "What I did was meant to save my sister's life. You dismiss the things you do, the murder Leland did, by telling me the circumstances were complex. Well, that's how it felt back then, like no one was listening, no one cared about J, when she fucking mattered to me."

I see, now, how badly I'd fucked up. How crazed I had become. But I regret nothing before the drones. The drones were a horrible mistake. But I don't say this.

"I understand," Momma says. "And, because I do, I'm willing to offer you a choice."

"What choice?" Tension and suspicion mount my shoulders.

"You can leave here with your memory and mind intact. You will undergo surgery to hide your identity and must agree to never come back to the States, and never communicate with anyone in this family or participate on any Guild operation."

"When you say don't participate on any operation, are you saying you'll help Honor, but I have to stay away from her and the mission?"

"Yes, to the mission. The Guild, as per your request, has taken on her case. I have no idea how long it will take to resolve, but once it is resolved, you will be free to join Honor under your new identity."

That could be years. "What's my other choice?"

"To be absolved of your betrayal and your attack on this family, to assure you can be trusted, you will undergo a procedure that blocks memory of your culpability in damaging the school and betraying your sister. After that, you will resume your membership in The Guild and assist us in organizing the operation with Honor Silva."

"What about my memories of Honor?"

"What of them?" Leland says.

Momma says, "We would not touch them, of course."

I really don't want them to fuck with my head, but this is a good offer, one I know I can make even better. "I'll do it. As long as Honor and her family are brought here, kept safe here."

"We can ask them, of course," Momma says. "But it will have to be their choice."

Chapter 48
Tony

I'm in a hospital gown, strapped to a chair that reminds me of a dentist office. A helmet with wires that dangle from a mechanical arm connected to the ceiling is on my head. Electrodes are attached to my chest, fingers, and torso. Wires flow to a machine with a large screen filled with graphs and lines of information.

Being in this Dr. Jekyll's nightmare is terrifying. That's saying something, considering I'd been pretty damn scary myself before coming into Neuro Room 3D.

It's unnaturally cold, with crisp white walls and a buzz of electricity. Suppose it needs to be cold for all the computers and technical mind-fucking crap.

Zuri, my older sister, walks around, checking equipment with a *click*, *click*, *click* of brisk heels. Her dark skin glows and her long braid flies behind with her brisk pace. She's in her element and has barely spoken a word to me, so, when she does, I startle.

"I have never"—her Kenyan accent makes the word sounds like *nevah*—"been so torn. On the one hand, I see the need for punishment." Her eyes pin me with accusation before softening. "And on the otha', I see the boy who would sit and let me read *The Lord of the Rings* to him, gently correcting my English."

I just liked the way she spoke, the way her accent gave special emphasis to words my tongue would mash, but I don't tell her that. I say, "What about Bridge? Did you feel conflicted when you did her?"

She pushes a button on the table of equipment, a large block with screens, sensors, and electric dials, then shrugs. "Do you mean the first time?"

I jerk forward in the chair, but the straps tug me back. "There was more than one time?" Bridget must have Swiss cheese for a brain.

"Yes. We've been working together to find a solution to a problem she had long wrestled with. You see, three years ago, Bridget asked me to remove the memory of her chemical addiction."

My heart breaks for Bridget who, before coming here, had purposefully been addicted to drugs to make her easier to manipulate. I suddenly wish she was home and not working overseas. I want to hug her tight. "I thought she had that under control."

"You misunderstand. She wanted me to see if I could devise a treatment for other addicts and was, therefore, willing to undergo treatment."

Gah, Bridge. I fucking love her. How can anyone be that damned giving? "Let me get this straight, you fucked with Bridge's head twice and both times she asked you to?"

Zuri frowns. "I did not *fuck*, as you say, with her head. I disrupted the place where her attachment to an emotional idea existed, in the hopes that her brain would then alter her memories, eradicating the attachment permanently."

"Dumb it down, Z."

She stops fiddling with stuff. "I've explained to you before that your mind is not a book, written and done. It is more a computer file, capable of being pulled out and altered. Using a chemical and electrical process, I can disrupt one memory, allowing the insertion of another."

Sounds painful. "Okay. So how you do you insert a new memory?"

"Again, I do little. You see, our perception of the world is already flawed, incomplete. Our mind, supported by belief and conditioning, fills in the blanks of our senses, creating what we think of as a stable representation of reality. It's not, and changing a key idea or feeling—in your case, that you were afraid for Justice's life—forces the mind to make sense of conflicting data. In other words, your own brain rewrites your memories, so that it aligns with the new information. It's amazing, really, how well our minds can trick us."

"Z, I've never been more afraid of you in my life."

Her brow creases. "Why—"

"So, if you just take my fear that J was going to get hurt, my brain will alter everything to fit?"

"Yes. Basically."

"And you won't be taking Honor from me? Puerto Rico?"

Zuri recoils. "I would fight anyone who would try to take that from you."

All the muscles in my body turn to liquid. One memory. Not really even a memory—an attachment, a fear, and this has been done before successfully. Except for her fascination with yoga and meditation, Bridget's okay. "Is Bridge the only one? Or have you M-erased other people in the family?"

Zuri pulls a flashlight from the pocket of her lab coat and examines my eyes. "Momma."

"You altered Momma's memory?"

"She wouldn't let me touch Bridget until she'd tried it herself."

"What'd *she* want altered?"

"Momma couldn't decide. She asked Leland to choose for her."

"Did he?"

She pockets her flashlight. "Yes. It worked out quite well. She had no idea that you were Leland's nephew until you put it into that letter."

Chapter 49
Honor

I lie on my stomach, looking over the edge of a huge cliff as Tony dangles by his fingertips. Puerto Rico is far below him, impossibly far, misted by clouds—as if this mountain is in the sky. Frantic, I reach for him. "Give me your hand."

With a growl, he swings up, stretches for me.

Arm aching, toes digging into the soil, hips scraping against the rocky ground, I reach back.

A helicopter passes overhead, the sound throbbing against my ears, scattering dirt into my face and tearing away Tony's tenuous grip.

He falls.

I wake up with a scream and jerk so violently that I nearly roll off the mattress.

The person standing by the side of the bed, grasps me by my forearms. "It's okay," she says, pushing back, so that I drop onto my pillows. "You're safe."

Safe? My eyes skim away from Dada's angular face, closely cropped hair, and honey eyes to the suite in the mansion I was transported to three days ago.

Light flushes through windows. Blue-and-tan silk drapery pools onto a lightly stained wood floor. There's a dresser, flatscreen TV, a sitting area, a small fridge, and a miniscule but spotless kitchenette. All signs that Dada's words are correct, and I am safe.

Except I'm *not* safe. I'm in some kind of voluntary witness protection, but the people protecting me won't tell me what I most need to know.

"This room is starting to feel like a prison."

Dada makes a sound of objection.

"Oh, not prison," I say, "I'm a *guest*. But I'm not allowed out of this room, can't open the door without some doohickie in my arm—which I'm not allowed to get—and had to be driven here blindfolded because you operate a secret society called The Spy Makers Guild, of which Tony is a member."

Dada nods. "As I've explained, we secreted you here after your agreement to keep you safe from Winthrop and what we suspect is a large network of cohorts. A safety no one else would provide since you have no proof of any of your claims."

"I would think the scene at Loco for Cocoa would be proof enough."

"And was it?" Dada doesn't say this rudely, but it feels like a slap.

I don't answer because she's well aware that the authorities think that my family and I have ties to drug smuggling. They're trying to put a case together against us, using Tito as a starting point. Of course, it will fail, but, meanwhile, the real villains are searching for us.

"When do I get to go out? When do I get to see La—Tony? You said he asked me to come here. I left my grandfather and my uncle—"

"They could have come, but are, nonetheless, safe in Puerto Rico," Dada says.

"I know that!" I snap, then take a deep breath. She's kind and sincere… and pregnant. She doesn't need me acting like a brat, but I'm beginning to lose my patience. "I appreciate the care and help you've given me and my family. I appreciate you taking Ford—my, uh, father—to his wife and daughter, and I really appreciate you keeping them safe, too. As much as I appreciate all of that and the rescue, I need to talk to Tony, and I want to use a phone to check on Junior. He's still in jail. I'm worried about him."

"As I've told you before, communication is impossible and there is a whole group of highly trained professionals on the case. Things are happening, even though it seems they are not."

"Fine. No phone, but why can't I speak with Tony?"

"As I've explained, he knows you're here. If he wished to see you, no one would stop him."

"I don't believe you. Why ask me to come here if he isn't going to see me? Why send for me only to lock me in this room?"

Dada looks away, pain pinching her beautiful features. "I wish I understood that myself." She stands. "Is there anything you'd like to be brought to you? How is your arm? Would you like me to send for the doctor again?"

"No," I wave a hand. "My arm is fine. I'm…" On second thought, maybe it's time to use my skills to make my own way out of here. "Actually, do you think I could get some supplies to make chocolate? That's what I do. I'm a chocolatier."

Dada frowns at my odd request, and I sense that she knows I'm asking for a reason other than making chocolate, but finding no fault or no escape plan in it, she says, "I'll have the things sent up."

I smile at her. "You're the best."

Chapter 50
Tony

Dressed in my workout clothes—the all-black uniform that feels like a call to action—I bound down the front stairs of the Mantua Home, humming a tune.

It's good to be home. That shit in Mexico—no one to blame but me, since it'd been my plan—it'd been intense, so intense I'd had to take a vacation, get clear of the family, meet a girl, and get laid.

At least that'd been the plan. My head flashes with pain. Ever since that M-erasure, I can't seem to shake this headache. I'd talk to Zuri about it, but don't want her anywhere near my head. Plus, there's too much to do. Leave it to me to go on vacation and walk into a case, a big one.

I double-check today's agenda on my cell. There's a meeting later downstairs to discuss the Winthrop case.

At the bottom of the stairs, I spot Veta and Cee still in their pajamas.

"Hey," I say, crossing to them. "It's nearly 7:45 and you guys aren't even in your gym clothes? Cee, you're new, so maybe you get a pass, but Elisaveta, you know better. You're morning run partners, right?"

Sure, it's Saturday, but life is getting soft around here. Came back just in time.

They stare at me.

"Get moving. I got a sparring session with Rome, then a meeting, but I'll be back here regular time to practice hand-to-hand."

"Tony?" Cee says, and I notice her lip trembling. "Do you still like me?"

"What? Yeah, Cee, I fucking love you."

Shaking my head, I start to turn. What is it Bridget always says? *When something makes you uncomfortable, pay even more attention.*

I pivot back to them. "Why'd you ask? What's goin' on?"

A blue streak through her hair—appropriate since she can talk a blue streak—Veta rubs the elaborate tattoo of a thorny vine with bright flowers that runs around the olive skin of her forearm and says, "They messed something up when they took your memory."

A kick to the balls would've caused less of a shock. As the words sink in, a jolt of pain threatens to crack my skull. "What are you talking about?"

In her soft Spanish accent, Cee says, "I heard Momma talking with Zuri. She said your resistance caused an emotional break."

"Resistance is futile," Veta says.

"Not fucking funny, V. And any issue with my brain is none of your business." Apparently not mine either. "Now get dressed and hit the bricks."

Chewing the shit out of my lower lip, I watch them walk up the stairs, whispering about if I'm in my right mind.

Truth? I'm not sure. Because something *is* different about the way I'm remembering stuff. Well, it's different from Mexico to Puerto Rico, to Honor, and Loco for Cocoa. It's like a layer of my memories is diluted. Not the actual events, but the emotions attached to the events. I remember feeling everything while there, but, now, I feel nothing. It's like watching a film that doesn't really capture your interest.

I thought it was temporary. Hoped it was. I was waiting for the condition to disappear, or, more accurately, reappear. That's the reason I haven't gone to visit Honor yet. The reason I asked Leland not to give her access to the home yet. She doesn't even

know my last name or about the family, and I'm going to face her, tell her all of that, knowing I feel nothing for her?
I shouldn't have asked to have her brought here.

The smell in the underground gym—an enormous space with state-of-the-art equipment, including an obstacle course and a dojo, might be my favorite thing in the whole world. Well, that and chocolate.

Chocolate?

But even being back here, being active and totally in flow with my body, can't keep me from a little brotherly annoyance. "Keep your head in the game, Rome." I offer the kid a hand up from his prone position on the sparring mat.

Pale skin slicked with sweat, black hair stuck to his head, amber-brown eyes bouncing around the room, he takes the offered hand with a mumbled "Sorry."

I pull him to his feet. "Maybe I should be sparring with your twin." Always feel weird calling Jules his twin because they look nothing alike. She's blonde with blue eyes and is six inches shorter than him.

With a brisk rub of one hand through his dark hair, Rome says, "I can get her for you."

Whoa. "Seriously, Rome, you're killing me with this. What's with you?"

"Nothing. It's just…" He looks away then whispers, "This sucks."

I'm done with this. I walk over and grab the cleaning supplies and toss them to him because the loser cleans the mat. "Look, whatever this is, you have to let it go. I agreed to the M-erasure just like Bridget. It was for the best."

I think.

Rome leans in closer. "I could tell you what they took."

No fucking way. "No. We all know the rules. We all play by the same rules."

I think.

So why does that statement feel wrong to me?

"Tony?"

I turn at the sound of that unexpected voice. Holy shit. "Victor?"

Dressed in all-black workout gear, looking tanned and toned—a lot healthier than the last time I'd seen him when he'd been shot up by bad guys—Victor rushes over and gives me a hug before swatting me on the ass.

"What the fuck, Victor?"

"Pendejo." Victor grins. "Gave you the best night of your life and you never called."

"I knew I didn't like you the moment I saw you in a G-string," I say. "You shouldn't fuck with someone who's had their memory altered."

Victor laughs. "Just checking, amigo. They said you were the same with just a small blip in the radar. Seems about right."

"It's not right," Rome says. "He's different. His girlfriend is upstairs and he hasn't even gone to see her."

I point at the mat. "Clean up and shut up."

The kid drops and begins to clean sweat from the mat, but his pronouncement of "He's different" strikes a gong of warning inside me.

Did they manage to do what I'd worried they'd do the moment I'd agreed to M-erasure—make me into the man they wanted at the expense of the man I was?

Chapter 51
Honor

Having no idea when someone from the staff will come with my supplies, I finish with the lump in my bed. It looks good, like I'm sleeping under the blankets. I even found a dark, hairy jacket—too trendy for me—in the armoire and used it to make it seem like a tuft of my hair is sticking out. Not bad.

Forty minutes later, the door beeps and clicks open. I quickly duck and hide behind the loveseat in the sitting area.

A twenty-something with blonde hair and a maid's uniform enters, pushing a wheeled metallic cart filled with some of the best chocolate-making supplies in the business. Seeing my sleeping form, she quietly takes items off the cart and puts them onto the counter in the kitchenette.

When she's done, she pushes her cart up to the door and reaches her wrist up. There's a click and a beep just like when Dada and the doctor, Zuri, or anyone from the staff leaves here.

She pulls the door open and wheels out the cart. As silent as a butterfly, I follow. I mimic her perfectly, but she doesn't turn around. She keeps going, and so do I. There's a turn ahead; I'll ditch her there.

The door begins to beep. The woman spins, and I just manage to keep pace with her, so that she doesn't see me.

She marches back to the door and so do I, because I can't make it down the hall without her spotting me. She waves her wrist over a pad by the doorway. A mechanical voice issues from the pad, "Verify that two people have exited the room. Authorization necessary."

The woman does a full 360, with me following her every move. She shrugs. "It's a trolley, daft machine," she says with a rather strong Scottish accent. She taps her foot. "Come on, home security, got work to do."

"Getting a visual," a voice says, and the pad blinks to life, showing the woman in the hall, the corridor, the trolley, and me.

The woman whirls on me with a scream as an alarm sounds.

I run, expecting the woman or someone else to chase me, but I keep running and no one does. The alarm cuts off.

A female voice comes over a speaker. "Hello, Honor. This is Martha with home security. No one will hurt you, and there's no need to run and no reason to risk aggravating your wound. Please stop there. Someone will meet you and show you around."

"Gracias, no!" I shout. "I'm not going back into witness protection."

Ay Dios, this place is huge, but I was taken through here before, and, even blindfolded, that weird part of my brain remembers. I run down another hall, turn down another, and find the front staircase exactly where I knew it would be.

I race down it with my arm aching and my shirt soaked in blood.

Again, Martha speaks up. This time, she seems concerned. "If you'd like to leave, that's fine, but please go slowly. You're injured and appear to be bleeding. Wouldn't it be better to allow us to show you around?"

She's probably telling me the truth, but I'll feel a lot better if I know I can get outside. I reach the front door, grab the handle, and pull. It doesn't budge. I try again and a mechanical voice says, "Exterior doors locked. Authorization required."

I drop the handle and fight back anger and frustration. Feeling stupid, not sure if Martha can hear me, I shout, "I want to talk to Tony!"

"That can be arranged."

I spin and am confronted by two women, one of whom I know. I point to her. "You came to my shop—money and an opinion. You were there looking for Tony?"

"Actually," she says, smirking at me, "at that point, I already knew where he was. I was there to feel you out, see what you knew about us, the family."

"The family?"

"See that?" She turns to the other woman "That, right there, can't be faked. I mean, I never bought the whole 'my boyfriend left me' thing, because your reaction was more melancholy, not heartbroken, but this... You really don't know who your boyfriend is."

"What are you talking about? Who are you?"

The dark-eyed woman walks forward, like stalking prey is her way of life. She holds out a hand. "I'm Justice Parish. Tony's sister."

I don't shake her hand, so she drops it. "And you?" I ask the other woman, a fair-skinned redhead.

"I'm Gracie Parish. His other sister."

"How many sisters does he have?"

Gracie snorts. "He has twenty-six sisters and one brother. All of us adopted."

I feel like an idiota for not putting the pieces together sooner, but when she mentions twenty-six adopted siblings, the name Parish finally clicks.

My gaze jumps from Gracie to Justice to the gym on my right. The doors are closed, but faces peer out from the glass. Kids and teens of a wondrous variety of skin tones are gathered there, staring at me.

"You're..." I can't say it. The Parish family. What I know of them, I know distantly through social media and tabloids. Which, to my mind anyway, means I don't know them at all.

Wait. I do know one of them very well. Tony Parish. That's Tony's whole name.

A knot made up of fear, pain, and stress forms in the back of my stomach. The door behind me clicks and I jump away as it swings open.

Two men enter, both muscular, both handsome, and both terrifying.

I take a step back. "Where's Tony?"

"It's okay," Gracie says. "He's downstairs, and we can take you to him." She points at one of the men. "The big guy is mine. His name is Dusty."

The big guy—big*ger* guy as they're both tall and muscular—says, "Warms my heart to hear you say that, Grace." He nods at me. "Pleased to meet you, Honor."

He has a nice voice. Southern. Congenial.

I don't respond to him.

"And the handsome guy, Sandesh, is mine," Justice says, earning her a swat from Gracie.

"Nice to meet you, Honor," Sandesh says. "I think you're going to want to come with us. We want to help you and your cousin, Junior."

My heart speeds up. "Junior?"

"Yeah," Justice says. "He was taken from the jail in Ponce."

"Taken?"

"If you want to know more, you'll have to come with us."

Hmm, these people have a habit of making ultimatums that sound like they're giving me a choice.

I point down the hall. "Lead the way."

What I know about the Parish family, bits and pieces I've read online and in the media is that they're a wealthy family, global travelers who like to pose for glamorous pictures, usually at charity events. I quickly discard all of it as unimportant. It's obvious there's a lot more to them than their carefully crafted media image. So, as I walk down the halls of their huge home, I put together the details most don't know. The Guild is an organization Tony is a part of. These people, his siblings, likely also belong to that organization. Tony said he'd tried to rescue his sister, but it had backfired. He'd said she'd never forgive him. Has she? Or was he right to run away from these people? Has Tony really been staying away from me or has he been *kept* from me?

"Although I have had a few bodyguards, I've never had my own security detail," I say, making note of the fact that these people have surrounded me as they walk me down another hallway.

"We're just making sure you don't get lost again," Justice says.

"I never get lost," I say, "In fact, you've led me around in circles three times, but you aren't fooling me. You can't fool me. I know exactly where we are."

"That's impressive," Dusty says. "Can you do that blindfolded?"

He's joking, and the others laugh, but I say, "Actually, yes."

No one says another word and neither do I because this house is intimidating enough without being led purposefully through gorgeous piano rooms, tea rooms, and art rooms meant to confuse my sense of direction.

I've never seen anything like it and I grew up with money. There's lush wallpaper, high ceilings, and stunning artwork. The scrollwork on the doorway is its own artwork.

We turn a corner and come to an elevator. I stop and look around. "This is down the hallway from the gym. Why did you drag me halfway around creation?"

"That's amazing," Dusty says. "Let's try that again."

"No," Justice says, and we get into the elevator. Inside, the others all put their eyes up to a reader of some kind, authorize an override for me, then spread their feet wide.

There's a change, a subtle shift in the tremor under the floor. *What's going on?* I transfer my weight to compensate just in time. The elevator drops.

The big man, Dusty, falls and clings to the sides with a, "Hate this thing."

The others in the square steel box—Sandesh, Justice, and Gracie—shift arms for balance.

I don't move. Which, judging by the looks I'm getting is as impressive as it feels.

The elevator isn't the only part of this ride making a shift. I sense the change in their estimation of me.

The elevator stops and I remain still.

Dusty rights himself with a, "You just became a legend, Honor."

Justice says, "That was weird."

"It made me swallow my candy," Gracie says.

"After you," Sandesh says, waving to let me know I can take the lead.

I'm glad they're no longer going to flank me, but I also don't think it's because they trust me more. I think it's because we're somewhere more secure than upstairs.

The elevator doors slide closed, and we walk down a gleaming white hallway until we come to a closed office door.

"Steady, soldier," Justice says, giving me an unexpectedly soft look as she knocks on the door. Somehow, I feel like her statement has nothing to do with Junior and everything to do with Tony.

Chapter 52
Tony

Bouncing on my heels despite this headache—it feels so damn good to be home—I knuckle-knock, then stroll into Momma's lower-level office.

She's on the phone, so I nod to Leland and wait. I've always loved this office. It's a warm place filled with color and kitschy decorations from around the world. Decorations that represent something from each of her children, even me.

Momma whispers into the phone.

I eavesdrop because that's why they pay me the big bucks, and I hear her say, "Yes. Keep her busy a few moments before you bring her to my office."

Hanging up, Momma motions me toward the couches set up in a conversation area.

It's meant to put me at ease, but it does the opposite. My radar goes up, and even more so when Zuri walks in.

I sit down with a, "This can't be good."

"You were always perceptive," Leland says and he's not smiling. He and Momma sit across from me, but Zuri sits next to me. She smells like chai and is holding a tumbler of coffee.

I've never seen anyone drink as much coffee as her. "I can't handle any drama right now," I say. "If there's a Band-Aid, rip it off."

Leland lifts his fingers almost dismissively. "Tony, we—"

Momma puts a hand on Leland's knee. He stills and they exchange a glance. It's a very familiar gesture, one that tells a lot about their closeness as a couple. And they *are* a couple. I've known it since that first moment I saw them together the morning Justice found me in the alley I'd taken to sleeping in, behind the restaurant where the family was having a birthday brunch. Of course, Leland and Momma had set up the brunch there, told Justice the alley was dangerous, and told her to stay out.

She'd done what Justice does: test boundaries. When I'd first found out they'd staged our meeting, I was beyond hurt. But then I'd thought about it. They might've set it up, but they couldn't have guessed that she'd grab my hand and say, "I know what I want for my birthday."

She'd claimed me and we've been best buds ever since.

My head starts to ache. Another headache. I breathe through it and focus on Momma as she lifts her hand from Leland's thigh and says, "Zuri has a theory on what has been happening to you since the procedure."

Procedure. It sounds so dainty, but I have a feeling it wasn't. I don't remember a thing about it. "You're talking about the fact that anything after Mexico is an emotional dead zone?"

Momma nods, Leland frowns, and Zuri shifts sideways toward me. "It's not dead as in gone forever. It's more... missing."

"Are you telling me my emotions from Mexico through Puerto Rico are MIA?"

She purses her lips. "I suppose that's better than dead zone. A more accurate representation would be that the emotions have been stored by your own subconscious in order to protect you."

"My brain is repressing?"

"I don't like that word ei—"

"Dammit, Z, *just* say it."

"Fine. You see, in order for memories to be reconsolidated properly, the subject must, to some extent, follow suggestion and willingly alter them. You resisted. That resistance caused a conflict that your brain couldn't correct, so it chose, instead, to protect you. That protection is a type of amnesia, an emotion-induced retrograde amnesia. It's actually quite common in trauma. The fault lies in the amygdala, and I believe I can correct it."

"No."

Zuri startles. "Hear me out. It's not as much medical as emotional tweaking. We simply need to spark the feeling that went along with the original memory. One session a simple hypnosis—"

I stand up. "No, Z. No fucking way." I back away from them, hands up. "That's enough. I'm calling enough. I might not be worthy of The Guild, but I sure as shit don't deserve this."

Do I? I'd assumed they altered my memory to save me from whatever awful shit had gone down in Mexico, something I definitely didn't want, but is that the truth? Did I do something wrong?

"Do you really feel you're unworthy of The Guild?" Momma asks.

Since I've already admitted it once to someone, it doesn't seem so hard to say it again. "Fuck yes. I screwed up. I… I knew my dad was hurting my mom. I didn't do anything to help."

"You were a child," Leland says, standing now, too. Something in his posture caved a little bit to the weight of grief. For me or for my mom, I don't know.

"He killed her, Leland. I knew it and I stayed quiet. First person I ever told was Honor." *Funny that, since I can't recall feeling the emotion of telling her, not like I feel the shame of it here.* "Keeping quiet was the most dishonorable thing I've ever done."

The room goes as quiet as a ship sunk in the deepest, coldest part of the ocean. That cold spreads through me. Now, they know.

Momma draws in a deep breath—probably to condemn me—but my ears tune in to that breath, focus on the flutter of her veil, and…

There's a knock and the door to her office swings open. Justice enters, along with Gracie, Sandesh, Dusty, and…

Honor.

Shit.

Her eyes swing to me and widen with a joy I can't ever recall seeing in anyone's face when it comes to me. Goose bumps wash down my body, or the memory of goose bumps, of looking into those eyes, of wanting her to kiss me.

I remember it, so I should feel it, but… there's nothing there now. I stand there, dumbfounded.

"You're safe," she says, then rushes over, throws her arms around me, and kisses me.

I don't intend to kiss her back, don't intend for my lips to lock on hers, for my arms to draw her closer, for that sound to roll through my throat, for my tongue to roll into her mouth, but when it happens, heat and desire unlock, and, for a moment—a flash—I feel *everything*.

The kiss goes on for a long, hot, and breathless time. I only realize this after we stop kissing, and I draw back from her to an empty room.

She realizes, too, and covers her mouth with her hand. "We cleared the room."

Fuck. She looks so happy. I'm such a jerk. An idiot. "I'm sorry." I take a step away. I feel that, feel the emptiness of her touch leaving me, feel the coldness of the space I created between us, feel wanting to kiss her again, kiss her senseless, kiss her until she melts under me, and no space exists between us, but that's lust. And I'm not that big of an asshole.

She frowns. "What's wrong?"

"I should've come to your room. Explained things. I've been a coward."

A sound like heartbreak and disbelief escapes her.

It tears a hole of shame in me as brutal and instant as lead through my gut.

She says, "So you *could've* come to my room? They *weren't* keeping you away?"

Chapter 53
Honor

I can feel the change in Tony, see it, hear it, breathe it. A thousand unmistakable cues—the way his body had felt against me, needy but not rejoicing. The way his eyes swept my face with acknowledgement but a lack of affection. The tone of his voice when he said he was sorry. The way he stepped back from me.

The way he's avoiding my question now. The way his eyes are darting around the room as if looking for a way out. Now who's the coward?

"Tony? What's going on?"

He draws a hissing breath through clenched teeth. "Yeah. That's the thing. I'm not exactly the guy you met in Puerto Rico."

"What happened to you?"

He does look at me then with surprise and a bit of wonder. "Why would you think something happened to me? Maybe I'm just different in a different space."

"What do you mean? I'm looking at your injured face." I take a step closer, and when he tries to step back, I fist the front of his black T-shirt and hold him there. "The fact that you can ask me that question makes me very nervous. I know you. Not everything about you, but the stuff that matters. What did they do to you?"

He squares his shoulders. "If by *them* you mean my family, you should back off from that."

"No. I've spent days locked in a room so secure the staff opens the doors with something embedded in their wrists. In a home that has a level to it that is so far below ground it almost gave me whiplash. Your sister Justice is scary as shit, and, you know what? She's not the only one! Someone took Junior from jail, and I have no idea where he is. I'm scared senseless right now. My whole world has changed overnight and not for the better."

"I'm sorry about Junior." His eyes soften. He massages the back of his neck. "Look, you come from a different world, different place, different rules, so this is going to sound crazy."

"Crazy, I can handle. You're a member of a global organization that does covert operations called The Spy Makers Guild. Got it. Anything else? Because it's the lies, the not knowing, that I can't put up with anymore."

"You're brave as shit. I remember that about you."

I hold back the sob that wants to break from my throat. I say, "Stop stalling."

"Okay. Well, first, it's not just a secret society. It's a global powerhouse of intellectuals and scientists, assassins and teachers, leaders, tech wizards, and spies, intent on making the world a better, fairer place."

"So, basically, you're telling me there are people out there other than law enforcement or soldiers fighting for what's right?"

"Basically. It's complex; a group that operates outside the law when powers-that-be don't have the interests of the most vulnerable populations in mind. And when you take on a mission that big, that far-reaching, the individual sometimes needs to sacrifice. That's what I did. Sacrifice. My sister, Zuri, developed a way to alter the memory of past experiences. Change them."

"She knows how to change people's memories?" I'm seized with absolute horror at the idea.

"In a nutshell, yeah. Z changed a memory of mine. Something that I needed to get rid of, something painful. I agreed to it. And that part went fine, but then something else went wrong. Not sure exactly what. Basically, everything that happened since the moment I arrived on Puerto Rico is an emotional blur."

My knees nearly buckle.

He reaches out and steadies me.

I look into his eyes, once filled with affection and warmth and remember something he'd first told me when I asked him, *"But if you feel bad, why did you leave?"*

And his answer: *"It was run or lose my mind."*

Oh. He'd been being literal. They've taken him from me and me from him. "Why would you agree to have your memory altered?"

"I don't remember."

"Then how do you know you gave them approval?"

"Because I know myself and my family."

"So, you remember me?"

"I do."

I'm crying. I can feel the warm wetness sliding down my face, and I honestly don't care. "But you don't remember how it felt to be with me?"

He shifts forward. "Don't cry."

I push his chest, so he takes a step back. I don't know why I'm mad at him, but I am. "Tell me."

"Yeah, you pegged it. I don't remember how it felt. Like, I have a visual, but not an emotional sense of it."

"Can it be fixed?"

"Maybe, but I'm not undergoing any procedures."

"Of course," I say, my heart squeezing into my throat. "You shouldn't. Is that the only way?"

When he doesn't answer, I look at him.

He swallows. "Zuri says it's like amnesia. The emotions are in there, so I guess it can come back. Maybe something can jar it loose. Maybe I just need the right experience to unlock it."

"Like the Cowardly Lion needed the right experience to unlock his courage?"

He smiles. "Sure. Why not?"

He's very blasé about the whole thing, but I guess that's the way it is if your heart isn't the one that's broken. Oh, I'm so mad at his family. "Can I help?"

"Think we just have to wait and see. You understand that, right?"

Understand? "No, I don't. The man I knew would've done anything to get back to me."

His face grows concerned, not with love or affection, the kind of concern a decent person would show for a fellow human being who is suffering. It hurts worse than if he'd showed me nothing. He says, "Could be fun to get to know each other again."

I shake my head. "I don't want *this* Tony. I want the one who was lost."

Chapter 54
Honor

After my meeting with Not-Laz, Un-Tony as I'm tempted to call him, Mukta Parish comes back into the room with a tall, gray-haired man who is introduced as Leland.

He wastes no time. "Honor," he says, "I know you've been through a lot, but in order for us to allow you to walk around the grounds, we're going to have to place a small monitoring device..."

He trails off when I hold out my wrist. "If that's the price for my freedom, you could've said so from the beginning."

Behind me, Laz—uh Tony, or whoever—says, "That was my fault."

I close my eyes and count to ten because it might've been Un-Tony's fault, but it's not *my* Tony's fault. I'm losing my mind. Pun not intended.

Ouch.

I gape at my wrist. "You could've counted to three or something."

Leland's eyebrows shoot up. "You closed your eyes."

"So, is that the signal to you that it's okay to push something into my body?"

"Okay." Laughing, Tony grabs my hand and drags me toward the door.

"I haven't given her—

"I've got her, Leland. She'll get all the instructions." Out in the hallway, he turns to me, "We have thirty minutes before a meeting with the team to discuss your cousin Junior."

"I can go?"

"You can sit in, sure."

That's a relief. I was certain they would try to keep things from me.

"Where would you like to go in the meantime? I can show you the gym, the cafeteria, the—"

"Stop," I say, because the cafeteria and the gym aren't the places I'd envisioned being with him again for the first time. And they aren't places I expect I can use to jar his memory, to bring back my Tony instead of Un-Tony. Wait. "Is there any place down here where we can be alone? No cameras? No monitors?"

He looks at me a long, long moment, then swallows and says, "You want to talk?"

That look he's giving me... He knows I don't want to talk. Desire, warmth and wet pools between my legs. "No," I say. "I want to fuck you, so that you feel something. So that you'll stop being this robot and come back to me."

He steps away. "I don't want to hurt you."

"You're not even willing to try? For me?" I sound as hurt as I feel.

For a moment, I'm sure he's going to say he isn't and I can pound sand.

Then he curses, grabs my hand, and pulls me down a different corridor to a secluded doorway.

This is bad, desperate, maybe even crazy, but I don't care. Need as sensitive and demanding as the urge to breathe pulses between my legs. I've lost everything: my business, my reputation, and part of my family.

At the steel door and the end of the corridor, Tony puts his wrist up and says, "There are only two ways into this stairwell, bottom and top. It goes up forever, and no one ever uses it."

There's a beep and a mechanical voice asking for the second person to identify themselves.

"Put your wrist up," he says, his voice tight with something that *definitely* sounds like emotion to me.

I do.

He pulls the door open, and we enter a stone tower with a spiral cement staircase going up and up, like something you might stick a missile inside of.

"For all it's high-techy-ness," he says, his eyes dipping down my body as he licks his lips, "The Guild has some archaic areas." He points up. "These stairs go to the garage. We used to have to run it as teens. Long way up. Gracie, back when she cursed, used to call it a shit-ton-of-stairs stairway."

I craned my head as we go up the stairs. "How many stairs?"

"Three hundred eight-six."

"That *is* a shit ton of stairs."

"You wanted to be"—he swallows—"alone. This is the place. No cameras. No recording devices. Come on." He drags me up the stairs. The silo resounds with our footsteps. It smells like concrete and water and compressed dirt.

"Here is good," I say, because even the feel of my G-string fabric against my slick clit is causing me to bite my tongue.

He growls a, "Trust me" and keeps hauling me up the stairs. We reach an alcove carved off the stairs, and he pushes me inside. Like the rest of the silo, the alcove is cement.

He reaches for me.

We crash together. The feel of his hard-on pressed against my body has my memory and my desire going haywire. He begins to tease my breast, unbutton my pants.

"No foreplay," I say, "Now."

I pull back from him, tug off my pants and underwear. On the way back up, I help him out of his black sweatpants and boxer briefs.

His eyes widen on a moan as I release his cock and grip it.

He says, "I hope this fucking works."

He lifts me, and I wrap my legs around him, crushing my wetness against his hardness.

"Now. I need you now." Is that my voice?

"I've got you," he says, and shoves himself inside me.

I cry out with relief and desire and so much feeling that I'm .oout to explode.

With a grunt that seems all he can manage, he presses me against the wall and begins to thrust hotly inside me.

The pressure of my orgasm is already there, *was* there the moment he grabbed my hand and began tugging me into this secluded spot, but, now, with him holding me protectively against the wall, rocking all of his hot strength deep, so deep inside me, I murmur hotly, "Yes. This. Yes."

"God, yes," he whispers as his thrusts pick up speed.

I cry out as my orgasm slams into me, and he goes wild, pumping into me at a furious pace, then kissing me as deeply and hotly as he penetrates me.

I kiss him back, dizzy with the sensations spiraling through my body.

He slams me so roughly that I grunt with each impact. He fills me so completely, he jostles every joyous nerve, searing his stroking flesh into me. I begin to come again.

The coil of energy, tight and throbbing, breaks over me, through me. I cling to his shoulders, feeling everything, helpless against his pace and the waves of pleasure.

He never slows. The wild rhythm of his body slapping into mine echoes through the stairwell as my core squeezes and pulses around all that fine, male hardness.

A moment later, he joins me with a, "Fuck," and, "Never want to stop."

Even after he's spent, he keeps rocking into me, and I know all it will take is a few moments more for him to grow hard again, for us to go again.

With a touch of my hand against his face, he slows, blinks, then grins at me like he's been caught with his hand in the cookie jar. He kisses me deep and rich, then lowers me to my feet.

Our heavy breaths echo in the stairwell, and I am so happy. I kiss his neck. "How do you feel?"

His breath is loud in my ears. "Uh—"

"Do you feel anything?"
"Uh—"
"Just say it."
"I feel satisfied." He shrugs, looks around as if for his pants. "And a little embarrassed."
I punch him.

Chapter 55
Tony

Seems like a lifetime since I conducted a mission briefing before Guild members. Standing in front of the room, I'm sort of seeing my world through Honor's eyes. Maybe it's because she's new and I'm curious about what she thinks.

Or maybe it's because of our connection in the stairwell. Best damn connection of my life.

Either way, I'm noticing tonight that the briefing room looks remarkably like a college classroom—cascading rows of seats, a podium at the front, and a huge screen behind me. Despite the school-like atmosphere, being here has to be pretty intimidating for her with nearly thirty strangers in the room. My unit—Dada, Gracie, and Justice, minus Bridget—are here, along with newbies, like Dusty and Sandesh. There's a bunch of people from internal security and seven other family members, Momma, Leland, and all three of the Troublemakers Guild.

Part of me wishes Honor weren't here. I'm not sure why because she earned her right to be here, and this is about her cousin, but there's still that voice that says her being here is wrong.

Maybe I shouldn't have had sex with her. It changed things for me in a way I can't understand. It didn't shake loose the feelings I'd had for her, but it sure planted some new ones. Maybe this woman, whose beautiful eyes turn silver like moonlight when she comes, has wormed her way into… my heart?

Nah. More like my sense of obligation or protection or both.

Once everyone has taken their seats and settled down—somewhat—I cross in front of the projected image on the large screen at the front of the room. "This is Kiki Hart—"

"Her name is Natalie Silva," Honor speaks up from her seat in the front row, taking me by surprise. Gutsy.

Seated next to her, Momma nods at Honor as if in approval.

"Sorry," I say, meaning it. God, she's beautiful. "Natalie Silva, from here on out known as Superhero Silva, made an in-depth documentary on an illicit cabal that's been operating for two decades inside and outside the movie industry."

Honor's eyebrows draw together. She knows this in general, but The Guild, thanks in large part to Ford Fairchild, has uncovered a lot in the last few days, so much of this is going to be news to her.

"We've recently learned that Carson Winthrop runs a secret organization called The Coalition." The screen flashes and a slide of corporate logos pops up. "The Coalition is a group of wealthy businessowners who manipulate government, law enforcement, and the media in order to carry out and coverup financial and sexual crimes."

There's a rumble around the room as it sinks in that The Guild might be facing its polar opposite.

"To keep members of this Coalition in line, Winthrop uses the carrot-and-stick approach." *Maybe we're not so different.* "The stick is compiling records of crimes members have been involved with. The carrot involves Winthrop's creation—then manipulation—of Hollywood stars. Apparently, no one is immune to Hollywood glamour."

"This is where my mom comes in?" Honor asks.

"Yeah. Superhero Silva found out years ago that Winthrop was grooming young actors. He made and collected stars the way you would make and collect trinkets."

"Made?" Veta asks.

"He'd identify promising actors/actresses looking for stardom. He'd groom then indoctrinate them into his business, promising and delivering the fame they sought.

"Once he'd made them famous, they became beholden to Winthrop. He has no problem directing them to endorse brands, be featured out with CEOs, or to engage in sexual activity with those heads of industry."

"Disgusting," Zuri says.

"Agreed. He owned these stars and made sure they knew it by branding them discreetly at the base of their hairline long before he'd allowed them any hint of success."

Shocked whispers float around the room.

"After they became famous, he kept them under his control through blackmail—which often centered on exposing shameful and degrading acts filmed by Carson Winthrop while they'd still been unknowns. He's a slippery fucker."

"Super slippery," Leland says. "He's been accused twice of rape. Both times, the charges were dropped and the victims paid or scared off."

Momma shifts in her chair and puts a hand on her side as if her hip hurts. "Carson Winthrop is a big donor to political parties and one of the wealthiest men in the world. No one looks into what he does because they are too busy trying to see how they can get into his pockets." She clears her throat as a few people giggle. "In addition to all this, he is a huge player in the shadow economy—laundering money."

Justice asks, "How come The Guild has never targeted this guy before?"

Momma's hands trace and retrace the edge of the desk in front of her. Her bracelets jangle. "Although we suspected him, it was decided that Winthrop was too powerful and too protected, and that going after him would endanger The Guild." She stops and glances over at Honor. "But our Superhero Silva took him on, despite how he tried to shame and debase her."

"Tell us about her film," someone shouts from the cheap seats, reminding me I'm supposed to be doing a job.

I point to Kyle from Internal. He sits at a large console filled with electronics at the center of the room. He presses some buttons.

The screen behind me changes, goes live to my sister Mila from Fantastic Five. Brown skin, playful brown eyes, and dyed curly red hair, she sits on a couch in a beachfront house in Puerto Rico. "Hello, darlings. I'm here at château witness protection with Ramon Silva and his brother, José."

"Abuelito," Honor says, leaning forward. "How are you? Are you well?"

Her grandfather moves closer to the camera, taking up a big chunk of the screen. "Estamos bien, mija. We're not allowed outside or on the beach, pero there are so many channels on the television."

"I prefer the beach," José grumps.

People in the room laugh quietly.

Shaking my head, I remind Honor, "This isn't Facetime."

She scowls at me, "Thanks, Un-Tony. I wasn't permitted a phone or even a phone call, so this is the first I'm seeing of my family in days."

Un-Tony? "Sorry about that. I'll make sure you get an encrypted phone."

Mila pulls Abuelito back so that we can see everyone. She says, "Hola, Honora. My name is Yamila, but everyone in the family calls me Mila. My wife and I are here with your charming grandfather and uncle. They've told us a lot about what went down in Puerto Rico."

"Sí, sí," Abuelito says. "Let me tell her of Ford's heroics."

Mila pats him on the shoulder. "Go ahead."

Abuelito nods once, sharply. "Honora, first you must see that I wanted to protect you."

"Not telling someone is still a lie," José says.

Abuelito frowns at his brother, and I'm sure they're going to get into it right here, but Abuelito relents with a one-shoulder shrug. "A few weeks ago, Ford arrived and informed us that your mother was..." He trails off, visibly becoming emotional.

"Was murdered," José finishes for him.

"Sí," Abuelito continues, wiping his eyes. "He also said that the man who killed her might be brought to justice if we could find a documentary your mother made about him."

Honor's face falls. She whispers, "How did Ford know any of that?"

"Speak up," someone from Internal says from the back, and I give the guy the stink eye. Internal can be so damn insensitive.

Before she can respond to the asshole, Mila answers her. "According to Ford, after Natalie found a star willing to talk on camera about Winthrop and his illegal activities, she reached out to Ford to get his help uncovering proof for her film. Ford risked his reputation, career, and life to help Natalie by giving her the financials and other information that would bring down his Uncle Winthrop and his wealthy and powerful cabal."

"And how is…" Sandesh, seated next to Justice, looks down at his tablet, reads, "Jesús Clemente, aka Junior, involved in this?"

"I asked him for help," José jumps in to answer. "Junior, my grandson, is very good with computers and puzzles. We needed someone to go through Natalie's files, pero, we didn't want Honora tied to such shady dealings."

"Really?" Honor says, and I have to agree with the outrage in her tone.

"Don't be angry, mija," Abuelito says.

José makes a shushing noise and continues, "After Junior found the film, Ford contacted Don Stoltz, a respected Pulitzer Prize-winning journalist," he says, holding up his finger like an exclamation point, "He told Don he would give him a copy if he would come to the island to collect because he dared not send it electronically."

"Of course," I jump in, "Winthrop already had a spy, Lanie, stationed there to get close to Abuelito and uncover the film."

"She was too young for me," Abuelito says. "I suspected her all along."

Not touching *that*. "When Ford first showed up, Lanie knew him and was suspicious, so she sent Winthrop a message.

Knowing of Ford's connection to Honor, Winthrop sent Ford a very specific message, threatening Honor's life if he dared move against him."

"Ford was very brave to come to us and tell us of Winthrop," Abuelito says. "Fearing for Honor, he also tried to get her to leave by secretly offering her money for the inn. He wanted to keep her safe from Winthrop and any fallout when we released the film."

"I would never have considered that offer if I'd known it was him," José says.

"Which is why he kept it a secret," I say, changing the slide, so it shows a picture of Bud. I run down his particulars and tell the group that he'd planned on hurting Honor on the trip as a message to Ford, and blame it on her own lack of guides. "Junior was warned something might go down on one of the tours, so, when the guides didn't show, including Tito—who was killed for refusing to quit his job—Junior was on high alert. According to Abuelito, Junior became suspicious of Bud because he kept asking questions about Natalie and Honor."

"Junior put that broken clip on him on purpose?" Honor says, slapping both hands to her face.

"He panicked," Abuelito says. "He didn't know what else to do. Ford had said something bad might happen. He feared the man would murder you like your mother."

"And when he drove into the lodge, was that panic, too?" Honor asks.

"It'll make sense in a sec," I say. Trying to keep not one but *two* families in line isn't easy here. "After the near accident on the climb, your grandfather and great-uncle—"

"Uncle is fine," José says.

"Your grandfather and uncle," I continue, "made a plan to hand off the film to Don, who'd shown up at Loco for Cocoa with his son, Cole, trying to make it look like he was on vacation."

"Why not call some authorities? The FBI?" Dusty asks, crossing his arms in front of his chest.

"Natalie didn't trust the authorities," Abuelito says. "She

was determined to put it out there first, so it would all be in the public eye, and I would honor her wishes."

I continue where I left off. "Enter our side player. That piece of the puzzle no one could've foreseen. Sick of his dad's helicopter parenting, Cole, who'd learned of his father's purpose for being there, intercepted Junior's note about meeting him in the jungle, sets outs to prove himself to his father, and goes to meet him."

"Oh, pobrecito niño," Honor says, putting a hand to her lip.

"That poor kid helped push everything out into the open," I tell her. "Not on purpose, but when he went missing, Lanie was paying attention. She did research on Don, discovered who he was, and realized she could no longer afford to work her way into the family's good graces, hoping to get the film. She needed to move fast. She sent someone to break into Honor's room."

"After that," José says, "we all became very afraid, but Junior most of all. He knew of the offer on the property—though none of us knew it was from Ford—and he tried to push you to accept by putting the snake, already milked of its venom, into your car. He thought you'd be safer if you took the money and left."

"I could've crashed," Honor says, incredulous. "And why make my car overheat?"

José shakes his head with a frown. "It's not his fault your car is no good."

"What about my store? Why put ants in there?"

"Lo siento mucho," José says, his cheeks going red and his voice lowering. "I thought you would be more likely to sell as well."

Honor rolls her eyes and I can't help remembering that I'd warned her it might be family.

She says, "So Junior *did* crash into the lodge on purpose?"

"He drove into it because he feared for his own life!" José says, and I can't recall ever seeing him so animated. He shifts forward, eyes bright. It's the first time he's ever reminded me of his brother. "You see, he knew Winthrop would now send people for the film. We all knew. But Junior was in the most danger because, to protect us, he'd destroyed most of Natalie's clues to find the film."

He sits back as if that settles that.

Mila interrupts with, "All, we're running up against our security protocols. I'm cutting this."

"Adios," Abuelito says. "Te amo."

"Te amo," Honor says, waving. The screen winks out.

Seeing the confused faces of my team, I recap, "What José was getting at is that Junior destroyed all clues to find Natalie's film, memorized them, and is now the only person who knows how to access it. He planned on leaving the day of the last tour—hoped, in fact, I'd be his replacement and he could take off, hide, and pass the film to Don. When I left, he panicked and drove the tour truck into the lodge, thinking he'd be safest in jail. And that's when... well, our family walked into the picture."

"Looks like someone walked into the picture all over your face," Veta says. There's laughter along with howls of protest.

I ignore it, because I don't want to explain that I got into it with Dusty after I accidentally shot Gracie with mace. I'd thought she'd been a danger to me and had reacted before I saw her. My training is usually much better than that. My head starts to pound, and I try to relax past it. Gracie forgave me, so it's all good.

"Do we suspect," Sandesh speaks up through the noise, "that Junior is on Winthrop's island?"

"That's the best guess," I say. "Junior smartly refused bail money from Ford, then later from some anonymous source we suspect was Lanie. The next night, according to authorities, he supposedly *escaped* from prison. No one can say how, because the cameras mysteriously stopped working."

"Someone was paid off," Honor says, "then took Junior from jail."

"Likely." The image on the screen flips to the island. I point to Gracie, who has her laptop open in front of her and is clicking away, a Jolly Rancher gripped between her front teeth.

She sucks the candy into her mouth. "Winthrop's island is outside of Estonia. It's sixty acres… looks pretty isolated."

"An isolated island? Go figure," Dusty says, jostling her shoulder, making her smile.

That catches me off guard and stops me for a moment. I'd never have guessed it. They're good together. Gracie smiles a lot with him and laughs, too. Like Honor and I did. A stab of loss hits me clean in the gut, knocking me for an emotional loop.

"So, what's our plan to rescue Junior?" Honor says, drawing me back to more important matters.

Our plan?

Chapter 56
Tony

Standing in front of the meeting room, I'm scrambling for a reply to Honor when the screen behind me changes to a different aerial of the island.

"Yee-haw!" Justice exclaims. "Always wanted to invade an island."

There's chuckling around the room. I'd forgotten how difficult it is to get through these meetings.

I say, "We have a rundown of the security on the island from Internal. Familiarize yourselves with it. The island has barriers, but also opportunities. Much easier to disrupt the grid because it's all tied into itself. Gracie has agreed to be our special operator by providing on-site drones."

Gracie does a raise-the-roof motion, with the palms of her hands pumping toward the sky.

I keep going. "Eugie from Internal will be stationed off-island, but will see to security and cyber."

There's a smattering of applause from some internal folks and Eugie clasps her hands into a fist, then pumps them over her head like a champ in a ring. There's always going to be that competition between Internal and family operators, so I ignore it.

"The tactical team won't need to be large, not with support from Gracie and Eugie, and we'll keep the Troublemakers as backup. So two volunteers from Internal, Justice, and I can—"

"Whoa, there, son," Dusty interrupts. "Sandesh and I are along for this ride. Don't count us out now."

"Wouldn't miss it," Sandesh adds.

I blink at them. I've never been on a mission with more men than women. It feels wrong. I want to argue that they're not actually Guild members. They're spouses, and I've never heard of a Guild spouse, other than helping with logistics or safehouses, being part of a rescue mission. But why take the heat? I say, "Momma has final say on the team. That's her call."

Momma nods thoughtfully. "I welcome their expertise."

"Really?" There's a ripple of laughter. "Fine, you maniacs. Me, Gracie, Dusty, Sandesh, and Justice—"

"Hold on," Honor says standing up. "What about me? You act like I'm not participating in the mission."

I open my mouth to gently and respectfully tell her that it isn't a good idea. That she isn't prepared. That she's still recovering. That she doesn't have the weapons training. But what comes out is, "That's because you sure-as-shit are not."

The room bursts with, "Whoa!" and comments like, "He told you!" and "Don't take that from him!"

These people. They love to turn the volume up on awkward situations. I probably could've used nicer words. I have no idea where all this anger is coming from.

Challenged, Honor puts her hands on hips. "I'm going. I owe it to my mother, my uncle, and my grandfather, to Ford, and to Junior, who repeatedly tried to scare me away to save me."

I rub my face and take a breath to calm myself. I like how, even though her family tried to scare her off, she understands why they did it.

Wait. My head is fucking killing me. I just need a second, so I can shut her down gently this time.

"Are you saying," Zuri says, standing from her spot, "that you wish to be considered for a place in The Guild?"

Really? "What the fuck, Z?"

Guild rule number one: if a woman rescued by The Guild asks to join, shows any real kind of potential, they are considered.

Honor's head spins from Zuri to me. She catches on quick

and her eyes go wide. "That's exactly what I'm saying. I wish to join The Guild."

"What could you provide the mission?" Momma asks.

Heat flushes along my neck and a dull throb starts in my head. Momma is seriously considering her?

Okay. Don't panic. Even if she became a member, she'd need more training. The Guild doesn't send lambs to the slaughter. That's another rule. That rule… Fucking headache now.

Honor turns to Momma. "I'm an excellent shot. Olympic level."

Exaggerate much? "You were an alternate on the Olympic *archery* team."

"My skills transfer to other weapons, and I've trained extensively with La—Tony. The real Tony."

"The real Tony?"

"Those skills helped me rescue my family from the middle of multiple armed men."

I can't help the annoyed breath. "Looks like *you* were rescued from where I was dropping in."

She sticks out her chin. "And I've been to the island."

She has? "You've been to the island?"

"When I was ten. Before my mother's second movie started filming, I was there with her for a working vacation. My mom worked; I hung out. We were there for a week."

"How much could you remember from that?" Justice says and I cringe. I'm sure Honor remembers all of it.

"I remember every inch perfectly, and assuming it hasn't been updated since, I can tell you things about the house you won't otherwise know. I know, for example, that there are three saferooms."

A ball of intense panic explodes in my chest. I have no idea where it came from, but the beat keeps time with the headache pulsing in my skull.

"You're injured." My breathing feels labored. "Your arm."

"As her physician, I think she can go," Zuri says.

I shake my head. I have to stop this. "Honor, do you really want to come on an extraction against highly-trained security, knowing how difficult it will be, knowing you could put the entire team in jeopardy and maybe get someone killed?"

I relax back on my heels. She can't push it now. Score one for peer pressure.

The room stills, waits for her to answer.

Not me. I know her answer.

She swishes her jaw as if considering. "It'll be dangerous with or without me."

"What?"

"I agree with Zuri," Momma says. "I'm going to approve this candidate for The Guild and give her full sanction for the mission."

I see red. It punches up through my mind and flushes through my body. My head starts to pound. This isn't right. I grind my teeth.

"No," I say. "I won't let this happen." Not after... my mom and... and..."

"Are you okay?" Honor asks, sliding over to me. "Your nose is bleeding."

I wipe it. Shit. I'm blowing a gasket. "Look, Honor—"

She puts up her hand up in a stop-talking-and-listen gesture. Softly, so soft I have to strain to hear, she says, "I can move silently through the house. A home I remember. Junior will recognize and trust me. I know you're confused, but, right now, without thinking too much about it, what does your gut say about me? Can you trust me?"

The heat in my face and head diminishes. Somehow, I trust this woman. I'd trust her with my life. Is that a feeling? Maybe. Or maybe it's just observation. "It says I can trust you."

She nods. "Hundred percent. Never doubt it."

Warmth suffuses my body. This has happened before. I remember it. More importantly, I remember the feel of it.

Honor goes back to her seat and I glace over at Momma. Is it my imagination or do her eyes look smug?

Chapter 57
Honor

Night. Darkness. The roll of the ocean. None of these things are new or unusual or disconcerting to me normally, but, normally, I'm not wearing full camo, crouched and straddling the side of an inflatable boat skimming silently though the ocean, heading toward a private island off the coast of Estonia.

In their helmets, dark clothes, camouflaged faces, and the spray of ocean, I can barely make out Justice and Gracie who are crouched low like me, holding onto the craft's tethers. Dusty and Sandesh are stationed at the front as some kind of counterbalance for people and equipment. Tony mans the near-silent electric motor. The only light is distant and comes from the coast of Estonia's rocky cliffs that are lit with regular life—homes, dinner, family, and safety.

This is more than I'd bargained for. Fear, dry throat, and pounding heart make everything slightly disorienting in the moonless, starless night.

What am I doing?

I'd started out feeling like I belonged on this mission because it was my family, my cousin, and my mother who'd sacrificed to see the truth get out.

But, as Tony cuts the motor, pulls the propeller out of the water, as waves lap and silence stretches and everyone grabs paddles—with me a second slower—I realize I've acted rashly, imagining myself better equipped than I actually am.

I shouldn't be here. I've underestimated this group's

organization, this mission, and my place in it. Training, experience with weapons, experience keeping panic at bay and my mind focused are all things I'm new at.

If it weren't for Junior needing me and Mukta's confidence in me, I might actually choose to stay on the inflatable.

I cling to Momma's words to me before I left: "I am an excellent judge of people, and I know there is nothing that will happen during this mission that you cannot handle."

I believe her. She's smart and has amazing connections, as proven by where our team launched from—the *Oceanic Voyager*, a marine biology research vessel that is part of Parish Holdings. All but a few of the crew were given time off, so the Parish "executives" could arrive and "survey" the project.

The seven team members still on the boat are either from Internal and serve as our tech team or are part of the Troublemakers Guild. I have to find out how they decided on the names for the family units.

"Almost there," Eugie says in my earpiece, giving us calm and professional instructions. "You're a hundred yards out. All quiet on the island."

Having this information makes me feel better, like I have a superpower since they're using satellite to give real-time information on island activity. It also helps compensate for the fact that, unlike the others, I'm not wearing night vision goggles.

Un-Tony tried repeatedly to get me to wear them, saying, "We have eyes in the sky. Small floating drones that will skim our paths, give us real-time information about what's coming up ahead. If you wear the NVG, that visual will be in the corner of your goggles."

I tried lowering them from my helmet to ride in front of my eyes, but they made me sick and disoriented.

The boat rocks up one last wave before Dusty and Sandesh jump from the bow and guide us out of the water. Once the rubber meets the resistance of the sand, I fling myself over the side with the others, grab one of the thick handles, lift and pull, along with everyone else. Even with six people carrying it into the tree line, this thing weighs a ton.

Under the cover of the trees, Tony pulls out weapons and tools from storage containers on the inflatable as the team dons protective body armor.

I've been told what to do, but I'm really watching everyone else to make sure I'm not screwing up. At least I'm keeping up, and when they stalk forward in silence, so do I.

Now that I'm back on land, I feel a sense of confidence again. I keep my eyes on the house in the distance, praying Junior is okay, praying we're not too late.

Hold on, Junior. We're coming for you.

Chapter 58
Tony

My still unmanageable anger at having Honor with us means I'm focused on her, on the economy of her movements, her instinctual application of aggressive and protective measures. It actually helps to calm me down. Does she even recognize how amazing she is? The rest of us have NVGs, and she's still keeping up with us.

When we reach the outskirts of the house, out of range of where the floodlights illuminate the dark, Sandesh and Justice move off to cover our exit point and to set J up as sniper. Dusty takes our six.

Getting ready to make our move into the house, I flinch when I hear Gracie giving Honor instructions that any field operative should know like the back of her hand.

Shit. There's that anger again. I'm so furious I seriously feel like I might puke. That's not going to keep anyone safe.

"Thanks," Honor says.

"You got this," Gracie whispers. Crouching down, she puts two small devices on the ground, pulls her handheld out, then signals for the light-refracting blanket.

I pull the square sheet from my pocket and spread it over her. She'll be invisible here as she operates the mini drones. The drones silently lift off and fly forward.

It takes only a minute or two before images appear in the corner of my glasses. Not green-gray images either—full spectrum, vivid images. I'm impressed. The drones are tiny, nearly invisible, so light they can land on a twig, and soundless.

"Where'd you get these things?" I whisper to her, squatting outside the blanket.

"Spoils of war from a prior mission."

"War?"

"Someone was trying to kill me. Working with Internal, I helped adapt these babies for our use."

"*Kill* you? Shit. I can't leave this family alone for a minute."

She snorts, then says, "Honor, you were right. There's a security-enabled doggy door."

In the corner of my glasses, the drone blinks red a few times and the doggy door swings open. Gracie flies the drone inside. If not for Honor knowing about that door, Gracie would've had to wait for someone to exit. It would've meant a bigger chance of the mini drone being spotted.

The interior of the home—milled beams, marble floor, white walls with expensive artwork—appears in my video feed. She's great at this. Still… "Don't get careless, G."

"I've been flying them on campus for months and was only spotted once."

"Veta?"

She huffs a laugh. "Yeah."

The mini floats up the staircase, turns down one hall, then a second. This is where thermal spectral analysis indicates Junior is being held.

I hold my breath.

"Got him," Gracie says. "Unless you can think of another reason for a guard to be posted at that door."

"Not without Winthrop or any family being here. They wouldn't waste the manpower." The island home is staffed year-round by fourteen security forces, with half of them working nights. Intel says they've added five more with Junior here, but those are likely to be centered around the prisoner. "Good job. Get that thing out of there."

"Nope. This one's staying." She parks the mini inside a plant in the hall. The second mini drone lifts off.

I click my mic. "What do you see, J?"

"A patrol just passed, so we have ten minutes before the next one hits. I've got a visual on the barracks. If things go south, I'll lay down enough cover fire that, unless they're walking stupid, they'll hunker down."

"I'll handle the walking stupid," Sandesh says.

"Sounds like we don't have to worry about reinforcements," Dusty says casually, like we break in and take on rich psychos every day of the week.

Okay, we've got experience.

"Internal, what's our status on the alarm and cameras?"

"I'm here," Eugie says, though the static on the line lets me know she's actually still on the boat. "I'll be jamming their tech in five, four, three, two…"

Taking the lead, I signal the go-ahead for my team. Honor follows and Dusty takes up the rear. Feels weird to be in full camo and heavily armed in a place like this, your typical billionaire beach house—lots of white, Hamptons-esque pillars, cedar shingles, large sliding glass panels. Well, typical if you don't take into account the guards with AK-47s.

At my lead, my team moves forward with AR-15s at the ready. Adrenaline pumps through my body, and I let my mind ride the focus without giving into the anxiety.

I skirt the back patio, move to the corner, pivot off my left foot, then round the corner.

Guard.

I nail him in the throat with the point of my weapon. He jerks back, and I hit him across his face with the butt of my rifle.

"Clear."

The others follow with Dusty stopping to drag the guard I took down behind a storage container. As we move, I have to check twice to make sure Honor is still directly behind me. Damn. Her stealth is worth its weight in gold.

Nearly at the entry point, I hold the team up when a guard

comes out the door to grab a smoke. His eyes still adjusting to the darkness, not to mention the flash of that lighter, he nearly walks into me.

He doesn't have time to even moan. I lay him on the ground and snuff out his dropped cigarette with my boot. So far, we are picture-perfect.

Beep! Beep! The alarm goes off and blast shields start to slide slowly down over the doors and windows.

"Eugie, the shields!"

The shields stop and the alarm goes silent. Through my earpiece she says, "You've got five minutes. Maybe."

An inside guard, responding to the alarm, spots us and opens fire.

Chapter 59
Honor

I'm in a firefight, crouched uselessly by the side of the house as Tony and Dusty try to shoot our way inside. I'm pretty sure I'm going to die.

Bullets ricochets off the quarter-lowered metal shields with white hot flashes of light. Gunpowder and salt coat the air, a mix of smells my brain can't seem to harmonize. I'm frozen in fear.

Tony tosses a smoke bomb to cover our movements. I have to get into the house and get to Junior, but I know in my bones that, if I try to get in this way, I will be shot.

Wait. There's another entrance near the laundry room—the exact opposite way of this firefight.

"Gracie," I breathe into my mic. "Doggy door."

"Smart. Drone's coming," she says.

I run and spot the drone, which is so tiny it almost seems like a play of light, a second before the doggy door opens. I crawl through, grateful the owner has a love for standard poodles.

Inside, I run down the hall toward where recon showed us Junior was being held. According to recon, the only people at the home right now are armed guards and Junior.

"Follow the bouncing ball to your left," Gracie says, and I trail after the small drone floating in front of me down the corridor. "And don't worry, Eugie disabled the inside cameras."

"That's what triggered the alarm," Eugie says. "I should've waited until I was sure you all had made it inside." She's admitting this to me, and I instinctually guess why. Because she wants me to know we all screw up, and that, even if I do, I have to keep going.

The drone disappears around a corner and Gracie says, "Hold up. There are two armed guards ahead. You can circle around for the back stairs."

The back stairs? That will take way too long. And according to intel, Junior is up these stairs, down one hallway, and a few short feet to the right.

I peek around the corner and see that the guards have their backs turned to me, looking at some kind of tablet between them.

I inch forward. Gracie's startled hiss tickles my ear, but I don't let her distract me. I move silently across the marble foyer, so close to the armed guards, I can see a loose thread on one of their uniforms. So close I can hear the swipe of fingers on glass. So close, if they turned right now, they could reach out and grab me without taking a single step.

I hit the stairs, proceed up to the hallway.

"You're amazing," Eugie says, and she sounds breathless.

It doesn't feel amazing. It feels like I've been given the basketball in a big game and am driving down the court with no idea how to make a shot.

Adrenaline pumps through my body. Sweat drips along my face and soaks into my collar. I inch up to the corner of the hallway where Junior is being kept.

A cry of pain that's both shocking and gut-wrenching fills the hall. It's Junior. I haven't heard him in pain like that since we were children and he broke his ankle jumping from a tree.

"There's one guard in front of the room," Gracie says. "Hold. Wait. Now go. Fire!"

Imagining I'm holding a bow, I bring my weapon around the corner and stop. The guard isn't looking my way. I don't have to fire. I inch forward, my heart thudding, the butt of my weapon raised. This is so stupid. I know it's stupid, but if I don't have to kill anyone, I don't want to. I slam my weapon against his head, and he falls to the ground.

Blood gushes from the back of his skull. My stomach pitches and saliva floods my mouth. As silent as the shudder wracking my body, I push down on the door handle. "G, it's locked."

"Search the guard."

Keeping my eyes from his pale face, I drop to my knees and search his pockets. Nothing.

"What's that around his neck?" Gracie asks.

Junior cries out again. Cold chills grip my body.

Hold on. I'm here. I'm here.

I grab for the security badge around the guard's neck, rip it off, swipe it across a pad at the door, and race inside just as Gracie yells, "Don't go in like that!"

Chapter 60
Tony

Whatever Eugie was doing to keep the blast doors open, it looks like they kicked her out. The doors start to lower again.

The good news is that Justice must be keeping the reinforcements from leaving the barracks, because the numbers are dwindling outside of Winthrop's island home.

Dusty and I face off against the last three guards. I take one out with a series of quick, bone-breaking strikes to his face and turn to see Dusty knock out one, grab the arm of another, and smash the guy headfirst into the side of the house. The guy drops as the metal shields fall close over our entry point. *Shit.*

My earpiece crackles. "Head south. I'm holding a gate," Eugie says.

Dusty and I run. There's gunfire behind me. "Go!" he yells, as he drops to his knee and brings up his weapon to engage.

I race toward the large sliding glass doors, and the sputtering shield that looks like it's fighting itself.

Please don't let that glass be bulletproof. I shoot and the glass shatters. I launch through the falling debris, flying like Superman under the grate as it slams shut on the back of my heel.

Fuck. Fuck. I twist, undo my laces, and yank my heel from my shoe. Thanks to the metal of my boot, I only lost a sock and a chunk of skin pulling my foot out, but I'm bleeding and it hurts like hell.

And I lost my earpiece. I push it back inside.

"Don't go in like that!"

Gracie? Gunfire. What's going on? I click my mic. "Gracie, you got eyes on the prize?"

Silence. I clench my teeth. "What's going on, G?"

"Keep the channel clear."

"G—"

"Shut the fuck up, Tony."

Did Gracie curse? Holy shit. Blood pouring down my arch, I run on the balls of my foot with my heart pounding in my throat. I shouldn't have let Honor come. I should've fought Momma harder on this situation—it's as fucked up as...

My earpiece crackles. "Go left. There's a hallway that leads to the front stairs. There're two guards at the top of the landing. They're waiting in case Honor exits that way."

In *case* Honor exits? I follow her instructions. Scanning, the stairs I spot the two guards and manage to shoot one from here before either sees me.

The other sinks to a knee and swings his weapon in my direction. With Gracie's drone hovering near him, I can see my attack point like a pool player can line up a perfect shot.

I fire low, lower than would normally seem wise, but, sure enough, there's a pop of red and a groan.

Gracie's drone confirms the guy is not only down but out.

I climb the stairs, stepping over the bodies, then run down the hall.

I'm so focused on the doorway where I know Junior is that it takes me a second to realize the wall to my right has swung open. There's an AK in in my face.

I grab the barrel, spin into the weapon, hit the guy in the nose, jerk the weapon free, and knock the man out with the butt of his own weapon.

Then I run down the hall and move into the room in time to see a man shoot Honor in the chest.

Chapter 61
Honor

Gracie's warning comes a beat too late. It's echoing in my ears as I enter the room and find Junior tied to a chair next to what looks like a gurney. His face is slick with blood. His hair is plastered with sweat. The smell of burnt skin and burnt hair is everywhere.

I rush to him, begin to untie him. I'm operating with a kind of panicked tunnel vision. I realize this and turn to clear the room. A fist lands in my face. I go sprawling.

No time to consider my actions or their impact, I roll out of the way of the next strike, pull my sidearm, and shoot the man under his jaw. Blood, like warm soup, splatters. I swing my gun around to the other man in the room. He has no weapon. He's holding a device attached to wires that run to tongs hooked to Junior's skin.

"*Honor, behind you*," Gracie says.

I turn to see the guard from the hall, with blood running down his face. You'd think I'd have learned my lesson before when I hit someone in the head on Tony's boat.

His hit cracks my cheek, sends me floating to the floor in a slow, stunned moment of absolute silence.

When I hit, I'm jolted into action. Fast as a storm, I kick with brutal force against the man's knee. There's a crunch of bone and a tear of ligaments. The man cries out and drops to the ground, curling in on himself in pain. I swing my gun around to find the last man, the man with the box, now holding a gun.

He shoots. There's a crack of noise then the jarring impact to my flesh as the bullet hits.

I fall to the ground when I hear Tony's yell at nearly the same instant he fires at Box Man—*bam, bam, bam.*

I'm on the ground looking up when Tony comes to check on me. Stunned, the impact of the bullets expanding in waves of pain throughout my chest, I try to catch air.

His hands are tearing at my chest. "Were you hit? Fuck. Fuck."

Still gasping for breath, I put my hands over his. Tony. Not Un-Tony. I know the difference. "Body armor…" I gasp as pain, worse than my inability to suck in enough air, lances my heart. "Help Junior."

His eyes wild, he pulls me tight, hugs me hard. "I love you, I love you, I love you." He kisses me over and over on my forehead.

"You came back to me," I want to say, but can't get the words out.

"Get this off!" Junior cries, and Tony lets me go then, crawls over to my cousin.

Junior moans as Tony detaches the electrodes pinching his skin before passing out. Tony turns to me. "I'm going to have to carry him. Can you take point?"

Pain rips through my chest as I get to one knee and rise to standing. I fight the spasms in my shaking arms and bring my gun around. "Yes."

With Junior in a fireman's carry over Tony's shoulders, I stalk down the hallway.

"Hall's empty," Gracie says. *"Head straight for the front door."*

I lead us down and stop at the front door. "Gracie, how do we get out?"

"Stand back," she says, "Far back. Dusty has the rocket launcher aimed at the front door."

Tony groans and we run back up the stairs. It's then that I notice he's missing a shoe and the back of his foot is bleeding badly.

At the top of the stairs, Tony falls to a knee with Junior swinging on his back like a sack.

I drop beside them.

BOOM!

Crashing glass, falling debris, and smoke fill the front hall.

My ears are ringing, and I'm coughing up a lung as I brush away dust and debris. Tony rolls to sitting. He repositions Junior then stands.

Trembling, I get to my own feet and stagger down the stairs. I have no idea how Tony manages to move with Junior, but he does.

At the bottom of the stairs, Dusty comes in. "Hand him over," he tells Tony, taking Junior onto his back, keeping one hand across Junior's unconscious body. He looks at Tony. "You good?"

"Fine." Tony snorts. "Could've carried him the whole way."

Dusty smirks. "Look after Honor. I got him."

Tony nods, but I have never seen him so pale.

In the earpiece Sandesh says, *"We're leaving the barracks, which means we're going to have company."*

We hustle out of the house and toward the beach.

Chapter 62
Tony

As we race back through the woods to collect Gracie and grab the boat, I barely keep control of the flood of emotions and memories.

Seeing Honor shot at, knowing I was too late, knowing I would be responsible for her death, had broken the wall in my mind. Enough that I remember everything—faking my death, trying to keep J alive, and falling in love with Honor.

I don't just remember it. I'm bombarded by feelings and images and truths. I remember.

The anomaly Zuri mentioned wasn't an accident; I'd fought her.

After Zuri had snapped the M-erasure shield over my face, no matter how I'd blinked, I hadn't been able to see a thing.

I'd heard Momma and Zuri working. They were good together, practiced, professional.

"I am injecting the serum," Zuri had said.

A strong hand had gripped mine. Not Zuri's. Not Momma's. Leland's.

The machine had begun to buzz, the medication had rushed through me, first, with intense pain, then warmth. I'd felt myself sinking, down and down and down, out of my body into a place of total blackness.

Zuri's soft, coaxing, cajoling voice had spoken to me through the darkness. She'd asked questions about Mexico. I'd answered, and the memories had floated in front of me, visually there, but, somehow, not part of me. Like watching tv.

I'd watched as I'd entered Walid's compound, watched as the alarm had one off, as the whole plan had backfired. Fuck.

I'd begun to panic in the M-erasure chair.

I'd promised myself when I'd come to the Mantua Home that I'd never stand by and let someone I love be hurt when I could do something about it. One for all. All for one. I'd had to save J.

Zuri had spoken calmly, told me it was okay. Justice could and would take care of herself.

A buzzing had increased in my head, distancing me from my emotions along with the images.

I'd suddenly realized Z was right; Justice could take care of herself. And the dream of her in danger and of me stopping it, of conspiring to stop it... None of that had ever happened.

I'd let it all go and it'd felt so damn good. It'd felt amazing not to have that responsibility. Amazing to watch as the movie had rewritten itself, changing everything. I'd let Zuri's soft, calm voice wash over me, reinvent history, because it had been so much better than the fucking guilt.

The movie had played before me, and I'd watched as I'd left my sisters with a hug and sailed off with their blessing.

Zuri had even said, "You sail to an island. To Dominica. A vacation—even from your identity. They called you Laz. You met someone. Tell me about her. Where were you when you first met Honor? When you first kissed?"

That's when I'd resisted. That's when I'd fought back. I couldn't let them change even a second of those memories.

I'd said, "I don't remember."

A shock had ripped through my head. I'd cursed, loudly. It'd really fucking hurt.

Zuri's voice again, soft and gentle, had said, "This is very important. Tell me about Honor, about being Laz."

"Go fuck yourself."

Another hot shock had hit that had sent me doubling down on my resistance.

She'd tried again and again, but I wouldn't give in. Frustrated, she'd pulled back and I'd won. Keeping Honor for myself had interrupted the procedure, kept my emotions from me for a time, but it's also allowed the break that let me get myself back, all of me. No more *Un-Tony* as Honor had called me. I have all my memories and I intend on keeping them.

Even if, right now, it's all a bit much. The rush of emotion nearly drowns me with the thought that now, after getting her back, I could lose Honor again. I won't fucking let that happen.

We run through the trees. Through my night vision goggles, the surreal world pitches with my strides, but my eyes stay on Honor's running form. *She's alive.*

The only thing that tempers my rage at Momma right now is that. And my love for her. Because I know, like I know my mother, that Momma sending Honor here was something she did to try to jolt my emotions, hoping to give me back what had been lost.

So like Momma. The end always justifies the means.

But not for me. Honor's life is worth so much more than that.

We get to the inflatable and Dusty deposits Junior into the boat.

Each of us takes a handle on the inflatable and, like a well-oiled machine, one that fears for its ever-loving life, we book ass out of the woods. We hit the sand and splash into the water. Not as smooth as when we'd come in, but a hell of a lot faster.

The resistance of the ocean swells pushes us, but we launch, jump into the boat, and grab paddles. We clear the waves quickly, get far enough out that I can engage the motor. I start it up and swing us around.

The *whoop* of the blades hits my ears a second before the copter swoops down, lights on, gunner out. We had intel that they had a helo, but I can't believe they got it in the air so fast.

Near simultaneously, from around a corner of the island, a boat full of guards—likely the pissed-off guards Justice held off—zips forward.

We're sitting ducks, caught between the helo and the boat. I'm pushing everything I can into the motor. It's not enough.

Justice brings her weapon around for an impossible shot at the boat, but then I hear a cheerful, "Hey, brother, get out of my way, so I can get at the boat on your six."

A stupid grin on my face, I veer left. "Go for it, Veta," I say, and speed up as the helo, flying low, stops the boat chasing us with a spray of bullets.

Epilogue
Honor

Eight Months Later

Fire dances and crackles in the deeply dug firepit as my toes flick sand and I snuggle closer to Tony. Moonlight stretches across the ocean. A warm breeze drifts along the Puerto Rican beach, carrying the smell of sautéed onions along with chicken, seafood, and pork from the house.

That's not the only thing drifting down from the house. I can hear Abuelito and José arguing over the paella cooking in a large flat pan over an open flame. I smile to myself as Junior berates them with, "¡Tomaría menos tiempo si dejaras de discutir!"

I laugh into Tony's bare shoulder because a lot of things, including the food, would take less time if it weren't for their arguing. "It smells so good," I say, and there are murmurs of assent from his sisters and their spouses sharing the fire with us.

Propped up by one hand in the sand, Tony runs a finger along the ring on my finger, breaths in deeply. "I can only smell cocoa and salt."

He's so cute. "That's because I've spent the last few days making chocolate for our wedding guests and we're sitting on a beach."

"No." He runs his nose along my cheek, nibbles my ear. "You always smell of cocoa."

"I have no idea if that's true, but there are worse things to smell like."

"Mmmm, that's true, Ojos Plateados," he rumbles into my ear. The growl in his voice when he calls me Silver Eyes sends an involuntary squeeze between my thighs. I have an almost Pavlovian response to *that* noise from *this* man. A well-learned response that I'm determined to repress until after the wedding.

I kiss his collarbone. "It's one more night," I whisper. "Stop doing that to me."

"I don't have to play fair. I'm not the one who made the ridiculous decision that has me in a bachelor bed until tomorrow night."

I have to laugh. He's right. I have no idea why I decided that we had to spend the week before our wedding in separate beds. Oh… *that* nibbling feels good.

I flick my head to the side, and he lets go of my ear with a groan. *Subject change.* "The investigation on Winthrop's cabal is still sending rats scurrying?"

He stares at me in a way that says he knows I'm trying to distract him. He shrugs. "More than ever since his trial started." He pulls me closer, as if hoping to ground me here. "As the daughter of the woman who broke this thing wide open, you're going to have to come out of hiding soon. You ready?"

Am I? For a time, hiding from the spotlight had been necessary. I needed the time to come to grips with what happened on the island, to spend time with Ford, his wife, and his daughter—my little sister, Suri. To help Abuelito and José fix up Loco for Cocoa to get it ready for sale.

Angelica, who, it turns out, José was dating, found us a real buyer, a local conservationist group. They're going to help me continue to bring cocoa trees back to the island and to produce my chocolate. If there's one thing I've learned from Tony and his family, it's that you need a team.

My team will do their part, and I'll do what I can to make dark chocolate from here a global phenomenon, which means dividing my time—our time—between the States and Puerto Rico. A plus for me since I'll have plenty of time with my family.

Abuelito and José have moved to San Juan to the home that Mila called Chateau Witness Protection—a home Momma sold to Abuelito and José for an incredibly reasonable price. I think she was trying to make amends for letting me go on that mission, though it will take more than that to get Tony over it.

That's another reason I needed time out of the spotlight—to help Tony heal and to get to know his family and The Guild. Enough time that I realized that I, like Bridget, am a member of The Guild, but not one who goes on special operations. I'd rather be a chocolatier. Well, among other roles.

"I'm ready to stand in Mom's shoes," I tell him. "I'm ready to accept that place, go in front of cameras, and tell people what we've learned about Winthrop's cabal, about Mom's death and Lex's death, as long as Junior is kept out of the limelight."

"He will be. There's enough evidence without his testimony," he says, touching my arm. He runs fingers up and down it, then kisses me lightly on my cheek. "Are you okay with your cousin being accepted into The Guild?"

"Not really, but it's his choice, and he does seem to fit in."

"He has some mad skills."

"Which, he'll surely tell you himself," Dusty says from his place across the fire.

We all laugh. It makes me happy that these people know Junior so well already and that my family fits in so easily with the Parish family, even though I could do without Junior being a member of The Guild.

I look over at Dusty, who's sitting in an Adirondack chair sunk deep into the sand with his wife, Tony's sister, Gracie, on his lap. I like him. Actually, I like all of them to one degree or another, even Justice—currently sharing a plaid blanket with her husband, Sandesh.

"Junior will be fine," Dada says, her baby boy cradled in her arms as she relaxes back against her husband, Sean.

I find myself calming with her reassurance. Motherhood agrees with Dada. It's given her a kind of centered peace that seems to flow from her.

"I saw Veta flirting with him earlier, so maybe better than fine," Sean says.

"Veta!" I start to get up.

Tony locks an arm around me, keeping me in place, as the others around the fire hold back laughter.

"She's not that scary," Justice says. This time the laughter is loud and long. "Okay, she is. But I think Junior might be able to take her on. If not for him and Superhero Silva, Winthrop would still be abusing the system and people for his own gain."

"Not just Winthrop," Sandesh says. "He might be taking most of the heat right now, but other trials are coming. It's going to be an interesting few years as the public adjusts to what's been hidden in plain sight."

"Agreed," Gracie says. "People who worked overtime to protect Winthrop are already being caught up in the scandal."

"Aye," Sean says, pulling the soft blanket around his son's face with a heartbreakingly loving look in his eyes. "Been something to learn about the celebrities, politicians, judges and the like under Winthrop's control."

"That's why Winthrop's perp walk was about the prettiest thing I've even seen," Tony says.

"Cheers to that," Justice says and the group around the fire lifts their glasses high before taking a drink.

A sadness rolls through me as I take a sip of iced tea. I wish Mom could be here for my wedding, meet the people who champion her and her work, the people who will become part of my—our—family. *You made a difference, Mom.* Ford, too.

"How's Ford doing, Honor?" Sandesh asks.

"He's well," I say, wondering if these people are learning to read me. They are all so observant. "He'll be arriving in time for the ceremony tomorrow, along with his wife and my sister."

No one says or asks why Ford isn't walking me down the aisle, and I have to admit that's one thing I love about this family. This group isn't bound to the traditions that some people assume are unbreakable in their importance, so no one second-guesses my choice of Abuelito to walk me down the aisle. Though I admire Ford terribly for all he did to help my mom and to break free of his uncle's control, a deeper relationship will take time.

"I would have recognized the threat in Lanie from day one," Justice says, and I tune in to the fact that she and Sandesh are privately dissecting the case. "Those yogis. Can't trust a one."

He laughs softly, but I can't repress my thread of unease. She's refereeing to the fact that Bridget, also a yogi, helped Tony when he'd been trying to keep Justice safe.

Bridget hasn't gotten her memories back. Of course, Tony insisted she be told what was taken from her, but, even after being told, she couldn't recall the memories, and she declined to undergo restorative treatment.

I understand why. She's happy the way she is. Happy in a way that I think few people ever achieve in life. Maybe that's why Bridget might be my favorite of all Tony's sisters and the only one I asked to be one of my bridesmaids. I can't say I have a particular sister I don't like. Still...

I lean into him. "How are Zuri's experiments going?"

His eyebrows go up. There's a tightening around his mouth. Any talk of Zuri, brings up what happened with his memory and our mission together. He's forgiven Momma for her manipulations, for allowing me to go on a mission I was patently unqualified for, but he hasn't forgotten. "Better than expected," he says. "Now that she's refused to use her technology to harm the mind, she's moving forward with using it to heal. She's closer to having it accepted as a treatment for those suffering through addiction."

A *whoop, whoop* slices across the sky as a helicopter passes overhead. "Group four will be here soon," Sandesh says.

I close my eyes as a small thread of alarm races through me. There are so many of them.

Tony leans closer. "You okay?"

"You mean am I going to be okay being with your entire family, all bazillion of them, at the same time?" I've met most of them by now—except for a few who live overseas—but I've never been with all of them at the same time.

He laughs softly, then kisses my cheek. "I meant, you okay being the center of attention? The bride walking down the aisle? Haven't changed your mind about marrying into this unconventional mess?"

"Never," I breathe. Actually, I think I'm beginning to understand his family and the very unique mosaic of cultures. They're the good guys, and so is he. The best. Reciting part of my vows that I should technically save for tomorrow, I say, "My mind and my heart are filled with you, so much so that, to me, we're already joined forever and our wedding is just the ceremony, the celebration of our always-connection."

He tilts my chin up, kisses me lightly on the lips, runs a hand along my face. "You're the best thing that's ever happened to me, Honor. My fairy tale come to life. I love you so much it hurts in all the best ways."

He kisses me deep and possessively.

Music blasts down from the main house, breaking up the satisfied comfort of the group on the beach.

"Party!" Tyler yells, running up from the water with Rome, Jules, and Cee trailing after him.

I'm pleased that I know all of them and can even tell who's who in the dim moonlight.

Justice shifts under the blanket, an annoyed look flashing across her face. "Damn Troublemakers."

"I see an opportunity for some fireworks," Tony whispers to me with glee, then louder, "Go get 'em, J!"

Her dark eyes, reflecting fire, swing to him. She shrugs. "I would, normally. But they *did* swoop in for the rescue when we were leaving Winthrop's island. Feel like I owe their crazy asses a bit more respect."

There's a chorus of surprised disbelief. Sandesh draws the blanket back over Justice's shoulders. "It's a calmer, nicer Justice."

Growling, she pushes him into the sand, sits on top of him, and says, "Not that nice," before bending down to kiss him.

"This is the perfect night," I say, capturing Tony's hand in mine. "But I think tomorrow night, the night we share our names, will be better."

"Couldn't agree more, future Mrs. Honora Parish-Silva."

I kiss him, and he kisses me back, possessing me. My head spins for love of him. I'm deliriously happy.

As his tongue teases mine, I silently claim every moment from here on out as ours, letting the past fade for what is in the present.

Us.

Acknowledgments

I'd like to thank my editor, Mackenzie Walton, for her incredible talent and insights. You transformed this manuscript, making it so much more than it would have been without your expert editing and spot-on insights.

A huge thank you to my copy editor and production editor, Judi Fennell. I sincerely appreciate all of your hard work and advice as I've navigated this self-publishing process.

To my incredible cover designer, Elizabeth Mackey, I can't thank you enough for your incredible artistic talent. You've managed to create a gorgeous cover for Daring Honor and for the entire series. Your covers captured my stories and my heart.

Another big and beautiful thank you goes to my Advanced Reader Team. You all provide me with valuable insight and support, and I truly appreciate your support.

A sincere thank you to everyone who has read this book and series. I consider it a privilege and an honor to be able to make this connection you.

About the Author

Diana Muñoz Stewart is a bestselling author who writes romantic suspense with a focus on diverse characters, action, adventure, family, and love. Her work has been praised as high-octane, edgy, sexy, and fast-paced.

Diana's work has been a BookPage Top 15 Romance, a Night Owl Top Pick, an Amazon Book of the Month, an Amazon Editor's pick, a Pages From The Heart Winner, a Book Page Top Pick, Golden Heart® Finalist, Daphne du Maurier Finalist, A Gateway to the Best Winner, and has reached #1 category bestseller on Amazon multiple times.

Diana lives in an often chaotic and always welcoming home that—depending on the day—can hold a husband, kids, extended family, friends, and a canine or two. A believer in the power of words to heal and connect, Diana has written multiple spotlight pieces on the strong, diverse women changing the world.

Sign up for her newsletter to receive the latest information on her new releases:
https://dianamunozstewart.com/newsletter/

Enjoy this sample of *It's All in the Hips* by Diana Muñoz Stewart

Expected Release Early 2024

CHAPTER ONE
Yolanda

Twelve years ago.

There was one in every group. Just so happens my one is a six-foot-tall, tanned and toned rich muchacho from the mainland. He's also quite drunk.

Coño. Do I dare to put hands on him to correct his form? My palms sweat with the thought. This is what I get for initiating beach yoga mere steps from a resort bar.

To be fair, the bar is part of my family's resort in Puerto Rico—the one we're desperately trying to revive after the hurricane. What else is new? If I had a dollar for every time La Vida Buena needed a dollar, I still wouldn't have enough money to keep it afloat. Except, we have a chance now. The insurance money and a recent loan could change everything. If we make the right choices.

Blond guy falls out, kicking up sand as he catches himself by one hand. His white-and-blue board shorts have dolphins jumping across a tight, muscular bottom. His long arms flare out as he stands back up, nearly slapping the woman next to him. "Whoa. Sorry."

The woman's glaring gaze doesn't seem very namaste. Her nose scrunches up as her eyes slip down, trolling the Celtic tattoo that winds around his muscled forearm. Ay. This situation needs my help.

"Bueno, Señora Centeno. Good, Mrs. Centeno," I tell her, automatically repeating the sentence in English, a practice my customer-oriented papi taught me long before I could even ride a bike. Mrs. Centeno is one of ten guests lined up on colorful yoga towels taking part in my beach yoga. I quickly wipe my palms on my shorts and make my move.

"Your form is shaky," I tell dolphin-board-shorts. *Understatement.* "Por favor, please, take a moment to rest in child's pose."

He stops his pathetic attempt at Warrior One and stares at me. "You're beautiful."

And you're drunk. "Let me demonstrate." I get down in the sand beside his towel and demonstrate the resting pose for him, sitting on my calves and placing my forehead on the warm sand.

After a second, I look back up.

Half his mouth quirks into a smile that is more than halfway to brilliant. This is a very good looking drunk.

"You're putting me in time out?"

I laugh, even though I really shouldn't. Muchacho blindsided me with that humor. And with those intense green-gold eyes framed by lashes so long you'd think he'd glued them on. Pero nothing glued on will survive this heat.

Standing, I dust sand off my shorts and try to exude inner power. Not easy. He's about a foot taller. Which has me worried. The bigger they are, the harder they fall… into someone else.

I gesture for him to try. "It's a resting pose, señor."

"Easton. Not sir. Sir is my dad. For now." He hiccups, wavers. Something shifts in his vulnerable eyes and a bone-deep sadness swims to the surface.

With that, Easton drops down like a puppet whose strings were cut. He places his sweat-soaked forehead on the mat with his arms by his feet, successfully completing a slightly misaligned child's pose. Sand is plastered across the wide shoulders of his white mesh tank top. It's all I can do not to brush it off.

"Ayudeme."

I turn to the mujer asking for help. She's younger than everyone else on the beach, closer to my age, and dressed in a pink thong bikini. I guide her through vinyasa flow. She smiles at me in gratitude.

When I'm done, I check on my downed pupil. Ay. My heart lurches. There's a tear stain, still wet, that has traced a line from the corner of one closed eye down his cheek. What was it he'd said about his father? *For now?*

My attention shifts as another participant falls out. She lands in the sand with a surprised *oof.*

I move to her side and demonstrate an easier way to get into the form.

The next fifteen minutes of the class pass without incident. Easton stays in child pose. His deep breaths indicate he's fallen asleep. He doesn't stir as I end the class. "Gracias for joining me today, pero—but—remember, tomorrow we'll be doing an exercise dance routine I invented. My brother. Mateo. will be providing live drums."

"Sí, voy," Señora Lopez says. Others chime in that they'll be there, too.

Mateo has a huge following. I've been told he's a hunk. I still think of him as my kid brother, a little goofy and a lot of trouble. Hunk? Nope. Now Easton on the other hand…

I help a few people shake out their colorful fringed towels and roll them up before returning to Easton.

Still down for the count.

Dropping into the soft sand, I put a hand against his hot, sandy back. Sensual awareness jolts through my body as unexpected as the gasp that comes from Easton.

He jerks up from a dead sleep, and I startle like I've been caught groping Sleeping Beauty.

Shouldn't be possible for my face to grow hotter in the San Juan sun, pero it does. I could fry an egg on my embarrassment.

Blinking, he looks around. He sits back and shakes out his legs. "My legs are asleep." His words are as groggy as his eyes. His forehead has a pink patch that he rubs absently.

"Kind of what happens when you fall asleep in child's pose."

"Ah, see, my bad. I didn't read the warning label on this yoga practice."

I laugh. Again, this muchacho has taken me by surprise.

"You're kind of funny, Easton."

The haze clears from his eyes and he full-out grins at me. We share a look that seems to open me up from the inside. It pours heat and possibility into me. Ay, Dios mio. He's cute, funny, *and* interested in me. That doesn't happen all too often. Sure, I get attention—usually from spring-breakers looking for a hook-up. The kind of interest he's showing goes beyond *I want to sleep with you before I head home*. It's like he's reaching out for something.

I wonder what—Nope. Nose to the grindstone. That's how I do it. But, this muchacho…

"East!" a dark-skinned guy calls from the edge of the bar's patio. "Time's ticking. You ready for your next shot?"

Easton flinches. He waves at his friend. "Give me a sec, Stone."

I sigh. Stone? Is that the guy's name? Stone and East. Ay. Dios. Where do these gente go to school? Harvard? New York City by East's accent.

I stand before he has a chance to engage with me again. One thing I'm really not interested in is a man who thinks getting wasted is a marathon sport.

"Hold on." Easton stands, hobbles, starts to tumble.

I grab him by the elbow and steady him.

He shakes out his leg. "Thanks. Pins and needles are stitching a sweater in in my calf."

Funny and clever. I'd walk away, let him tumble, but Easton is drinking at my family's resort, La Vida Buena, and I've grown up with that ironclad mantra of treating guests like familia. Or, actually, better than familia; we wouldn't tolerate drunk and falling over from familia. So says the eye roll my cousin Haydee sends me from where she's serving drinks around the bar.

When he's steady, he holds out his hand. "I didn't get your name." He grins at me. The sun has less warmth. "And I assume you don't go by Beach Yoga Teacher."

I press my palm to his and his hand covers mine. *Possesses* mine. I feel as hugged as I've ever felt from a handshake. "Yolanda Vasquez." Time to put some cool formality between us. "Teaching is only one of my roles as owner of La Vida Buena, the resort where you're drinking."

Technically, I'm a partial owner, but I'm not interested in exchanging histories, only shutting this flirtation down.

He doesn't drop my hand, just stares into my eyes.

I slide my hand away.

As if the action breaks some kind of spell, he blurts, "I'm not a barfly." He waves toward the bar. "Just drinking here, like you said. I mean, I'm staying here. In the Covento Suite."

He's in the most expensive room we have—Haydee's idea to charge two-thousand dollars a night. Mierda. I'm glad the hotel is making money, but this means my cousin's plan to turn the place into a rich-kids' spring break haven is working. Which would be good if it didn't go directly against the plan I've been proposing for four years—turning the resort into a health and wellness destination.

"Muchísimas gracias, thank you very much, for choosing La Vida Buena. Let me know if there's anything you need to make your stay more comfortable, Easton."

"East. Call me East."

I don't give him a chance to engage further. I smile and glide away. I'm not trying to be rude, but I need to get away from him. He's the exact type of person I don't want at the resort.

Download the next four chapters for free here:
https://bookhip.com/HRCDAWQ

Made in the USA
Middletown, DE
03 November 2023